A Shocking Affair

Gerald Hammond

A Shocking Affair

MACMILLAN

First published 1999 by Macmillan
an imprint of Macmillan Publishers Ltd
25 Eccleston Place, London SW1W 9NF
and Basingstoke

Associated companies throughout the world

ISBN 0 333 73279 0

1 3 5 7 9 8 6 4 2

A CIP catalogue record for this book is
available from the British Library.

Phototypeset by Intype London Ltd
Printed and bound in Great Britain by
Mackays of Chatham plc, Chatham, Kent

I am very much obliged to retired pathologist Dr Bill Hendry for the help and advice pertaining to his former speciality and to my son Peter for correcting details of executry in Scotland.

Chapter One

The pleasures of retirement had worn a bit thin that morning. Weighing idleness against boredom in the scales of discontent, boredom was undoubtedly the weightier. I quite realized that my life was one for which many tired workers would have given at least one leg and possibly both, but the monotony of repetition would eventually have palled on anyone. The passing years, and a strict application of the rules, had forced me to retire from a life of responsibility, reward and, I liked to think, service. I did not take kindly to becoming a nonentity.

My wife, Isobel Kitts (née McPherson), being a zealous partner in Three Oaks Kennels, is usually out of the house and walking the mile and a half through the village to the kennels before I am properly awake. But then, although no chicken herself, she has nearly two decades in hand.

Though Isobel's stake came from me and I am kindly allowed to help out in times of stress, I have no official connection with the firm and so am privileged to absent myself whenever I feel like it. Life, however, would be desperately boring if it were not for regular involvement with the younger and more vigorous activity at the kennels.

We had moved to Fife from Edinburgh after my retirement so that Isobel could be within reach of her few surviving relatives, only to see them depart, one for Canada and two others for unspecified destinations in the hereafter. We might have moved again, but by that time we had put down roots and made friends locally and soon afterwards Isobel was introduced to John Cunningham who, after reaching the rank of Captain in the infantry, had been retired on health grounds and was setting up as a breeder and trainer of working springer spaniels. It was vaguely envisaged, I think, that Isobel's contribution would be as an investor, a strong back and a qualified vet, but she had then discovered an unsuspected talent for handling dogs in competition and the unflappable temperament to go along with it. The predictable outcome was that she was busy and fulfilled while I could tag along if I felt like it or stay at home and lump it. To be fair, Isobel had not consciously contributed to my discontent and was quite unaware of it.

Strictly speaking this story had begun many years earlier, but on the day when I choose to begin it I pottered grumpily, as usual, with such few domestic chores as Isobel had left undone and timed the start of my walk to Three Oaks so that the pub would be open as I passed through the village. It was a fine morning in late spring, my well-worn joints moved with comparative ease and when I called in for a large Macallan and a chaser of Caffreys my malaise had evaporated and I was in a mood for celebrating another day rather than drowning any sorrows. As it happened, I bumped into an acquaintance in similar mood and I was later than usual, and walking very tall when I left the village and tackled the half-mile to where I could already see my destination on the crest of the hill.

I turned in at the gate to the former farmhouse where lived the Cunninghams and which formed the hub of the kennels. The traditional stone buildings, more than a hundred years old, had been lovingly (and expensively) restored. Paint shone in the sun and such of the garden as was not given over to dogs was bright with flowers.

As usual, the place was bustling with activity. Away to my left, one of the kennelmaids waved to me from among the tight groups of kennels and runs, and I waved back with my stick. On the gravel in front of the house was John, a spaniel sitting to attention at his feet. I told him once that without at least one dog at his heel I might not recognize him. To the uninitiated, one springer may look very like another but I had no difficulty recognizing Spin. (Short for the Spindle Tree, *Euonymus europaeus*. At Three Oaks, male dogs were usually named after trees, but the supply of varieties was running short.) I had shot over Spin on many occasions during his training, walked him as often and searched him for ticks and fleas now and again. He was a talented male liver-and-white springer of nine or ten months old, more liver than white, solidly built and with a cheerful and biddable disposition.

John was talking with a scarecrow figure with a mop of silver hair and a shabby kilt. The scarecrow, I presumed, was the driver of the large Japanese jeep-type vehicle standing nearby. This latter, judging from the registration letter, was less than a year old but already it was almost as tatty as its driver and quite as battered.

John looked round as I approached. 'Here comes one possible solution to the problem,' he said.

The scarecrow also glanced round. From behind he had looked faintly familiar. I could now see that he was at least as old as myself. My memory for names and faces has become less positive with the passing years but alcohol, for some reason, seems to put a fresh if temporary edge on it. 'Good Lord! Peter Hay!' I said.

'Good God!' said the scarecrow. 'It's Henry. Henry Kitts. Right?' The high, slightly neighing voice rolled back the years. I remembered more. Despite his eccentricities, I had always liked him.

'Quite right,' I said. 'Well done, both of us. Right first time after what? Twenty years?'

'Almost.'

We shook hands.

John was beginning to fidget. I could tell that he was dreading being trapped by a spate of do-you-remembers. 'We can catch up with the news later,' I said. 'For the moment, what's this problem I'm expected to solve? We can deal with that first and let John go. I know he's busy.'

Peter Hay nodded towards the spaniel. 'I've just agreed to buy this feller.'

'You could do a lot worse. I've always felt that he was among the best of his litter. But I thought you used to be a devout Labrador man,' I said.

He nodded again, this time in agreement. 'I've always had Labs,' he said. 'I get on with them. Spoil them, Keith says. Well, you can get away with being soft on a Lab, more or less, if you don't expect too much. But I've always had a hankering to have a springer and if I don't do it now I never will. I made up my mind to get a well-trained one of good stock and keep him up to the mark. So I spoke to Joe Little, your neighbour, who's always supplied my Labs in the past, and he recommended Captain Cunningham.'

'Mister. Just Mister Cunningham. Good of him,' John said. 'The problem, Henry, is that Mr Hay is on a business trip and has to go home by way of Stranraer. He won't get home for a couple of days, which would be hard on the dog.'

'More than that,' Peter Hay said. 'It must be hard on a young dog anyway, suddenly being snatched away by a stranger. What I'd like is for the dog to be brought to me by somebody he knows, who could then stay for a day or two, work with us and introduce me properly to the commands and . . . and so on. For a fee, of course. The estimable Joe Little has always managed to oblige me in the past when I've bought from him. But then, he has a cousin who lives down my way.'

John was looking pleased. But for the influence of his two partners, any prospective owner who gave deep thought to the well-being of his purchase could have asked and got a substantial discount. 'It's the counsel of perfection,' he said, 'but we're at the height of the training programme, preparing for the improvident folk who suddenly decide they want a trained dog about two days before the first shoot of the season. Add to that a few commitments to judge or compete in working tests. Also I promised to do a demonstration at a game fair. We honestly couldn't spare anybody. However, Henry, if you could oblige Mr Hay . . .'

Sir Peter Hay had always been modest about his

baronetcy except when it gave him a useful leverage in business. 'If it would help Sir Peter out – ' I began tactfully. I saw John flinch minutely at his own gaffe. 'It would depend on whether Isobel could manage without my services as chauffeur. You're still in Newton Lauder?'

'Of course,' Peter said. He sounded surprised. He was a feature of the place.

'I didn't suppose that you'd moved the family seat,' I explained. 'I just wondered whether you wanted the dog brought there or to your place up north.'

He smiled. His teeth were whiter in his weathered face and more regular than I remembered them, but with the passing of time I too had converted to dentures and he was probably as disconcerted by my flashing smile as I was by his. 'I got rid of that mouldering mausoleum years ago,' he said. 'It was costing me more money than it was worth and I'm trying to simplify and streamline my affairs. I unloaded it on a lottery winner who fancied setting up as a Highland laird. He soon found that being a laird isn't all it's cracked up to be.'

I seemed to remember that Peter's wife had been devoted to the 'place up north'. I had never been there but I had gathered from her that, far from being a 'mouldering mausoleum', it was more of a stately home with above average sporting facilities. 'And how is Lady Hay?' I asked.

'Her La'ship went and died on me some years ago,' he said without showing more than token grief.

That, I supposed, explained that.

John, who had faded away, reappeared. 'Isobel says

that she can manage without you or the car,' he said. 'One of the girls can always drive her around.'

I nodded. One of the 'girls' – the two kennelmaids – would have had to drive her anyway if I were absent. Her licence had been taken away, to my relief. Sober, she was a hazard to those around her. She was partial to a glass or two whenever she got into sociable company, after which her driving improved.

'If there's a car shortage,' Sir Peter said, 'I could send Ronnie to fetch you.' He nodded towards his vehicle and I saw for the first time that a large individual in a chauffeur's cap was sitting stolidly in the driver's seat. 'I'm not trying to save on your charges for transportation. I just want to make it easy for the wee chap to adapt.'

'Then he'd be better in a car that he's travelled in before,' I pointed out.

'That's so.' He considered for a moment. 'I'm away until the weekend. Shall we say Monday? Stay for a few days. And bring a gun. We can chase the rabbits about a bit, by way of settling him in. And you could fetch along a trout-rod. Before I go, should I make my number to your good lady?'

'She's spaying a bitch for one of Joe Little's clients,' John said.

'Then I can do no more than ask you to give her my regards.' He settled himself beside his chauffeur and was borne noisily away.

John kept me busy for what was left of the morning, firing blank cartridges and throwing a variety of dummies – canvas, furred or feather-covered – while he instilled steadiness and a delight in retrieving in a succession of juvenile springers. It was a relief when Hannah came out into the field to call us for lunch. I had been on my feet for rather a long time and my old joints, which had carried too much weight too far for too long, were beginning to complain.

At Three Oaks, lunch and all other meals take place in a big kitchen, around a large old table ruined as an antique but made practical by the addition of a more recent Formica top. That table epitomized the whole room – a traditional farmhouse kitchen refurnished with modern equipment and old furniture so that Windsor and basket chairs were seen against a background of white goods such as the microwave and fridge-freezer.

Sam, the Cunninghams' son, was at school, but for once we adults all sat down together – John, still skinny and pale after the illness which took him out of the army; Beth, his wife, in her thirties and looking like a pretty teenager; the two kennelmaids, Daffy and Hannah, suitably dressed for a day's hard and dirty work but, to my old male eyes, still managing to exude glamour; Isobel, round and matronly and bespectacled, a mother figure, but with more energy than any two of the others put together. And, of course, yours truly, not a member but a regular attender all the same. As usual we looked after ourselves, devising whatever combinations we fancied of toast, rolls, oatcakes, pâté, cheese, pickles, lettuce, chopped herbs, honey, fruit and whatever else Beth had thought to put out.

'They tell me that Peter Hay was here,' Isobel said. 'A voice from the past.'

'There you go again,' John said peevishly. 'Peter

Hay, Peter Hay. That's all he seems to be called, even on his cheques, so of course I called him *Mister* Hay. Nobody bothered to tell me that he was a Sir.'

'I dropped you the hint,' I pointed out.

'Too late for Mr Cunningham,' Daffy said. There was laughter in her voice.

'Baronet. He wouldn't be offended, he doesn't mind being Peter Hay around Newton Lauder and probably in his own mind too. He sent you his compliments, by the way,' I told Isobel. 'He bought Spin and he wants me to take the dog down to him and perform introductions on what will become the dog's home territory.'

'Best way to do it,' John said, nodding. 'It's not like taking over a platoon or a new business. Dog and handler don't start with a common language. As Sir Peter said (got it right at last!) the change must be traumatic enough for a young dog without being handed over cold to strangers in a strange land.'

As the morning's refreshment wore off I was becoming less and less keen on the errand. 'Agreeing with all that,' I said, 'I can't say that I'm in a hurry to go off and try to sleep in a strange bed and adjust to somebody else's house – a house which, as I remember it, was a cold and draughty dump even in summer.'

'Well, if you said you'd do it, you'll have to,' Isobel said firmly. 'We don't go in for mind-changing and letting clients down.'

'But I'm not a member of the firm,' I said.

'As good as,' said John. 'And he offered a good fee for the service. We can credit the fee direct to Isobel.'

'If I do it, you can credit it direct to me,' I retorted. I gave a sigh. 'Well, it needn't take me away for too long. I can go down on Monday and come back on Tuesday.'

John looked at me as though I had uttered a scandalous interpretation of the doctrine of virgin birth. 'That you will not!' he snorted. 'I always stress to new owners not to try and shoot over the dog for several days, until it's settled down. Just for once, we have the chance to do it right. What are you complaining about? You're invited to spend a few days shooting rabbits, catching trout and probably boozing the evenings away in the company of an old friend who seemed, on short acquaintance, to be just the kind of company you enjoy and probably with an excellent cellar.'

'And I seem to remember something about a fire,' Isobel said. 'So if there isn't a new house, the old one must have been largely rebuilt and modernized.'

'They all want to get rid of me,' I told the ceiling.

'*We* don't,' Hannah said, smiling. 'We rather like having you around and we slaves will miss the help you give us. How do you come to be friends with a member of the aristocracy?'

'It's old history,' I told her. I pushed my plate away and accepted a cup of coffee. 'We first met up during the war, in the army. We both did our basic training in Lanark. He really was just Peter Hay in those days.' I decided not to mention that we had together been caught out in a disgraceful episode, as a result of which neither of us had ever been commissioned. 'We lost contact for years, until I was in the merchant bank. A friend of his had come up with a new system for exchangeable tractor attachments. Sir Peter is or was a wealthy man, owning great tracts of the Borders, but he was ploughing all his income back into the land and he wanted to capitalize the invention without having to sell property, while still keeping the new jobs strictly local. He came to me and I organized a loan and we floated a company. I believe it's done very well – at least, they wanted to pay off the loan ahead of time.'

'But you wouldn't let them?' Daffy asked. She has a nose for these quirks of business.

'Of course not,' I said. 'Once you've got somebody on the hook and paying a very satisfactory rate of interest, you keep them there.'

'And no doubt Sir Peter made another million,' Daffy said. She also leans to the left, politically.

'He made a few bob,' I told her. 'But that isn't why he went into it. The first clause in the agreement was that a new factory would be established in Newton Lauder. That created a little difficulty with investors but it almost wiped out unemployment locally. You don't mind if I take it on?' I asked Isobel.

'Mind?' she said. 'I insist on it. Not that I don't love your company,' she added more kindly, 'but you need a change or you'll turn into a human vegetable.'

The last remark was so close to my own earlier thoughts that I put aside my reservations. 'All right,' I said. 'I told him I'd do it and I will. Just don't forget that you owe me.'

Isobel, whose sole recollection of Sir Peter was from an occasion when we were entertained by him to a lavish dinner in a club where he was obviously well known and treated with great respect, was in a ferment to ensure that I was clean, sane, sober and properly equipped for a visit to what she envisaged as a stately home, complete with footmen and a butler. During the succeeding days I was sent to have my hair cut and to buy new socks while, in between her other activities, she managed to select from my wardrobe what she considered to be suitable clothing to take with me. She even made me phone the baronet to enquire whether a black tie would be called for, which seemed to cause him some amusement. If we had guessed just how infelicitous the question would turn out to have been, we would have been horrified but he would doubtless have been even more amused.

Early in my retirement, Isobel and I had arrived at a simple understanding about my clothes. I buy anything that takes my fancy and she immediately impounds it and puts it away as being too good for wearing around the garden, the countryside or the kennels. As a result, I am usually clad in the old, tatty and comfortable. Although I have been known to point out that the only way to get old clothes is to wear new ones, the arrangement generally pleases me very well because I had more than enough of the black jacket, striped trousers and restrictive collar image during my time with the bank. Meanwhile, more respectable clothes accumulate, ready for a sedentary old age which, I sincerely hope, will never arrive, sometimes to be released grudgingly when the garments in ordinary use threaten to disintegrate altogether or when some occasion calls for best bib and tucker. In the Scottish countryside, where gorse and brambles soon make the toughest and smartest garments look second-hand, it is the dandy who is subject to scorn and derision – behind his back.

Isobel, however, now decided that the moment had come for all this finery to be put to good use and I found, heaped on every flat surface and ready for packing, more clothes than would have gone into all our suitcases combined. As I told her, the baggage required would have left no room in the car for the dog or myself. I rejected three-quarters of the new clothes, also threw out my heavy tweed shooting suit and sneaked back in some comfortable slacks, corduroy breeks, a few sweaters and a kilt as old and tatty as any of Peter Hay's.

Thus equipped, but neat and tidy for the moment, I drove off on the Monday morning with a mere two cases on the seat behind me, several pairs of boots loose on the floor and Spin peering hopefully through the dog-guard and thrashing with his tail every time he caught my eye in the driving mirror. The weather was holding; the sun almost too bright for comfortable driving in a southerly direction. Without hurrying, using the motorways, I made Edinburgh in little over an hour, lunched with an old friend and did a minor errand, watered Spin and walked him and set off again. After we cleared the small satellite towns to the south of Edinburgh our route led for a while through moorland on top of the Lammermuirs. Then we descended again into the fertile farmland of the Eastern Borders.

It was many years since I had passed that way but I remembered the route well. I turned off the main road, ran parallel to it for a few miles and came to the pleasant little town of Newton Lauder, nestling in its valley with the main road grinding past along the face of the hill above, where the heather began. I was nearly there. I climbed out of the town towards open country beyond and after a few false casts found a stone archway almost covered with creeper and swung in onto a driveway of gravel between spreading trees.

In a sense it was like encountering an old friend and yet something was monstrously different, as though the friend had lost hair and teeth and all his limbs. I had been expecting the loom of a stone-built pile complete with turrets and battlements and all in the worst of Scottish Victorian Gothic taste. But instead there was sky at the end of the avenue where the pretentious structure had stood and, as I came nearer, I saw that on its site was a garden on many levels. The foundations of the old house had been kept to provide the retaining walls and over them dripped and tumbled a glorious mixture of alpines and rockery plants. At the centre of each bed was a specimen tree, usually a cherry in full blossom. It was the ideal season of the year for that display, but even so I could see by the shrubs and especially the rose bushes that it would still be a place of beauty when spring was only a memory.

A hundred yards after emerging from the trees, the drive ended in a circle of gravel where the front door of the old house had been. Now, to one side stood a modern house, spacious but nowhere more than two storeys high, largely built, I was sure, of stone retrieved from the original house but with panels of cedar alternating with the picture windows. Beside and behind the house a broad lawn reached to a wood of mixed pines and silver birch, but the house itself fronted onto a view down to where, in the distance, the slated roofs of Newton Lauder shone purple-grey in the sunlight. Though modern, the house fitted into its surroundings as though it had been there first and the landscape then arranged thoughtfully around it. I can't explain further except to say that it just looked right. Within a few seconds, the image of the old house was eradicated.

Two figures rose from a half-hidden flowerbed and approached – Sir Peter, kilted as always, in the lead. I got out to meet them.

'You've made it,' Sir Peter informed me as though I might have been in some doubt. 'And right on time.' He showed me his hands. 'I won't shake until I've had a chance to wash but be assured that you're very welcome. Of course, this looks a bit different from the last time you were here. We had a fire, you know.'

'I heard,' I said. 'Should I commiserate?'

He shook his grey head. 'Best thing that ever happened. You've brought my new companion? Ronnie must meet him. You met Ronnie, or at least you saw him, when I visited in Fife. Ronnie,' he explained, 'used to be my ghillie and stalker. He still does a bit when it's called for. But nowadays he's mostly my chauffeur and butler and valet and general handyman and deputy gamekeeper. His wife's the housekeeper. Ronnie and I keep the gardens between us, although we call in outside help when it gets too much for us or when either of us is too busy.'

Ronnie had already taken my cases out of the car and was awaiting instructions through this lengthy introduction, standing loosely to attention. He was a large man. He had never been a beauty, but now, aged around sixty, he was gnarled like driftwood and had lost all his hair except for a silver fringe. He looked, frankly, a bit of a bruiser and not at all the type to be manservant to a nobleman. I wondered whether he was in fact a bodyguard but put the thought aside. Nobody could want to harm the amiable baronet.

'Well, now,' Sir Peter said happily, 'let's have a look at the little chap.'

I opened the back of the car. Spin waited until I gave the word and then jumped down, relieved himself against one of my wheels and came to sit beside me.

'I have his pedigree with me,' I said, 'and Kennel Club registration and certificates of vaccination.'

Sir Peter had squatted down to fondle the spaniel, who rolled over on his back, grinning affably. 'And I see that you brought his own basket and bowl.'

'And the whistle that he was trained to. We always do that,' I said. 'It helps them to settle in if they have as much as possible of their own environment with them. It's included.' I found that I was speaking like a member of the firm.

'He seems in fine fettle. What do you think, Ronnie?'

'Braw wee beastie,' Ronnie said. 'But will he be good at the job?'

Sir Peter grinned and looked at his watch. 'We can find out,' he said. 'We've plenty of time to hunt down Long Strip for rabbits before dinner.'

'I'm afraid not,' I said. I thought back to John's last words to me. He had read me a serious lecture before allowing me to remove one of his ewe-lambs. 'When he's been through all his training exercises with you and got used to being handled by you, and most of all when he's got used to the idea that you won't let him

16

play you up – ' the baronet looked doubtful and his henchman frankly amused ' – then it'll be time enough to reintroduce him to live quarry. Anything else would be to invite disaster.'

'He's no' wrong,' Ronnie put in.

'Tomorrow?' Sir Peter said hopefully.

I shook my head. 'Maybe the next day if you get on well tomorrow. Believe me, I'm not trying to spin out my invitation—'

'But, my dear chap,' he broke in, his voice and his eyebrows rising together, 'stay for as long as you can. I don't see enough of old friends, especially to shoot with. And by "old friends", I mean friends of about my own age, content to proceed at a gentlemanly plod and give the dogs time to work, not youngsters like Ronnie here who want to dash about all over the place. Ah,' he added, 'now's the time for the new boy to meet the rest of the menagerie.'

Two black Labradors, both of them male, were approaching from the direction of the house. One, evidently the older, was white-jowled and walked with the stiffness of age. The opaque milkiness of cataract was beginning to dim his eyes. The other, not very much younger, showed traces of grey at the muzzle and I had the impression that he would have hurried to inspect the newcomer but held back for the sake of his aged companion. The two came on together. Spin, daunted, retired behind my legs and then rolled onto his back again, miming non-threat.

'Meet the other residents,' said Sir Peter. 'The geriatric is Nick, now known as Old Nick – unfairly, because he's long past any devilment. Old Nick's twelve. Royston's eight and a bit. I had a younger one coming along but he developed a cancer at the turn of the year. That's when I began to think that I might have been offered my last chance to try myself out with a spaniel. I doubt if I'll ever get another dog.'

With the pecking order established, the two Labradors sniffed and then backed away. Spin righted himself, made a couple of play pounces, took his turn for a sniff and then raced in a circle around the other dogs. Old Nick, beyond such capers, settled down with a grunt at Sir Peter's feet, but the younger Royston accepted the invitation and gave chase for a few seconds. But he was no match for a young spaniel and he soon returned to his master, with an air of having been amusing the younger generation but not wanting to show off. Disappointed, Spin raced once around the lawn and then came back, sniffed again and lay down beside the others.

'That's a relief,' said Sir Peter. 'It looks as though they'll get along.'

'As long as jealousies aren't allowed to develop,' I suggested.

'Good heavens, yes! And I wouldn't want to hurt the old boys' feelings. We've had too much fun together over the years. Tact called for. But I mustn't keep you standing here. Ronnie will show you your room. Would you like tea? Or a rest before dinner?'

I realized that I was tired after my long drive and I had missed my customary afternoon nap. But Peter, I could see, was champing at the bit and only restrained by good manners. 'I'll take a rest shortly,' I said. 'First, don't you want to start the – um – induction process?'

His face lit up, crinkling with pleasure lines. 'If you're sure,' he said.

'You can't begin impressing your leadership too soon.'

So the two Labradors were put into the house and we spent a happy half-hour on the lawn, putting Spin through the basic exercises while I coached Sir Peter in the different language and attitudes of the springer spaniel as compared to those of the Labrador. Spin sat and heeled and stayed and came and retrieved a variety of dummies and even seemed to be enjoying himself. But *little and often* is the motto. When I suggested a halt, Peter seemed well satisfied and I gathered that even the dour-looking Ronnie was impressed.

Sir Peter turned back into the perfect host. 'Let Ronnie show you your room,' he said. 'Have your rest. I might have a snooze myself. You'll be called in plenty of time for dinner. I have guests coming, by the way, but we don't dress up any more, or only a little bit. Had enough of that in her La'ship's time.'

Ronnie carried my cases while I tagged along with my gun and my trout-rod. I kept Spin with me. Ronnie dumped my luggage on the floor in a bright and comfortable double room and immediately relieved me of the gun-case. 'This goes in the gun-safe,' he said gruffly. 'Rule of the house.'

'Of course.' I wondered whether to tip him but he seemed not to expect it and I decided that the time of my departure would be soon enough.

The house, I judged, had about six or eight bedrooms, each with its own bathroom and the whole place was finished to a very high standard. I showered and lay down for what should have been a brief rest, but the bed was soft and I was tired and I fell deeply asleep until roused by a knock on the door and a cheerful female voice warning me that dinner would be served in an hour.

As I descended the stair with Spin sticking close to my heel Peter Hay met me in the hall, standing in a slightly newer kilt with well-worn evening appurtenances.

'We feed the dogs about now,' he said. 'But first . . .?'

I knew what he wanted. At his suggestion I bestowed my car between the battered four-by-four and an even more battered Land Rover in a garage which still had space for several more cars, and then we spent another ten minutes on the lawn in a fading light while again Spin happily sat and heeled and came and went, retrieved a dummy or two and resisted several carefully plotted temptations. Then, in the kitchen, while the three dogs ate from their separate dishes in relative amity, I was introduced to Ronnie's wife Mary, Sir Peter's cook-housekeeper. She was about ages with her husband but either she had worn better or, more probably, she had been prettier to start with. She was helped by Joanna, a cheerful girl with beautiful skin and a roguish eye, who was maid of all work.

I decided that Isobel must never see that kitchen or she would never be content with her old one. It seemed to have been built, furnished and equipped regardless of cost. Sir Peter seemed quite at home in it and would have been happy to have lingered over a chat with his staff, but we were interrupted by the gentle sound of a doorbell. Joanna brushed crumbs off her apron and went to answer the door while Sir Peter, hurrying almost guiltily, led me through into a sitting room which seemed to be all polished parquet and sweet-pea colours and as generously designed as the rest of the house. It was a strangely old-fashioned room for a modern house, furnished with chintzy wing-chairs and a few good antiques, but it took me back immediately to my youth in my parents' house and I found it comforting. The dogs remained in the kitchen and Spin, now that he had been reassured that this was a proper house where good and timely meals were provided, made no objection to being left with his new companions.

The other dinner guests, ushered in by Joanna, proved to be a foursome – parents, daughter and son-in-law. The father, Keith Calder, must have been nearly sixty but carried himself very well. He was a fine-looking man but outshone by his ladies. Mother and daughter resembled each other in being dark, softly rounded and devastatingly attractive with good complexions and eyes that a man could happily drown in. Over drinks, I learned that Keith was proprietor of the local gun shop, a dealer in antique weaponry and an occasional dog trainer. The son-in-law, Ian Fellowes, was a typical Border Scot of the sandy-haired style, and was, I was told with a mixture of pride and apology, a policeman – the local detective inspector. There was yet another generation, because Sir Peter asked who was looking after his godson.

A good meal was served – again by Joanna. I began to think that Ronnie must be more chauffeur and gardener and ghillie and stalker than butler or valet. With the meal we had two respectable but not pretentious wines. The company was enjoyable – and amusing in more senses than one. I guessed, from his questions, that Keith Calder had been invited or had invited himself in order to satisfy himself that I really did know what I was talking about when it came to dogs. He was very knowledgeable but, having owned and handled gun dogs for most of my life and after dancing attendance at Three Oaks kennels for the past seven or eight years, I was well able to keep my end up. The discussion even provided me with material with which I intended to amaze John and his household on my return.

I had been wondering why an extra place had been set at table. Halfway through the meal our forks paused in mid-air at the beat of what sounded to me like a motorbike engine in the drive, followed by feet on the gravel. Sir Peter got up quickly and excused himself. The others resumed conversation hastily. Keith Calder asked me a question to do with the removal of sheep-ticks to which I was sure he knew the answer perfectly well. I managed to elaborate on the theme, quoting liberally from Isobel, but the voices in the hall were not quite drowned.

I heard a girl's voice, subdued. Then Sir Peter spoke. 'Yes, this is your home. But it is my home first of all. You are very welcome in it, but I have told you before that that young man does not come in here.'

The girl's voice spoke again. Then I heard Peter clearly. 'That decision is your own, my dear.'

The front door slammed. A minute later my host returned to the room, rather red and white about the face. He was followed by Joanna who removed the extra place setting.

When the guests had left, I expected Peter to hint

that we were not as young as we had been and that perhaps it was time for bed. But he led me back into the sitting room and we settled before the fire with another brandy apiece. The three dogs were admitted and curled up companionably together on the hearth-rug. My host produced a brace of cigars, medium sized but of first quality.

'Should you?' I asked doubtfully, mindful of my hardened arteries and the pacemaker which, he had admitted, had kept him ticking over for the last few years.

He grinned at me. 'No, of course I shouldn't. Nor should you. That's why I waited until now. Molly Calder would have read me a lecture if she had even smelled smoke. But I've sent Joanna to bed and Ronnie and Mary have gone home for the night, otherwise they would have looked at me disapprovingly and dropped hints about heart disease and lack of will-power. Which only makes a good smoke all the more enjoyable, placing it among the forbidden delights which are so much better than any other kind.'

'Stolen fruit being sweetest?' I suggested.

He blew a perfect smoke ring. 'Of course. It takes me back to sneaking out of school for a smoke in the Head's potting shed. Anyway, I'd rather have a few good years than rather more but austere ones. "One crowded hour of glorious life is worth an age without a name", and all that. Don't join me if you don't want to. Are you ready for bed?'

His philosophy rang an only slightly muted bell with me. So I accepted a cigar and we puffed com-panionably, two naughty old boys enjoying themselves together while others' backs were turned. 'Society is forgetful on the subject,' Peter resumed, puffing smoke at the ceiling. 'When you and I first met, we were offering our lives to our country. And a grateful country rewarded us with pennies but filled in the long hours of boredom by providing us with cheap and sometimes even free tobacco. Many years later, when we are good and hooked, society does an about-turn and decides that we are evil and that tobacco will kill us. We are not even accorded the rights traditionally given to other persecuted minorities. Not a word now about lands fit for heroes to smoke in.'

'It's time that they made up their minds,' I agreed. 'But perhaps the pendulum will swing back again. Many things that we used to be warned away from are now found to be good for us after all.'

Our conversation roamed, setting the world right. At one point I thought that he was about to explain the unadmitted visitor but we were distracted. An eye-watering smell seemed to fill the room. There was no doubt where it came from. Spin looked uncomfortable. Even the two Labradors seemed surprised.

'Oh dear!' Sir Peter said mildly. He held his cigar high above his head, but whether for fear of contamination or of an explosion I could not tell. 'This may put a crimp in our future relationship. I like a dog to be company as well as a worker.' I was feeling my drink but he was no more than mellow.

'At Three Oaks, the dogs are in outside kennels. John wouldn't know if a dog suffered from flatulence.'

'Well, I can't have him in here with me if he's going to do that all the time. And I don't suppose he'll be welcome in the kitchen. Or is there a cure?'

I sipped my brandy while I thought back to advice

that I had once heard John give to a horrified client. 'All is not lost,' I said. 'I don't know whether it's a palliative or a cure, but diet certainly helps. Charcoal biscuits. And the addition of bran to the feed.' I mentioned the name of a proprietary compound also recommended by John.

'I can believe charcoal,' Peter said. 'But bran? Who was it said that a fibre diet is never quiet?'

'Not I.'

Peter stubbed out his cigar. 'Many a true word spoken in jest. But you give me hope,' he said. 'Ronnie can go shopping for me in the morning. But for now, my new friend seems to have made this room uninhabitable. We'll give the dogs one last turn in the garden, and then I suggest bed.'

'I was going to have Spin with me for the first night,' I said as we went out into a warm spring night. 'But now I'm not so sure.'

Sir Peter humphed. 'The sooner he learns to sleep with the other two in the gun room, the better. Labradors don't mind a bit of a niff. Hope it doesn't corrode the guns.'

Chapter Two

I can never sleep late in a strange bed. In my youth I was able to drop into a deep sleep and snap awake, fully refreshed, seven or eight hours later, but with age has come sleep of a different order, deep at times but rising near the surface at others. During those periods of partial wakefulness I was aware of the unfamiliar softness, the different texture of the sheets and, later, filtered daylight of a different quality from that at home.

Sleep soon deserted me and I got up and went through my morning ritual. It was early, but I found Peter already working his way through a plate of bacon, eggs and fried bread – all the things loaded with choles-terol, in fact, that a man with a heart condition should avoid. Despite my sympathy with his stand against those embargoes which, taken all together, would soon ensure death from starvation or boredom, I contented myself with my usual breakfast of cereal and a slice of toast.

Spin had met me in the hall, but his greeting was no more than the usual 'Good morning!' rather than the frantic relief of a worried dog. The omens were good. He felt at home.

Some minutes later, Peter leaned back to look

under the long table where, I now realized, the other two dogs were curled together, awaiting handouts. 'Spin seemed to be making good progress yesterday,' he said. He buttered another slice of toast, cut it into thirds and distributed it under the table. 'And there was no howling in the night. I suppose it's still too early to shoot rabbits over him?'

'It is, if you care how he settles in,' I said firmly. 'Now is the time, before you've impressed him permanently with your status as pack leader, when he may begin to wonder if he doesn't know his job better than you do. Don't rush him. Keep up the training exercises today. See how he does and if all seems set we'll try him tomorrow. And don't look at me as though I'd stolen your rattle,' I added. 'He's your dog now and you can do as you like. I'm only here to advise.'

He gave a bark of laughter that fetched the dogs out from under the table. 'I'm sure it's good advice,' he said, 'and I'll stick with it. But nobody was ever thanked for handing out good but unwelcome advice. Patience never did rank high among my virtues and it seems to get scarcer as the days become more precious. If you've finished, shall we move?'

He had already given the dogs a morning walk and put Spin through his paces, he told me. We walked out into a cool, bright morning. 'If we can't shoot, shall we fish?' he suggested.

'I can go along with that,' I said.

A small lorry with a trailer behind it was coming up the drive. Peter clicked his tongue impatiently. 'It's the local builder,' Peter said. 'McAnderton. I do want a few words with him but I'll tell him that I can't waste time on him today.'

I fetched my rod and other gear. When I came out again, the builder's lorry was turning out of the archway and Peter was soon on my heels with a ready-assembled rod over his shoulder. We left the dogs. The Labradors seemed to understand that the presence of fishing rods meant that nothing of any interest was on the programme. We crossed the lawn and took a path through the wood. As we went, he said suddenly, 'That was my granddaughter who turned up during dinner last night. I suppose the Calders told you?'

'They didn't say a word.'

'Amazingly discreet of them, but it's really no secret. She is the daughter of my late son. She's all the relatives I have left, apart from a remote female cousin in Tasmania, so the baronetcy will die with me.' He broke off as we crossed a stile and then resumed. 'She's a student at Edinburgh University. Stays in a hall of residence. You might say that she's the reason I bother to go on living. I believe, sincerely believe,' he said fiercely, 'in giving them the freedom to learn from their own mistakes, but not if the mistakes are heading them towards disaster. She's taken up with a boyfriend – a lover, I suppose one has to assume these days – who I simply can't stand at any price. It broke my heart to turn her away but that lout does not cross my threshold and that's that. If he thinks he can seduce his way into a fortune he can think again.' He had been working himself up. His hand shook and I could hear a similar tremor in his breathing. 'Forgive my crudeness, my dear chap,' he added more gently. 'It gets me hot under the collar to think about it.'

'I understand,' I said. I tried to lighten his mood.

'I'd probably feel the same way. Fortunately, I don't have to.'

'God spared you?'

'Exactly. There was a time when Isobel and I felt cheated because we had no children. Now, as we see our friends driven to distraction, we realize that fate was smiling on us.'

He stopped suddenly in the middle of the path. 'Perhaps you really are the lucky ones. There's so little one can do. To be so impotent . . . Tell me something,' he said. 'You're almost ages with me. Do you find life still worth living?'

He meant it as a serious question and I gave it serious thought. 'It's not something I think about very often,' I replied after a moment. 'I accept the aches and pains and not being able to do everything that I used to do. On the other hand, I've settled into a good sort of life and I take full advantage of the privileges of age. Sometimes it gets boring but I've no real complaints. And you?'

He started walking again. 'Sometimes I feel that the aches and pains curve is about to intersect with the joy of living curve and it's time I was away. And I've no stomach any more for the hassle of business. Perhaps I'm tired, tired. You see, it's always been in my nature to look forward, but now there's so little forward left and looking back I seem to remember nothing but my mistakes. I can't start anything and be sure that I'll be around to finish it. But then I come to a morning like this and go fishing with a friend, and I'm damned if I won't struggle on for a few more years.' He was looking more relaxed. His colour had improved.

I found that I was flattered that he should think of me as a friend.

The wood was more a series of glades and tree strips. Well-grown pheasants, the survivors of last year's birds, were scuttling about in the undergrowth. We spent the next hour on the banks of a small loch. It was half-hidden among the trees but these had been kept back from the waterside to allow for careful overhead casting. The presence of fish was attested by occasional splashy rises, but they seemed totally uninterested in my various offerings. Peter, on the far side of the loch, I noticed, was casting skilfully with a beautiful old split-cane rod, laying a long, straight line dead to the centre of the previous ring on the water, but with no better result.

Before long, we were interrupted. From across the water I heard the beep of a mobile phone. I knew that he carried one but had assumed that this was for the same reason that I carried mine – in case of another heart attack or other emergency while alone in the countryside. Peter walked around the loch to join me. He looked tired. 'I have to go into Newton Lauder,' he said. 'I tried to clear a few days for fun and games but business still calls and sometimes I have to listen. Unless you have other ideas, I suggest that you fish on and then join me for lunch at the hotel, around one.'

I said that that sounded a reasonable programme and he nodded. 'I'll tell Mary that we'll both be out. If you get there too early, you could call in at Keith's shop across the Square. It's always good for a browse. If I hurry I'll have time to put Spin through his paces once more before I go.'

I was left to my own devices. A trout rose nearby.

The only insect life seemed to be the midges on the water so I made up a team of three Black Gnats and persevered. Either the selection was right or my luck had turned. By noon I had three acceptable brown trout on the bank. What seemed like a few minutes later I glanced at my watch and found that I had left it rather late. I hurried back to the house, patted all three dogs on the way through the garden, delivered my fish to Mrs Fiddler, made myself comparatively respectable and drove into the town.

Parking in the Square, I cast a regretful glance across to the shop – almost dwarfed by the small supermarket next door – where a display of knives, pigeon decoys and fishing tackle on a foundation of cartridge boxes caught the eye of anyone with a sporting bent. There was no doubt that it was my sort of place. But the CLOSED sign was already in the glass door and my host would be waiting. I hurried into the hotel.

I found Peter Hay in the cocktail bar. He was deep in discussion with a fat, bald little man of about my own age, but he spotted me through the gathering of lunchtime drinkers and the two came to meet me.

I shook hands with Ralph Enterkin, the stranger. 'How was the fishing?'

'Improving. I got three after you left,' I told Peter. 'Just under a pound each.'

He seemed genuinely pleased. 'Well done,' he said. 'Mary will be delighted. Trout is one of her many specialities. I'm afraid my mind wasn't really on the job. I've booked a table. Ralph is lunching with us. Shall we go through? You can have your drink at the table. We'll be more private.'

He was right. The bars had been almost packed but

we had the dining room to ourselves. Most of the locals, it seemed, preferred a bar snack to a full lunch on a weekday. The other two were in abstemious mood but Peter invited me to order whatever I wanted to drink. I said that I would be satisfied with a pint of beer and it was brought through from the bar by a cheerfully plump lady whose attractiveness managed to shine through the layers of fat. I wondered whether Newton Lauder was renowned for the beauty of its female population or if perhaps, now that I had reached the age at which my sexual activities were usually limited to mere voyeurism, all female persons had started to look beautiful to me. I was relieved when our food was delivered by a waitress who could by no stretch of my imagination have been called beautiful.

Mr Enterkin was on easy terms with the more attractive waitress. He did not seem to be the sort of man to be 'carrying on' with a barmaid and this became even less likely when he excused himself for a moment and Peter explained that he was the premier local solicitor. Enterkin and I soon discovered that our reminiscences intersected, as he had had some involvement on the legal side in several major cases of fraud in which my bank had nearly or actually suffered. He had even prepared the defence of one of the fraudsters who I knew for a fact to be as guilty as sin and, to my indignation, had stage-managed his acquittal, a minor miracle for which Enterkin showed no shame. In his view, he said, if the law said that somebody was guilty or innocent then it was so, even if he personally knew the reverse to be the case. During the course of a pleasant lunch I was drawn out on the subject of my experiences in merchant banking and it may be that an attentive and flattering audience led me into being too expansive on the subject.

When the meal was finished Mr Enterkin withdrew, remarking that he could be found in his office for the rest of the working day. I thought that he had exchanged with Peter a glance, the significance of which was lost on me. Peter looked at me searchingly for a few seconds.

'I have something to ask of you,' he said seriously. 'It seems that the hour produces the man. Ralph Enterkin handles all my local business and family affairs. He also has charge of my will, although he gives it a fancier name. He, individually, is named as one of the executors. But although he's a good lawyer he'd be the first to admit that he has his limitations. He knows company law but he has little experience of the machinations of high finance. And as far as he's concerned the value of farming is entirely scenic. He can carry out the conveyancing or draw up a lease, but if he was asked a question about good farming practice, he'd be lost. On the other hand, I seem to remember you saying that you were brought up on a farm and you certainly seemed to be familiar with estate management when we were associated in the past.

'The other executors of my will were an Edinburgh firm of solicitors who have been handling any broader business matters and also factoring the farms. Unfortunately, I've had to drop them and I need a replacement as co-executor, somebody who I can trust and who has wide financial experience. I'm making provision for a substantial fee. So what do you think? Would you care to act?'

'I've been retired for a good few years,' I said doubtfully.

'But you've kept up with the world of business.'

'How would you know that?'

'I watched you at breakfast with the newspaper. You turned to the business pages first and the news afterwards.'

'The news is filled with disasters and politicians doing the expedient thing,' I explained.

'Can you separate the two? You've just put your finger on the reason why, apart from two ventures onto the Regional Council, I've steered very clear of politics.'

'You never thought of parliament?'

'I was invited to stand, more than once. I couldn't have faced the hypocrisy of it all. I see that a recent survey found that eighty-six per cent of the public mistrusted all politicians. What I want to know is, where are the other fourteen per cent? I never met any of them.' He laughed shortly and then returned to the original subject. 'And it would have meant being away from here for longer than I'd have liked. Life's too short for that.'

His words were a reminder. 'I could predecease you,' I pointed out.

He shrugged. 'In that eventuality I should have to look around yet again. But I think it unlikely. You've had one minor heart attack, I think you said?'

'True,' I said. 'But who's counting?'

'I am. I've had four and two bypasses,' he told me, not without a touch of pride, 'and now I'm on a pacemaker.'

The exchange had given me time to think. I had

been admitting to myself that retirement, although pleasant, had seldom offered any mental stimulus. Perhaps this was my chance to savour again the challenge of responsibility. If, that is, Peter should ever die. Despite what he had said, he seemed immortal. And although I was ostensibly there on business I was in fact the guest of a generous host and I had been wondering how to repay his hospitality. 'I'll be happy to be named,' I said.

'That's splendid! I'm immensely grateful, my dear fellow. I must just pop in and see Ralph again for a few minutes. Why don't you go back to the house? Have a walk or a rest or a cup of tea or something. Go fishing again if you like. I'll be with you again shortly and we can think what to do with whatever's left of the afternoon.'

We parted in the Square, which was really a triangle. Peter headed for an old-fashioned three-storey block of what seemed to be offices across the narrow end of the triangle. The programme that he had suggested seemed reasonable but first I headed for the gun shop. I was served with cartridges by a thin, grey-haired man with a slight stammer, who I took to be Keith Calder's partner and who was helpfully knowledgeable about the best trout-flies for the time and place.

I carried my purchases out to my car and drove back up the hill.

As I headed up the avenue towards the house I saw that a group of people were clustered around the front door and a motorcycle, crowned by two helmets, was standing on the gravel.

'Here's Mr Kitts,' Mary Fiddler said as I walked to

the door. She and Joanna seemed to be barring entry to a young man and woman, both of who were dressed in leathers. 'He'll know. Mr Kitts, is Sir Peter coming back?'

'Not just for the moment,' I said cautiously. 'He went to see his solicitor.'

There was a passing flicker of movement or hesitation, I could not be sure which. The girl, who was pretty enough in a soft but rather sulky way, asked the sky, 'Who is this man?' Her hair was on the borderline between blonde and brunette.

'Yeah, who is he?' echoed the youth.

'Mr Kitts is staying here as Sir Peter's guest,' Mary said firmly.

They weighed me up. 'Well, I'm his granddaughter,' said the girl as though trumping my ace. 'This is my home but the servants won't let me inside.'

'I'm sure you're very welcome to come in, Miss Elizabeth,' Mary said. 'But Sir Peter's orders were clear. The young man stays outside.'

'Did you ever hear anything so ridiculous?' the girl asked me. Apparently I was now to be the mediator. 'This is my fiancé and he can't come into my home while I collect a few things.'

'I'm sorry,' I said, 'but I can't help. What your grandfather says goes around here.'

'That's right,' Mary said approvingly. 'Just ring when you want to come inside, Mr Kitts. You too, Miss, if it's just you.' And with that the two women withdrew inside and the door was closed and locked.

'I guess they mean it,' said the girl. 'You'd better kick your heels out here for the moment, Dog-face.' She rang the bell and after a moment was admitted. I heard an angry voice through the timber but the words were unintelligible. I could have entered the house with the girl, but I must confess that curiosity made me linger outside.

'What does the old man have against me?' the young man demanded. I looked at him for the first time. He was tall and well built, but his frame was topped by a face with inappropriately delicate, almost feminine, features. An attempt at a smile revealed prominent incisors. His eyes seemed ready to settle anywhere except on mine. He seemed to be sweating, but it was a warm afternoon for motorcycle leathers. On the basis of a first impression, gained in the first few seconds, I could understand Peter's suspicions.

But I could hardly say so. I temporized. 'I don't know you well enough to make a guess,' I said. 'From long experience, I can tell you that it can be a revealing mental exercise to compare the people who like you with those who don't. You're doing well if you're liked by the people you like and vice versa.'

He thought about that for a few seconds without seeming to derive any pleasure from his thoughts. 'Well, I don't care about that,' he said at last. 'I'm going to marry his granddaughter and the old man can like it or lump it.'

'I think you'll find that there'll have to be a few changes before he'll give his consent,' I told him.

I could almost see the wheels turning in his head. Really, he was a most unintelligent young man for a student, if that was what he was, and charmless with it. The girl, I supposed, must have seen something in him, but the mating instinct can foster more delusions than the DTs.

'The granddad'll come round,' he said.

'He might,' I said. 'Eventually. But if you're thinking of speeding up the process by means of a touch of pregnancy, I think you should put it out of your mind. I've known him for about half a century and my bet would be that he'd hire a hitman to deal with you and then marry her off to some suitable young laird. He's got the money, he's got the contacts and from what I've seen of him in business he's got more than enough ruthlessness when his blood's up.'

'He wouldn't,' the young man said, without any very great conviction.

'I don't think I'd advise you to bet your life on it. He hates to have his hand forced.' I lowered my voice. 'If I were in your shoes and I couldn't restrain myself, I would practise the safest sex since family planning was invented. And I suggest that you take your own precautions. Girls have been known to omit taking the pill . . .'

He opened his mouth several times without finding an answer so I rang the bell. When the door opened to let me in it also let out the girl Elizabeth. She passed me with a look of disdain and soon afterwards I heard the motorbike roar off down the drive.

I settled in one of the comfortable wing-chairs in the sitting room and, as has been my habit over the last few years, promised myself a five-minute nap. When I awoke an hour later, much refreshed, Peter was resting in another chair. He stirred when I did and we yawned in unison. We gathered our wits in silence for a minute or two.

'Mary tells me that Liza was here with that young lout of hers,' he said disgustedly. 'And she left you to deal with the pair of them. She shouldn't have done that. You're a guest.'

'I didn't mind,' I said. 'I only hope you approve of the line I took.' I recounted the whole short confrontation.

Peter chose to be very much amused. 'You certainly struck a blow for family planning,' he said. 'Proper little Marie Stopes. But I'm glad you put a spoke in that particular wheel. My innocent mind would never have thought of insemination as a weapon of blackmail.'

'Nor of a hitman to counter it?'

'As to that, no comment. And this conversation never took place. If – what did she call him? – if Dog-face should happen to be found embedded in a Glasgow flyover, I wouldn't want you remembering that we had discussed any such possibility as a solution to a thoroughly unsatisfactory liaison. Ho-hum! Why do the young always think that they invented sex?'

'I was only guessing as to which way his little mind was working. I may have wronged him.'

'I doubt it. Anyway, that type can do with a good wronging now and again. And now,' he said more cheerfully, 'one or two of my tenants have been complaining about pigeon damage to the young wheat.'

'We should certainly do something about that,' I said.

'By the time we could get set up with decoys, they'll be thinking about going to roost. So do you fancy a roost-shoot? Or would you say that Spin wasn't ready for that yet?'

A pigeon shoot, carefully handled, would not

expose a young dog to a tenth of the temptations presented by a rabbit hunt. 'I think it's a good idea,' I said.
'If you can keep him sitting beside you, not on a lead,
while you drop a few woodies, I'd say that he was
ready to take the next step.'

'Then let's go! *En avant, mon brave*! School's out!'
With these and similar cries he hustled me to my feet
and out of the room. By the time I returned downstairs,
in shooting breeks and boots and with cartridges in
a game-bag over my shoulder, he had the guns out
of the gun room. I had brought gloves and a peaked
cap with me in my pockets – nothing spooks an
approaching woodpigeon like the sudden movement
of a white face or hands or a balding head.

At my insistence, we paused on the lawn to put
Spin through his paces yet again and as we walked I
had the two Labradors on leads while Peter walked
Spin at heel, leaving him sitting now and again and
whistling him up after we had gone out of sight. It
never does any harm to have the young dog freshly
reminded of his subordinate status when setting out,
or a new owner reminded of the need to maintain
discipline. Peter had already provided himself with a
pocket full of charcoal biscuits which he dispensed
to all three dogs. Seeing the guns, the Labs roused
themselves from their habitual placidity and even Old
Nick had a semblance of a spring in his step.

Our way diverged from the path to the trout-loch
and led us through a long finger of woodland. We clattered through a short tunnel under what seemed to be
an old railway embankment. As we emerged I heard
a cock pheasant rocket up, clocking indignantly.
Immediately, a figure appeared from the direction of

what looked like a release pen. He was a tall man, slightly stooped. His head was almost entirely covered by a beard and whiskers with a mop of hair to match, so that a small face seemed to peep out from the middle of a ball of brown knitting wool.

'This is Hamish, my keeper,' Peter said. 'Hamish, this is Mr Kitts. He's staying with me. We were . . . we're going to wait for the cushies to come in to Langstane Wood. I take it that that's all right?' he asked anxiously.

Hamish had a firm, strong handshake. 'Aye,' he said. 'Fairly that. Until the young birds go out in July. Any of the old buggers around from last year will sit tight or come back later. But keep clear of the corner where the big oak stands. There's two hens nesting in the hedge nearaboot.'

'We'll be careful,' Peter promised. We walked on. 'Sometimes I wonder who works for who,' he said when we were out of earshot. 'I don't know why I stand for it, except that he's a bloody good keeper. Single-handed, too, though Ronnie helps him out when he's busy. As good as his father, who was another Hamish.'

Our path joined a track which brought us uphill to the edge of the trees and a metal gate in the surrounding fence. I found that we were looking across fields roughly bowl shaped to farm buildings on the further rise.

'Home Farm,' Peter said. 'The others are all tenanted. I used to farm this one myself but now I leave it to a manager.'

The two Labradors moved in close to me. When Spin strayed a yard from Peter's heel, the baronet called him back sharply. 'You be careful too,' he added in my direction. 'Most electric fences around these parts are fed from a battery, and if the battery isn't freshly charged you could sit on one of them without feeling more than a tingle. But Geordie Jennings, my farm manager, doesn't waste time with batteries.' Peter pointed to the group of farm buildings on the far slope. 'The tractor shed's close to the boundary, so he uses a transformer off the mains to power a fence that goes right round the fields he uses for stock. It can give you a jolt, I can tell you. I let my gun barrels touch the fence once while I was opening the gate and I thought for a moment that I'd been shot. There's a damn sight more than twelve volts going through the fence. How he hasn't killed any cattle yet I do not know, but when I tell him about it he blinds me with science about volts and joules and ergs and things. The ground's always damp here, too.'

I nodded my understanding. Cattle are very vulnerable to electrocution. A faulty milking machine has been known to decimate a herd. An electrified cattle fence is rather more sophisticated than Peter was implying, but this was not the time to set him right. Peter opened the gate and we passed through carefully. The top strand was insulated from the timber fence posts by black rubber insulators and the wire crossed the gateway in an underground sleeve. The field before us was given to young oilseed rape which showed signs of serious rabbit damage, but beyond was a large pasture.

We headed left, following the edge of the wood, climbed a stile and crossed another grass field. Cattle watched us from the far end, wondered whether to panic or to come in search of food and decided not to bother. We passed through a wooden gate in a plain wire fence into a wood of tall deciduous trees, all of a hundred years old, in bright young leaf. The trees had either been thinned or they were planted well apart, because enough sunlight reached the ground to have encouraged an undergrowth, bramble and nettles predominating.

'You take that end,' Peter said, nodding to our left. 'Anchor those beggars or they'll run in, sure as anything. I'll go the other way.'

I led my two charges towards the corner of the wood. And there I encountered a familiar dilemma. If I retreated to a position where I would be hidden from incoming birds, they would be hidden from me. If I gave myself a good field of fire, they would see me from far off. In the end, as usual, I was forced to compromise. An alder which had taken root in one of the glades offered me a degree of concealment and I had only to sway aside to get a fair view of the sky. I attached the two dogs to the base of the tree and prepared for action. I did not have long to wait. Pigeon are the first birds to head for their night-time roost just as mallard are usually the last.

I have experienced some tricky shooting in my day – red grouse on the moor, ptarmigan on the high tops, driven partridges bursting over a hedge, or geese a long gunshot overhead – but I believe that woodpigeon coming in above the treetops are among the most difficult of quarries. High, deceptively fast birds, they must be swung through and led, but the human tendency is to check the swing of the gun as it passes every trunk and branch. I have seen a champion clay-pigeon shot reduced to tears of frustration until he learned to adjust his mental approach.

The streamlined shapes might have come in a single flock and clattered out at the first shot, but in fact they came in their twos and threes, in a trickle rather than a flood, but a slow trickle which lasted for nearly two hours. To make it more difficult, they were coming out of the sun and I suspected my crafty friend of knowing it and giving himself an advantage. I wasted my first few shots and then began to connect.

The light was beginning to fade when Peter came out of the trees, carrying a heavy game-bag and with Spin at heel. I broke open my gun.

'All's well,' he said. 'Steady as a rock. And between us we've picked up twenty-six.'

'I think I've nineteen down,' I said. 'It's difficult to be sure.'

He nodded. 'They're out of sight a millisecond after you've pulled the trigger,' he said. 'We'll have to pack up now or Mary will get worried and send Ronnie to find us and then he'll be aggrieved that his supper's been spoiled. Let's go and make her day. She does a pigeon pilaff that you'll have to taste to believe.'

I had picked up those birds that had fallen nearby and in the open as we went along. I unleashed the Labradors. Spin and Royston worked with a will, but when they came back and lay down, as if to say that that was all that there was, I was sure that I was still one short.

Peter looked at his watch. 'You probably missed it,' he said. 'We'll have to be going.'

'You could be right,' I told him. 'But I saw one fold up and fall over there and I haven't seen one brought from that direction. As you say, I could be wrong, but I'd hate to risk leaving a runner to suffer.'

As I spoke, I pointed into the trees.

That was enough. Old Nick, who had been reclining under the alder, watching his juniors perform with rather the air of an emperor overlooking his slaves, sighed and struggled to his feet. He walked stiffly through the weeds for some fifty yards. I heard him grunt as his head went down and came up again with a pigeon, dead, in his jaws. He came back as slowly, handed me the pigeon and then sat. He looked disinterested but I thought that there was about him a touch of smug triumph. There was life in the old dog yet.

Peter patted him and then stooped to fondle Spin. 'Never you mind,' he said. 'You did your best. Oh Lord!' He looked up at me. 'His coat's full of burrs.'

'That's what you get when you take on a spaniel. I hate to break it to you but you'll spend the rest of your days picking them out. And ticks don't show up as they do on a Labrador, you have to search for them.'

'Any more bad news?'

'John always says that God made spaniels and sponges on the same day. A Lab sheds the water but a wet spaniel is a wet, wet pet.'

'A soggy doggy?' Peter straightened his back. 'I didn't know that you could get burrs so early in the year,' he said glumly. 'Well, you're never too old to learn.'

Chapter Three

I was woken next morning by the sound of whistling and occasional words of command. Peter Hay was putting Spin through his paces on the lawn below my window. I would have liked to take it as a sign that he could be trusted to maintain discipline after I had left him to his own devices, but I suspected that, rather than zeal as a trainer, his noisy activity was due to his eagerness to have me up and about. I knew exactly what was in his mind and so I put on the oldest clothes that I had with me. Spin was to be tested on the rabbits. Peter had already taken all three dogs for their morning exercise.

I thought that in some ways Peter, despite his years, had retained a schoolboyish zest for the fun things in life. But in matters of business he was still the crisp and methodical man I remembered from long ago. There had been no guests the night before and after dinner he had taken me into his study, a room where the latest office electronics contrasted strangely with the comfortable chairs and book-lined walls, and there, with the dogs around our feet and another brace of cigars tainting the air, he had insisted on demonstrating how to explore the ramifications of his business interests. I had begun to wonder what my rash agreement to be named as co-executor had let me in for. Not only were those interests wide and apparently handsome, but Peter's insistence that I should know how to access every scrap of information made the whole exercise seem real instead of a mere token courtesy to a friend. It was lucky, I thought, that the assistance I had given to Isobel in connection with her computer programs had kept me at least partially in touch if not absolutely familiar with business technology.

However, the evening had not been all gloom and foreboding. Peter remained a charming and witty host. Moreover, there had been only one more sudden smell, and that of a relatively minor potency, barely detectable in the haze of cigar smoke. I had suggested that those of the previous evening might perhaps have been due to no more than a passing upset or a change of diet, but Peter swore by the efficacy of the charcoal biscuits and continued to dispense them to the dogs as he might have given sweets to a child.

Peter curbed his impatience and worked alone in the study until I had finished my breakfast, by which time the guns and gear were waiting in the hall. To be frank, I was almost as anxious as Peter to see whether the ingrained discipline had been properly transferred along with what one can only consider to be 'leadership of the pack' but, mischievously, I dallied until I thought that he was probably ready to burst. Then I put my head in at the study door, catching him with a ferocious frown on his face and, 'Come along,' I said. 'I thought you wanted to shoot.'

He looked at me pop-eyed. I thought that he was looking even older than usual. Then he laughed and stored his work onto the disc. 'I do. And Hamish has been warned, so the sound of a shot or two won't bring him down on us.' He switched off the computer and almost leaped to his feet.

But we suffered another delay. We were in the hall and gathering up our gear when Peter looked out through the glazed screen that fronted that part of the house and said, 'Ten thousand damnations! The stars in their courses are fighting against me! I'll have to ask you to hang on here for a minute. And if I come in to collect my gun before she's gone, don't let me have it.'

He hurried outside. I saw that a woman was getting out of a shining car. She was too far away for me to make out any details or to hear any words of the exchange, but it was clear from the body language that an altercation was taking place. Peter's posture was rigid. Once, the woman gestured towards the house and in his reply Peter several times pointed down the drive. After a few minutes of argument the woman acceded, got into the car and drove round the circle and away.

Peter returned, breathing heavily through dilated nostrils. 'Some people,' he said, 'can't take no for an answer. And when I decide to give the handling of something over to my lawyer, I don't expect to be badgered in person.' With an effort, he relaxed and even smiled. 'But never mind. If I imagine that harpy's face on every rabbit, my marksmanship will improve beyond recognition.'

I took up my bagged gun and my game-bag, but my attention was more on the camera in my pocket. If all went well, Peter might like a record of the day. The two Labradors were indignant at being left behind, but there were to be no distractions on this testing occasion. Ronnie let it be seen that he, too, was hurt at being left out. Three reproachful pairs of eyes followed us out of sight.

We followed the same path as on the previous day. The sound of hammering from the direction of the release pen suggested that Hamish was preparing for the delivery of pheasant poults a little later in the year. Peter walked on until the sound was coming from rather behind us and then unsleeved his gun, a Churchill Premier. I left my W&C Scott in its sleeve slung on my shoulder and, instead, produced my Leica. 'I'll follow behind you,' I said. 'Before I join in the fun, I'll record your first triumphs.'

'Or tragedies,' he retorted. He stooped to pick up a piece of paper, the wrapper from a chocolate bar, and slipped it into his pocket. 'I don't grudge the public access to the land, as long as they behave and don't let their dogs run wild,' he said, 'but I do wish they'd take their rubbish home with them.'

'You really love your land, don't you?' I said.

He thought about it. 'I suppose I do,' he said. 'I never stopped to consider it before. My life's been bound up with it. It provides my daily bread and keeps me off the streets.' He was smiling. The boyish expression was making a comeback.

'And it provides you with your shooting,' I pointed out.

'Of course it does. But you don't farm for the shooting, that's a sure way to lose money. At least, it used to be before this age of set-aside and diversification. But when the work's done and the harvest's in . . .' He blinked at me. 'It's just another form of harvesting. The fact that it's a very *companionable* one is a bonus. But man found it necessary to co-operate and organize in order to hunt his meat, for ten times as long as he was ever a farmer. Even wild animals do the same. I suppose that's why we still find it necessary to elect leaders even when we'd be a damn sight better off without them.'

'And that's why your dog has to know that you're the pack leader,' I reminded him.

'Heavens yes!' He looked at me vaguely. He raised his hand and Spin sat obediently. Peter's mind was miles away for the moment. 'What the women and the townies don't understand,' he said, 'is that man has always had to be the defender and the hunter. I don't suppose that he sought those roles, he just fell into them. So of course aggression and hunting both come naturally to him. Starve the hunting instinct and the other makes an appearance.' He stirred. 'Oh well. Let's get on with it. We came out to enjoy ourselves, not to philosophize.' He was smiling again – at himself, I thought.

Peter cast Spin out. The cover was open and I watched the pair of them. I could see that already Peter was elated. I hoped that he was not in for a fall. In dog training, the safest thing to expect is disappointment.

The spaniel settled into his to-and-fro hunting pattern, moving at a speed disconcerting to Peter who was used to the more deliberate gait of the Labrador. He was slow with the 'turn' whistle and Spin, sensing hesitation, might well have started to take advantage. But I saw the nose go down as he met a trail and soon he was hunting a scent across our front. Something raced through the dead grass and low bilberry bushes.

50

Peter mounted his gun and fired. Spin dropped and sat tight, waiting for the word. But Peter walked forward and looked down. Then he raised his voice. 'Hamish!'

His cry was acknowledged from a distance. Soon, the keeper appeared at a fast trot. He looked down at Peter's quarry – a large, ginger tom-cat now lying dead. 'M'hm,' was all that Hamish said but there was a world of approval in the sound.

Peter called Spin to him and gave him a pat and a charcoal biscuit. 'Got the bugger at last,' he said. 'Just shows what a difference a good spaniel can make. We've been after this one for a year,' he added to me. 'Seemed to get in and out of a release pen as easy as going through a cat flap, electric wires and loose overhangs notwithstanding.'

'Aye,' Hamish said. 'I'll fetch a spade.'

'Take him with you,' Peter suggested. 'Save coming back.'

'Right.'

Hamish bent and lifted the ginger corpse by the back legs. As he did so, a figure appeared round a clump of holly from the direction of the gate.

'Oh God!' Peter said softly. 'Here's trouble. Our local cat lover. Lives near the farm. Name's Snot, or something very like it. Pray God this isn't his.'

'We should be so lucky,' Hamish muttered. 'And his name's Synott.'

The new arrival was a tall man, thin apart from a small pot belly, dressed in bright-green corduroys and a yellow shirt. He had a small, sand-coloured beard around a weak mouth and hair of similar colour was draped across his bald crown. My first thought was that he did not look like the sort of person whom I would

welcome into my circle of friends. 'Have you seen – '
he began. Then he paused and his eyes bulged. He
seemed very close to apoplexy. He pointed a shaking
finger at the dead cat, which Hamish was half-
heartedly trying to hide behind his leg. 'You've killed
Xanadu!' he cried in tones of disbelief.

'Is . . . was this your cat?' Peter enquired.

'He certainly was. My favourite. Why would
anybody do a thing like that?' he asked the branches
overhead. 'How could you bring yourself . . .? The most
gentle . . . loving . . .' His wild eyes came back to Peter.
'You must be evil. But you won't get away with murder.
I'm going to the police.'

'We'll go together,' Peter said, his voice tight but
controlled. 'We've been after that bastard for a year or
more, because of the damage he's been doing.'

'Xanadu would never have hurt a fly,' Synott protested.

Hamish uttered a snort of derision. 'I've seen that
orange bugger take pheasant chicks, aye, and song-
birds. It was him took that firecrest you was in such a
tizzy aboot.' He turned the carcass over and looked at
its mouth. 'Aye. The bugger's had another pheasant
chick. Look at it, the wee feather.'

'You've just put it there, to exonerate yourselves!'
In his fury, Synott's voice had become a squeal.

I decided to interfere, even if I had to embroider
just a little. I had taken a strong dislike to Mr Synott.
'I photographed the whole incident,' I said, lifting the
camera. 'Nobody put anything near the cat's mouth.
We'll see what the photographs show.'

'I don't believe any of it. I've never known him
stray far from home before.'

Hamish laughed bitterly.

'You were quick enough to come looking for him here,' Peter pointed out. 'I think you knew damn well where he was in the habit of hunting. Over the last couple of years he's taken . . . how many birds would you say, Hamish? A hundred?'

'Double that,' Hamish said. 'At the very least.'

'Worth about twenty quid each in a bag at the end of a let day,' Peter resumed. 'Not to mention my keeper's time and expenses trying to protect his birds against your pet. And then, of course, the extra mesh and electric wires . . .'

'We had to bring in a fencing contractor,' Hamish said, apparently to remind his employer. I could see that the pair of them were improvising wildly and enjoying it.

'That's so,' Peter said gravely. 'Now that I can prove whose cat was doing the damage, by his own admission in front of three witnesses, I must consider whether I go to law about it. If you want to live in the country, you must accept the responsibilities that go with it. Certainly, if you stir up any trouble you'll force my hand.'

Synott's face, already pasty had turned very white. He shook his head and began to back away.

'Here,' Hamish said. He held out the remains. 'Take your cat. No doubt you'll be wanting to hold a burial. Or have it stuffed and mounted.'

To the unaccustomed, anything dead but not yet turned into parcels of packaged meat can be a frightening reminder of mortality. Synott uttered a squawk of horror. He turned and fled.

'You conned the poor man,' I said. 'You wouldn't have a hope in hell of recovering damages at law.'

Both men grinned. 'By the time he finds that out,' Peter said, 'he'll be too late to cause trouble. And you know damn well your photographs wouldn't have proved a thing. Come on. Despite a shaky beginning this could be turning into a very satisfactory morning.'

After all the disturbance, any rabbits in the neighbourhood would have fled or be safely underground. Peter called Spin to heel and we walked on down to the metal gate.

We came to a halt. 'You see the farm buildings,' Peter said, pointing.

I said that I did.

'You see the small house just to the right of them?'

The farm buildings were near the skyline opposite us, two fields away. Beyond and to the left there were more houses in the distance, but after a moment I picked out a roof, almost lost among trees, near the farm buildings.

'That's where Snot lives,' Peter said.

'Synott,' I reminded him.

'I keep forgetting his real name. Freudian, I suppose. At my age, the memory for names gets unreliable – especially for names one would rather never hear again. That was the original farmhouse, but the farm manager before Geordie had an enormous brood so I built him a larger house, a quarter of a mile the other side, and let Snot have the smaller house – on a long lease, unfortunately, but that was before I discovered what a pain in the backside he could be. He illustrates children's books, quite prettily, and rashly I assumed that anyone whose work had so much charm

couldn't be all bad. I was wrong,' he added. 'I was
looking for a favour in return at the time, so perhaps
I was predisposed to be taken in. Well, let's get on.'

We passed through the gate. Spin walked at Peter's
heel though he still showed an occasional tendency to
switch to mine. Peter led us away to the left. We passed
the wood where we had ambushed the woodpigeons
and took to a track which curved round the shoulder
of a low hill. We climbed a stile over the electric fence
which Peter said marked the boundary between two
farms. The far slope was of grass, patchy with gorse
and the scrapes of many rabbits. As we came over the
crest I saw the flicker of many white tails bobbing for
cover. There was no doubt that the rabbit population
was too high. Left to nature, the balance might be
redressed by myxomatosis or predation but I agreed
with the view that the shotgun was more humane.

It was obvious that Peter had shot the ground many
times. He knew exactly which clumps of gorse contained rabbit holes and which were over rock. I was
still not shooting but my presence was enough to turn
a bolting rabbit just the same. Peter placed me near
the holes and himself where he could best intercept
rabbits running for cover. Then he set Spin to work.

All went well. A bolting rabbit is a temptation for
a dog to chase which is almost irresistible. Almost, but
not quite. A perfectly trained dog will seldom if ever
commit the dangerous and disruptive sin of 'running-
in', though the time of transfer of ownership, while
the dog is testing the mettle of its new handler, is a
time of danger. But Spin was well trained and, although
I was sure that Peter was usually an indulgent owner,
under my stern eye he gave a credible imitation of one

who would stand no nonsense. Spin hunted the bushes, sat whenever the rabbits bolted and fetched the slain when directed. He was in his seventh heaven – there is no dog so happy and fulfilled as one that is doing what it was bred and trained for. When I had all the photographs that Peter was likely to want, I put the camera away and joined in the work.

By mid-morning we had a satisfactory row of rabbits, neatly paunched and laid out in the shade of a clump of hawthorns. We two old gentlemen had walked further than we would have dreamed of walking in ordinary circumstances, but it is amazing how a gun under the arm pulls you along. We took a rest on a low wall while we wiped our hands on the grass and then on paper tissues. Spin lapped from a cattle trough and then sprawled at our feet.

'We could start back soon,' Peter said. 'Don't want to exhaust the little beast.'

'He could keep up that pace all day,' I told him.

'Well, I couldn't.' He beamed. 'All this hard work has made a happy man feel very old. We'll leave the rabbits here. Ronnie can bring transport round later and collect them. We keep some for our own use and give the rest away to anyone who wants them. A lot of them get fed to dogs, but at least they're not wasted. I can't abide waste of good meat.' He bent down and gave Spin a pat and a tug of the ears. The spaniel's short tail rustled in the grass. 'We're going to get along like a house on fire,' Peter told him, 'as long as I don't spoil you the way I've spoiled those other daft beggars. I'm too soft, that's my trouble.' The tail thumped again. Spin, without understanding the words, knew that he was being spoken to kindly.

After a few minutes' rest, we were ready to move. Peter whistled cheerfully as he walked. But as we passed Langstane Wood, where we had shot the pigeons, he said suddenly, 'But, my dear chap, I've been very selfish. You've hardly had a shot.'

'I've enjoyed myself,' I said truthfully. I steadied the camera on a fence post and took a shot of the scenery.

'So have I. But that's not the point.' We arrived at the tip of the long finger of woodland. Peter placed me carefully. 'You stand here,' he said, 'and for the Lord's sake don't touch that fence. I'll take the little fellow round to the gate and we'll push back down towards you through the trees. You'll find that they come out there or there.' He pointed out the rabbits' favourite exits and the routes which they habitually followed.

He set off, pausing to wave to a distant figure. He and the spaniel turned the corner of the wood and were out of my sight. I loaded my gun and waited. Patience was no hardship in that gentle sunshine. The countryside was looking its best. Even the cattle looked as if they had been shampooed.

I had noticed a pair of blackbirds nesting near where Peter had shot the cat. I listened for their shrill alarm call but it never came. After what seemed an eternity I decided that something must be wrong, or else Peter had been delayed. I walked round the corner of the trees.

As soon as the gate came into view I saw a shape on the ground beside it. I broke into a run, or as close to a run as I could manage, carrying my gun and the weight of the years.

Sir Peter Hay was lying beside the gate, showing no signs of life.

By the time I had reached him and lowered myself to my knees – not a process to be hurried any more – I had my priorities roughly ordered in my mind. I thought that I could hear a vehicle somewhere but there was nearer help than that. In the hope that Hamish was within earshot I let out a bellow that made my head swim. A check for pulse and respiration gave me no reassurance. Peter might have gone down ten seconds or ten minutes earlier, I had no way of knowing. I gave him the kiss of life for a full half-minute, ignoring as best I could the unnatural feel of slight stubble between us, and then tried the procedure for heart massage, one-handed, while I fished out my mobile phone and keyed the Emergency Services.

I resumed the kiss of life, but the emergency operator answered almost immediately and in a few more seconds I was connected with the ambulance service. The voice was helpful but we were almost immediately at a standstill because I had only the vaguest idea of where we were and no idea at all of how an ambulance would get to us. But a hand came over my shoulder and took the phone, and there was Hamish like an answer to a prayer, giving concise instructions as to where an ambulance should park and what route the paramedics would have to take on foot. I resumed my attempt at resuscitation, but after a minute Hamish pulled me gently to my feet, handed me my phone and took over the alternating kiss of life and heart massage. His ministration seemed more competent, or at least more confident, than mine.

Left with no contribution to make to Peter's survival but anxious not to stand around like an idiot, one idea occurred to me. It seemed probable that Peter's heart had let him down at last. On the other hand, when he was moved, a bullet might be found in him, fired by some careless hunter a mile away. I had been present at scenes of sudden death in the past and my clearest recollection was of being asked many questions to which I had only the vaguest idea of the answers. Memory, mine at least, tends to record with remarkable distortions at times of emergency. So I took out my camera and recorded the scene from a variety of angles until my film ran out.

'I'm thinking it's no good,' Hamish said. 'But I'll carry on. You go and meet the ambulance. Follow the fence a hundred yards and you'll come on a stile that takes you over the fence and down into an old railway cutting running in the direction o' they plane trees. There's a road just beyond and that's where the ambulance will be coming.'

I put my gun and cartridge bag carefully aside and hurried off in the opposite direction to the way we had gone earlier. Plane trees, I knew, were sycamores, but whether I would distinguish a clump of sycamores from all the others at a distance was another matter. The edge of the wood, at that point bursting with hawthorn in blossom, brought me to another stile in the corner of the field. A well-worn track led down into the railway cutting, a continuation of the line running through the wood. It led in the direction of trees on the skyline.

It was not very far but the path was slightly uphill and, although the sleepers had been lifted long before, the way was still uneven with the stones which had formed the original ballast. The cutting was devoid of air, or else my heart was not pushing around enough oxygen for the effort I was making. I hurried and stumbled along as best I could. Above me on my right, pine trees gave way to sky and then suddenly the tops of the sycamores. I tackled the embankment, followed a path through some broken ground with scattered gorse bushes and arrived at the road just as an ambulance came to a halt nearby. I was desperately out of breath and could not have spoken to save my life, but I led the two ambulancemen to the lip of the cutting and managed to point out the two figures against the strip of woodland.

'We see them,' said one, 'but we'll know what to take wi's if you can tell us whit's adae.'

I waited until my gasps became deep breaths. 'Don't know,' I managed to say. 'Didn't see him go down. Could be heart. He's on a pacemaker and he's had bypasses.'

'Right,' said the other one. He looked at me hard. 'What about you, Granddad? Will you be all right?'

I was far from certain but I nodded violently. He led me to a tree and settled me with my back to its trunk. 'You bide here,' he said. 'The doctor will be along in a wee minute. You can point the way. Then, if you're no better, you can come in with us.' His mate returned with a folded stretcher and a case and the two of them set off at a steady trot.

I waited. My breathing slowed but my legs were still shaking. The doctor arrived. I pointed out the huddle around the prone figure. He too set off at a trot. I followed more slowly. When I caught up with him, Peter's body was on the stretcher and a blanket was being laid around him. I saw that there was an oxygen mask over his face although I could see no sign of breathing.

Hamish and I watched the sad procession heading back towards the road.

'You don't look a whole lot better than Sir Peter,' he said. 'Will you wait here while I get the Land Rover?'

'I'll manage,' I said. 'It's not far if I go back through the wood.'

'M'hm.' He looked at me doubtfully but decided that I might survive for a little longer. 'Leave the guns. I'll fetch them up to the house later. We'll not see the laird again, I'm thinking. It'll be for you to tell the staff. And Miss Elizabeth.'

'I suppose so,' I said. That aspect had not occurred to me.

'Well,' Hamish said, 'if that was the end of him, and I think it was – '

'I agree,' I said.

' – at least he went out happy. I don't mind when I last saw him so blithe. It was being sae well suited wi' the wee dog, I'm thinking.'

'Very likely,' I said. I looked around. 'Where *is* Spin?'

We whistled and called but there was no sign of the spaniel.

Chapter Four

I made my way slowly back through the wood, uncertain and miserable. Perhaps I should have stayed to help search for the dog. It was a lonely journey without Peter's company. The medics had been going through the motions but I was in no doubt that he was dead. Not long before, I had been wondering why such a fuss was made about the sanctity of life. Death was all around us. Man was the least of the predators. Millions of creatures were born every day only to be eaten by some other creature before another day had dawned. When death became inevitable, nature's anaesthetics took over and it was accepted with resignation if not with grace. It had seemed to me to be a gross piece of impertinence to set a higher value on human life. People grew old and died. They fell ill and died. They were in accidents and died. And sometimes they were killed. It would come some day, the only question being when – which, it seemed to me, did not make an enormous difference. But now I knew that death mattered, not for the one who died but for those who were left to suffer the shock and to grieve.

The first thing to do, I decided, was to share or shed as much responsibility as possible. I sat down on a log, took out my mobile phone and after a short wrestle with Directory Enquiries called Mr Enterkin's office.

The female voice that answered his phone was unco-operative. Yes, he was in, but who would she say was speaking and what was it about? I asked her to pass on a message. Would he meet me at Sir Peter's house as soon as possible? With mounting impatience, I stressed that it was urgent but the voice refused to promise anything without knowing a good reason.

I lost patience. 'Tell him that Sir Peter Hay is dead,' I snapped.

When I emerged from the trees, I found that the massive and rough-hewn Ronnie was orbiting the lawns on an equally large and rugged motor mower. I signalled to him to follow me into the house. The absence of his employer must have struck him as significant because he stopped the mower where it was and was almost on my heels as I entered, ringing the doorbell as I went through.

The maid, Joanna, came out of the kitchen. 'Bring Mary to the sitting room, please,' I told her.

They joined me in the sitting room and I invited them to sit down. Mary Fiddler was wearing a bright floral apron which jarred on me. For the occasion, it seemed skittish to the point of irreverence. There was no easy way to break the news. When I had the three of them sitting in an anxious row on the big settee, I told them simply that their employer had been removed to hospital, presumably dead. 'If it's any comfort to you,' I added, remembering Hamish's words, 'his last hours were supremely happy.' Then, because they seemed to expect it, I described the events of the morning. There was silence when I had finished. They immediately accepted the fact of his death. They must have been half expecting it for years. It occurred to me that I would look the world's biggest idiot if some miracle of medicine were performed and Peter came home again.

'He was a guid man,' Mary said at last through her handkerchief and the others made murmurs of agreement. It seemed to be as fine an obituary as anyone could ask for. 'What'll we do now?' she asked.

'For the moment, just carry on as before,' was all I could find to say.

There was another silence. Ronnie felt the need to break it. 'The wee dog was good?' he asked.

'Very,' I said. 'But that reminds me. When I found Sir Peter, there was no sign of the spaniel. He hasn't come back here?' They shook their heads. 'He probably will,' I said. 'Dogs can be sensible that way. Many a person has spent hours searching for a lost dog in strange territory and then found it sitting beside the car. Anyway, Hamish is out looking for him.'

Ronnie nodded and then got to his feet. 'I'd best go and collect those rabbits,' he said. 'Then I'll help Hamish to look. You'll let us know if he's found?'

I gave him my mobile phone. 'If he comes back here, I'll phone you,' I promised.

The ladies went back to the kitchen, probably to enjoy a refreshing weep while secretly beginning to relish their position at the forefront of pathos and drama. Ronnie strode off. For some reason it seemed desirable that everything should be as little changed as possible, as if that would delay Peter's final departure. I was alone and too restless to sit still but my hips ached too much for walking. I wandered out to the mowing machine. The controls seemed simple. A minute later I was in the saddle and paralleling Ronnie's neat lines while burying some of my grief under the sweet smell of newly mown grass.

It was some little time before Ralph Enterkin's old but highly polished car arrived. I assumed that he had been with a client who had delayed him, but I learned later that he had spent the whole time en route. The law moves very slowly and the solicitor drove at a similar pace. I stopped the mower and walked to meet him.

He was looking very grave. 'This is terrible news,' he said.

'I may have been precipitate. He collapsed. I'm assuming that he was dead.'

'You may have been precipitate but he did indeed die. I phoned the hospital before I left the office. He had been pronounced and certified as dead.'

My last, faint hope faded away. 'I see. I've told the staff, nobody else.'

'You've told the whole world,' he retorted. 'My amanuensis may be a treasure who can take dictation at a thousand words a minute and knows as much law as I do, but she is the world's worst gossip. The word will have gone round Newton Lauder by now and will reach Edinburgh within the hour.'

'She wouldn't put me through or give you a message without good reason,' I explained.

'You should have invented something. But never mind that,' he said testily, as though I had been trying to evade the subject. 'You'd better tell me what happened. Shall we go inside?'

I led him indoors. It seemed appropriate to use

Peter's study rather than the sitting room. When we were established in two of the deep, leather chairs I told the story again, much as I had told it to the staff.

'I'm not happy about this,' he said when I had ground to a halt. 'I don't mean about the loss of an old friend and favourite client. Of course I'm saddened by that. But let me ask one or two questions. How did he look?'

I thought back. It seemed a strange question. 'He looked dead,' I told him.

'He *was* dead,' Enterkin said testily. 'I'd expect him to look it. But how was his colour?'

'Not noticeably different.'

'I was with him when he had his first heart attack. He was chalk white and his lips were purple.'

'Nothing like that,' I assured him.

'H'm.' His scanty eyebrows began a long climb up his forehead. 'Tell me, did he have a visit from a woman, small, dark, about forty, with sharp features and a penetrating voice?'

'He had a visit from a dark-haired woman. I didn't see her face or hear her voice. He told her to see you. How did you know?'

The solicitor ignored my question. 'You and I are going to have trouble with that one.'

'Me?' I said, throwing grammar to the winds.

'Of course. You're my fellow executor.'

'But he only asked me after lunch yesterday whether I was willing.'

'And signed the fresh trust disposition and settlement an hour later. He was very anxious to get the change formalized, in case some sudden accident should put the previous will into effect. I take it that you would not go against the wishes of a dead friend?'

Hypnotized, I said that I would not.

Enterkin learned back in his chair and put his fingertips together. 'You see, that woman – ' again the solicitor made the two words sound like a curse ' – that woman is Dorothy Spigatt of the firm of Weimms and Spigatt . . . Solicitors, I'm ashamed to say. Head office in Edinburgh but branches throughout the Borders. Sir Peter trusted them utterly. Indeed, until very recently I would have done the same. Nothing was known against them. They handled his major business affairs – with my full agreement because, as Sir Peter no doubt told you, although I have a grounding in Company Law I have no head for the subtler ramifications and machinations of big business. And Ms Spigatt had charge of the local office and did some factoring of the farms, although she has had to take over the Edinburgh office now, for reasons which you will soon understand.

'Recently it emerged, partly due to some questions of my own,' Mr Enterkin said modestly, 'that Henry Weimms had been dipping into Sir Peter's money to play the stock market on his own account. Unfortunately, he was not very good at it and was deep in the red. Even more unfortunately, those questions of mine that brought the matter out into the light of day also gave him warning that the – um – mess was about to hit the fan. He helped himself to a further sum which brought the total deficit to nearly three hundred thousand and then headed for pastures new.'

'Surely,' I said, 'the firm's insurers would have to make good.'

'Professional indemnity assurance covers negligence,' Enterkin said sternly, 'but not dishonesty. The Scottish Solicitors Guarantee Fund may make good the loss in the end, but the innocent partners are thereafter liable for making good the losses to the Fund. What's more, the Law Society has power to insist that the wronged client pursues a civil claim or initiates criminal or disciplinary proceedings.'

I began to feel rather sorry for Ms Spigatt. 'So the lady's head is on the block,' I commented.

'She is not a lady,' Mr Enterkin snapped. 'She is trying every legal and semi-legal dodge to evade her responsibilities. I suspect that she even offered Sir Peter the doubtful pleasures of her flesh to forget the matter, although fortunately they were both beyond the age at which such a bargain might have been attractive to either party, and particularly at such a price.

'But you are quite correct. Unfortunately for her, instead of being left as sole proprietress of a thriving firm, she will have to strip the firm of a large part of its assets if she wishes to remain in practice. Her house will also have to go, but it comprises only a pair of converted cottages in this vicinity and is unlikely to fetch more than a fraction of the missing sum. And if she endeavours to meet her obligations by further borrowings from clients' accounts, it will be the accounts of other clients. I have seen to that. Sir Peter had already made it clear that the matter was in my hands. She had no business approaching him direct – no doubt in an attempt to influence him against my advice.'

'He said something of the sort.' It was already clear that, in hastily accepting a duty that I had supposed to be so far off as to be discounted, I had bitten off as much as I could chew. 'So what do we do?' I asked.

Mr Enterkin noticed the 'we' but acknowledged it only with a lift of an eyebrow. 'Leave that with me for the moment,' he said. 'The matter will roll along a prescribed course.'

He would have said more, but his earlier words had only just rung a warning bell in my mind. 'Did you refer to the will as a trust?' I asked.

'Trust Disposition and Settlement. Yes. In addition to being executors, we are his granddaughter's trustees.'

The mouthful was becoming ever less digestible.

'So,' Enterkin said with emphasis. 'The death comes just a little too pat. Coincidence it may be, but rather too many people are better off, or had reason to think that they might be better off, with Sir Peter out of the way. No doubt the death was perfectly natural but, just in case of questions in the future, we had best take all reasonable steps. Which doctor attended the scene?'

'I didn't get his name, but he was tall, with black hair and glasses.'

The solicitor did not seemed to be cheered by the information. 'I must see what I can discover by telephone,' he said slowly. 'The phone in the sitting room is on a separate line. While I make use of it, perhaps you would advise Miss Hay of her grandfather's death.'

That seemed to be well within my capabilities. There were two phones on the desk in the study but a small light on one of them indicated that there was an extension in use. I discovered Elizabeth's number in a leather-backed address book and found myself speaking to a hall of residence at the university. I left a message asking her to call or come, as a matter of urgency.

If the little light was to be believed, Enterkin was still on the other phone. I keyed in the number for Three Oaks. Isobel's voice came on the line. She sounded surprised to hear from me. I had been calling her at home in the evenings.

'Does this call mean that you're coming home?' she asked.

'The reverse. I had rashly agreed to be one of Peter's executors—'

'You told me that,' she said sharply. I guessed that I had caught her with a patient on the table. 'So what's changed?'

'Everything,' I told her. 'He's just died.'

'Oh dear! What of?'

'We don't know yet. He went down quite suddenly. Heart perhaps.'

There was silence until I began to wonder whether we had been cut off. 'That's a shame,' she said at last. 'He wasn't what you'd call a charmer and yet I remember him as one of the most charming men I ever met. He seemed eternally youthful. I can't imagine him ever dying. Say all the proper things from me to anyone who could possibly give a damn. Is there anything we can do from this end?'

'Not just now, except to manage without me. I may want advice later – it seems that I am also joint trustee of a young girl, God help me! I only called to break the news and to explain that I may have to put in a lot of time on this. My movements may be unpredictable.'

'Understood. Mind you don't knock yourself up, trying to do too much too quickly. Try to visit home

70

soon for clean laundry and some proper clothes,' said my ever practical wife. 'And let me know when the funeral will be. I'd like to come to it.'

Her words had reminded me that I was still dressed for informal rabbiting. Enterkin still seemed to be on the phone, so when our call was finished I slipped upstairs for a quick wash and change. I helped myself to a black tie from Peter Hay's wardrobe, telling myself that he would have understood and approved. His bedroom was large and very masculine. I supposed that his granddaughter would be sleeping there some day and no doubt there would be changes, though I could not imagine what they would be.

When I came downstairs, it was clear that the staff had also been struck by the need to dignify the occasion with a change of clothes. I saw Joanna in a grey dress although with coloured stripes while Mary Fiddler, red of eye, had changed into a black dress which might have been more suitable for a cocktail party. She had even managed to find an apron of more muted tones.

They were bringing a late lunch on two trays into the sitting room. 'My suggestion,' Enterkin said apologetically when we were alone together. 'But we could hardly demand a cooked meal in a house of bereavement. And there is much to be done. Sir Peter's own doctor is on holiday in Florida at the moment. His partner, who attended the scene and who knows little of Sir Peter's medical history, has certified death but is unable to certify the cause of it. But that is of little moment since I was considering whether to suggest that the estate should order a post mortem examination. You would agree to that?'

'I think it's a good idea – in case of future questions, as you said.'

'Good. We might engage the services of Professor Mannatoy, the Professor of Clinical Pathology. One of the foremost men in the field. At the same time, we must have proof of death. And a notice in the press. And people to be informed.' He sighed and began to jot down a list. 'There is much to be done.'

I nodded agreement. 'Did Peter not have a secretary?' I asked. 'It would seem to be usual.'

'He had an excellent secretary until about a year ago when the young woman married and moved abroad. Her successor proved to be a disaster and he found that by making full use of modern technology he could manage perfectly well without anyone. Anything of great importance he brought to my office.'

'If you tackle that list,' I said, 'I could go back to the study and start cancelling his appointments and notifying his business contacts.'

He agreed immediately, with the proviso that I limit myself strictly to business contacts, consulting him if in doubt. 'And leave Weimms and Spigatt entirely to me,' he added.

At first glance, Peter had kept several days more or less clear, presumably for the benefit of myself and Spin. Thereafter his business diary was fairly full for the next fortnight and then progressively less so, but on further study I saw that several of the appointments were with Mr Enterkin, presumably to meet with other parties, and it seemed hardly necessary to include him among the persons to be notified. Fortunately, Peter's entries were not in the sort of personal shorthand adopted by lazier folk like me, and reference to his address book soon identified the individuals and busi-nesses. In a long spell on the phone I left one message on an answering machine but managed to notify all the others and to make brief answers to a number of shocked enquiries. More than once, I found myself speaking to former acquaintances, now risen high in the world of finance.

The computer on Peter's desk was not familiar to me but it turned out that the word-processor program was an updated version of the one used by Isobel. After a little fumbling and several false starts I managed to produce a set of draft letters confirming the sad news and either outlining or seeking proposals for future action. These I took, with my list, through to Enterkin. He agreed them with only two minor suggestions.

He nodded to a chair and I seated myself. For a modest man of unimpressive appearance he had a compelling manner. 'Matters are taking their course,' he said. 'The doctor had a word with the fiscal, who has ordered an autopsy, thus saving the estate the cost. I have had a word with the Professor, however, and he promises to conduct it himself.

'I shall have to leave shortly. Important though these matters are, I do have other clients. In an emer-gency I can be reached through my office or, later, at home. We will resume in the morning. In the mean-time, I must leave you to hold the fort.'

One question had been niggling at the back of my mind. 'Should I remove to the hotel?' I asked him.

His sparse eyebrows, almost as bald as his head, shot up again. 'I fail to see why you should. The house is here. The staff must be paid. The additional expense of keeping you here will be little more than the cost of raw food and laundry. Why burden the estate with unnecessary hotel bills? Besides, there may be occasional phone calls to be dealt with. I will explain the position to Mary Fiddler as I leave. I'll have these letters re-typed – they would be better ostensibly coming from my office.'

'Would it help if I gave you the disc I stored them on?' I asked. 'Then all your typist would have to do would be to change a few words and print them again on your letterhead.'

He seemed amused. 'Thank you for the kind thought, but we have only just arrived in the age of the electric typewriter. I would invite you to dinner this evening but my wife might be discommoded by the short notice. Perhaps tomorrow, or some time next week? Meantime, you may care to while away the evening with a perusal of the will. Sir Peter's copy of it must be around the place somewhere.'

He spent some little time in conclave with the staff and then drove very slowly down the long drive. As a consequence he was barely out of sight before it became clear that his forecast of 'a few phone calls' was a gross underestimate. His other prophecy, that word of Peter's death would spread rapidly, was more accurate. There began a succession of phone calls, from desolated friends, anxious tenants and business contacts, concerned acquaintances and some which I could only assume were from the just plain inquisitive. I could do little more than list most of them for sifting and dealing with later. The local paper phoned and I fobbed them off with the briefest of statements and promised them a notice and an obituary in due course.

The telephone messages were nearing a climax when I was distracted by the arrival of a car and a ring at the bell. I was surprised to see a cup of cold tea and a biscuit at my elbow. I had not glimpsed the visitors but Joanna tapped at the door and told me that Keith Calder and Ian Fellowes hoped to see me. I kept them waiting for a minute while I put a suitably subdued and mildly discouraging message on Peter's answering machine.

Joanna removed the teacup and gave me a reproachful glance before going to fetch the visitors. It was a measure of their respect for Sir Peter that each had found time to put on a black tie. They shook hands formally but with an air of doubt which I put down to uncertainty at what to say. Commiserations were hardly appropriate, when they had known the deceased, if not longer, far more continuously than I had. Instead we all agreed what a sad occasion it was. I decided to break the ice. The afternoon was almost gone. 'As co-executor,' I said, 'I feel entitled to offer Sir Peter's refreshments.'

They brightened. 'Why not?' Calder said. 'Peter aye kept his cupboard well stocked with the best. We wouldn't want it to fall into the hands of that apology for a man that his granddaughter's walking out with, would we?'

'Certainly not. Unless you're on duty?' I added to Inspector Fellowes.

He smiled sadly. 'If I am,' he said, 'I may be forgiven. Tradition requires a stirrup cup for the deceased.'

Joanna had been waiting for just such instructions. I asked her to fetch whisky and a jug of water. Calder and Fellowes murmured a few affectionate words about Peter Hay. They were stilted words but I felt that they were more sincere than any eulogy.

When we were settled with our drinks, Calder said, 'How did it happen?'

'I didn't see it.' They listened intently while I told the story. The account seemed bare so I went on to quote what Mr Enterkin had said about it. 'But you must know all this,' I said to Fellowes. 'An unexplained death would have been reported to you.'

'Reported, yes,' he said. 'There's no substitute to hearing it from the best witness. There's been no further word about the dog?'

'None that reached me.'

'We'll see what we can do about that.'

'I think Ralph was wrong about Peter's colour,' Calder said. 'I was with them both when Peter had an attack – the second or third, I forget which. His face didn't change colour. Ralph's remembering the faint that Peter threw, a couple of months after he came out of hospital from the first one. Lack of blood to the brain or something. So it could perfectly well have been another heart attack. I don't know anyone who has survived five.'

'I was wondering whether the electric fence was to blame,' I said.

'And so was I,' said Fellowes.

Calder was shaking his head. 'Electric fences are intended to turn cattle back, not kill them. A twelve-volt battery is usually enough power source but the current then goes through a transformer which steps it up to short pulses of a very high voltage. That fence comes off the mains through a transformer. I don't know what voltage it can reach but – '

'But we can find out,' Fellowes said. 'It might even have been faulty. Short-circuiting or something. And, after all, Sir Peter had a pacemaker.' He looked at me. 'From his position when you found him, did it suggest that he'd been touching the fence? Or the gate? Or neither?'

I forced myself to think back to a scene which I had been trying to forget. 'The gate, I think.'

Calder frowned. 'The gate should be insulated from the fence. You can't be sure?'

'No. But I took some photographs . . .'

Both men stirred. 'You did?' said Calder. 'Have you sent them away for processing yet?'

'I'll do it in the morning,' I told him.

'No. We can do better than that. My wife has a good photographic set-up. She does all her own processing and gets better results than the lab. Give me your film and we'll have good prints by morning,' Calder said blandly, apparently oblivious to the fact that he was committing his wife to working all evening and probably part of the night. Molly Calder, I decided, must be a softer touch than Isobel.

I fetched my camera and was winding back the film when Joanna put her head round the door. 'Ronnie's here,' she said. 'He'd like to see you.'

'Ask him to come in,' I said. 'You don't mind?' I asked the others.

Keith grinned. 'He's my brother-in-law.'

'And my wife's uncle,' Ian Fellowes said.

The rugged bulk of Mary's husband came through the door. He took up a stand on the hearthrug, nodding a separate greeting to each of us. He looked close to exhaustion. 'Hamish and I have searched and searched. We whistled and shouted fit to raise – ah well, you'll ken the saying fine. There's no' a sign of the wee dog. He's not caught in a snare, I'll swear to that. Likely he bolted for here, or for his old home, and lost his way.'

'I doubt that,' Calder said. 'Peter and the dog had been getting along well?'

'Very well indeed,' I said. 'They seemed delighted with each other.'

'Then the dog's instinct would be to stay with its new master if he collapsed, or look for human help.'

'But . . .' said Fellowes. 'But suppose the dog got a shock off the fence, or off his master if the dog touched the man while the man was still touching the fence. What then?'

'That might do it,' Calder said slowly. 'He could think that Peter had struck him. Dogs' minds work in mysterious ways.'

'We're putting the word out among the farmers and we'll be gaein' out again after supper, wi' the lamp,' Ronnie said. 'So I'll keep your phone just now.'

I nodded. 'Hold on, then. You'd better have the battery charger.'

Calder took the film. I fetched the charger for Ronnie and gave him a dram to toast his employer's memory and give him energy for the task ahead. The party broke up but not before Fellowes had put a great many questions to me. Calder and Fellowes left, promising to return in the morning. I was far from sure whether Fellowes was acting as a policeman or as a concerned friend and there may have been doubt in his own mind. He promised to report the missing dog to all his fellow officers. Spin would not languish in some pound until re-homed or put down for lack of identification.

Chapter Five

The answering machine seemed to be coping with the phone calls. It seemed unlikely that any of them were of tremendous urgency. My need to get a grip on my new responsibilities was probably greater. I decided to leave the messages for the morning, by which time some of them might, with luck, be obsolete, and instead take Mr Enterkin's advice and begin digesting the will.

I found Peter's copy of the will, or *Trust Disposition and Settlement* in Ralph Enterkin's words, in a drawer of the desk on top of a neat stack of bank and credit-card statements. It was dated the previous day.

I settled in one of the comfortable chairs, flipped quickly through the opening paragraphs which were concerned with the legalities rather than actual bequests and then skipped to the salient paragraphs. There were few surprises. After a number of personal legacies to staff and friends, Peter had left the balance of his estate to his granddaughter Elizabeth, in the trust of his executors until she reached the age of twenty-five. His dogs were bequeathed to Hamish the keeper. His guns were to be distributed among certain close friends and shooting companions. His personal clothes were to go to charity. There was a long list of items which were to be sold and the proceeds given to charity. One or two dispositions puzzled me, but no doubt Ralph Enterkin would be able to elucidate.

The will also made provision for the disposal of certain properties, most of them remote from the main estate. The intention seemed to be a consolidation of the estate and simplification of its management. I found a local map and began to pick out those properties. Such was the concentration required that I heard nothing until Joanna materialized suddenly beside me. Miss Elizabeth, she said in hushed tones as if speaking of the dead, had arrived with 'yon lubbard'.

Another distressing task was looming over me. 'Can you bring her in but leave her boyfriend outside?' I asked.

She nodded more cheerfully. 'Easy. He's sitting on his machine in the drive.'

When Miss Hay flounced in, she looked puzzled rather than distressed. I guessed that the news had not reached her in Edinburgh and that the couple had swept contemptuously through the neighbourhood without pausing to gather news. During our one previous encounter, I had been too much concerned with the overtones of hostility to notice the finer details of her appearance, but now I saw that, behind the sulky look, she had her grandfather's fine bone structure. She was dressed inexpensively, in tune with current fashion but with taste.

'What's this about, then?' she demanded. 'And where's my grandfather? Why do I have to speak to you?' She threw herself into a chair without bothering to control her short skirt, as though I were a person of no more consequence than a eunuch. Charitably, I decided to attribute her attitude to my age. Joanna was on the point of closing the door but I asked her to wait.

'I have bad news,' I told Miss Hay. She must have guessed where the bad news lay from the fact that I, rather than her grandfather, was breaking it. I saw her lips whiten and she braced herself. 'Sir Peter died suddenly this morning. Apparently it was another heart attack, but we don't know yet for sure.' I paused to give her a chance to speak but she was frozen. I blundered on. 'If it's any comfort to you, though he had been seeming a little depressed from time to time, his last few hours were extremely happy ones and the end came quickly.'

She remained motionless. I thought that she was going to accept the news matter-of-factly. But suddenly her face began to crumple and look much as I thought she must have looked as a distressed child. She put her hands up to cover it and rocked to and fro, mewing like a kitten. My first sensation was of relief that I had asked Joanna to wait. I would have been helpless, but Joanna stooped to put her arms round the crying girl and made sounds of comfort, softly. Elizabeth turned her head into the other girl's breast and wept for her grandfather.

After several minutes, Elizabeth Hay straightened up and shook Joanna off indignantly, as though liberties had been taken. Her face was soaked with tears so that I knew her grief had to be genuine. She was making an effort to pull herself together.

'Thank you, Joanna,' I said. 'You can go now.'

'One minute,' Miss Hay snapped. Her voice was choked but the old mixture of complaint and imperiousness was creeping back. 'I want Roland with me.'

'If you mean – ' I began.

'Roland Chatsworth. My fiancé.'

The name seemed too good to be true but I let it pass for the moment. I shook my head. 'You can go,' I told Joanna again. She closed the door softly behind her. 'We can go out to him, if you like,' I said.

Miss Hay was recovering her poise and temper. 'Who the hell are you to tell me who I can bring into the house?'

'Mr Enterkin and I are joint executors of your grandfather's estate,' I explained.

'Then you'll know that it's my house now.'

I sent up a short prayer that I might know what I was talking about. 'Not yet,' I said. 'Not until we have Confirmation.'

'Confirmation of what? That he's dead?'

'Confirmation in Scotland is the same as probate in England,' I explained. 'As things stand, I haven't even had time to read to the end of the Trust Disposition and Settlement.' I felt rather pleased with myself for remembering the terminology. 'He has certainly left you the house as well as a great deal of property, but there are many bequests of contents to others. It would be irresponsible on my part to let a stranger inside, against the strongly expressed wishes of the deceased.'

'But how long—?' The same word that had belatedly caught my attention now brought her up short. 'Did you say "trust"?'

'Yes. Didn't you know? Mr Enterkin and I are your trustees.'

'That's iniquitous!' She got to her feet and stalked around the room. I had heard the expression 'like a caged tigress' used to describe such pacing but never before had I realized just how apt was the cliché. I waited, prepared to duck at any sudden movement. But when at last she halted in front of me she seemed to have thought the matter through and decided that not alienating one of her trustees was more important even than venting her temper. 'Does that mean that you can allow me to marry?'

'We could. But if you had that young man in mind – the one you addressed as Dog-face or something similar – I think we'd be much more likely to implement your grandfather's wishes.'

'Until when?'

'I think the figure mentioned was age twenty-five.'

'But that's another seven years!'

I wished that Mr Enterkin were at hand to guide me, but now that the subject was out in the open I felt that I had to go on. 'Of course, if the young man became an acceptable member of society, took his degree, got a job and was in a position to provide for you . . .'

'But he wouldn't *need* to provide for me,' Miss Hay pointed out, as though to a simpleton.

'No,' I agreed. 'Except that we wouldn't release more than a bare living allowance to you if you married or . . . or cohabited with somebody who depended on you financially and was incapable of earning a living, with the possible exception . . .'

'Yes? What exception?'

I gathered my thoughts. 'With the possible exception of an artist or writer of acknowledged talent or an athlete preparing for major competition. Those, at least, are my views as I think they would have been

84

your grandfather's and I expect them to be supported by Mr Enterkin.'

She sat down again, more carefully this time. 'And you expect Roland to put on a dark suit and join the ranks of the ordinary breadwinners?'

'Not "expect", exactly,' I said. ' "Hope" would be a better word.'

Of course, it was too much to hope that that would be an end to it. She kept her temper but spoke vehemently for some minutes, making reference to 'little grey men', 'proletariat', 'stultification of the expanding soul', and much else which was beyond my comprehension. I nodded occasionally, while keeping a judicious smile on my face, but my mind went off on its own. The danger, as I saw it, was that the girl might decide for herself that the solution to her dilemma might lie in a touch of pregnancy, real or fictitious. Women, I was aware, sometimes resorted to that expedient. In Miss Hay's case the threat of a hit man, as well as being a fiction of my own, would no longer carry conviction after the death of her grandfather. I decided that it was time to make as much peace with her as I could, at the same time edging her away from any such measure.

I waited for her to run out of steam before adopting my most avuncular tone. I probably sounded insufferably patronizing, but did seem to earth some of the electricity out of the air. I avoided starting out by saying that she was very young. 'Time is very much on your side,' I began instead. 'If you desperately want to marry now, it must be because you're not sure of him, in which case he isn't worth it.'

'I'm absolutely sure of him,' she protested.

'In that case, you have time to mould him into what we and you would want you to marry. Unless you really want to be tied for life to somebody your grandfather wouldn't have let across the doorstep, and forced to do so on a small fraction of your real income.'

Instead of exploding again, she looked at me thoughtfully. 'How would you suggest I do that?' she asked.

'Women always do find ways,' I said. I drew a quick mental analogy with spaniel training and realized that it was valid. 'Don't ask me to explain the mysteries. Thinking back, I believe it's a long slow process of applying gentle pressure and then showing less or more affection according to whether or not the lesson has got through.' As I spoke, I had a sudden revelation in which I recognized that Isobel had treated me during most of our marriage in just such a manner. 'If you're so set on wedding bells,' I went on, 'keep in mind the first three steps in the wedding ceremony. You walk up the aisle. You arrive at the altar. You sing a hymn.'

'Yes?' She was puzzled.

'Aisle . . . altar . . . hymn,' I said. 'Think about it.'

It took a few seconds for the penny to drop. 'Very funny!' But I could see that she was amused. I decided that there was hope for Miss Hay yet.

Moments later she was all seriousness. 'I really did love the old boy. We fought. But he wasn't always going to be there and it was the rest of my life I was fighting for. Do you understand? And now he isn't there any more and I'm sorry. Because I didn't mean some of the things I said and I don't think that he did either, and now we can't take them back and say that we're sorry and tell each other . . .'

I had a feeling that her grandfather had meant every word that he had said about the insufferable Roland, but it did not seem to be the time to say so. 'I shall be staying here for the moment,' I said. 'Except probably at weekends. You might find it convenient to move back for now, until we've sorted out the estate.'

'But Roland doesn't come inside?'

'You've got it.'

'I'll get back to university. I'll need my degree if I've got to support both myself and Roland.' Her surly alter ego resumed control. 'What do you need me here for anyway? Don't worry, Joanna will look after you, just as she did for Granddad. You realize that, one way or the other, I'll be a wealthy woman one of these days?'

I held onto my temper or the occasion might have become a screaming match. 'I'm long retired, so threats of that nature mean very little to me.'

'Then you might pass the word along to chubby-chops.'

'Are you sure that you want to make enemies of us just yet? We could probably arrange things so that you wouldn't see a penny of your money until after we're dead and buried.'

'I don't give a damn,' she said, but her voice was less certain.

She left shortly after that. I promised that she would be contacted again as soon as the Trust Disposition and Settlement had been studied.

The custom of the house, I discovered, was that Mary Fiddler, who lived with her husband in a cottage rather nearer to the town, would prepare Sir Peter's dinner and then go home, leaving the meal to be served by Joanna who was then responsible for all domestic duties until Mary returned in the morning after completing her own housework. (In compensation for her long hours, Joanna was given considerable latitude regarding time off during the day.) The arrangement seemed to have been long-standing and satisfactory to all parties, so I saw no need to interfere.

I spent as much as I could of the time remaining before dinner in delving deeper into the Trust Disposition and Settlement. Peter Hay had dealt with each aspect in as straightforward a manner as possible, but his interests had been large and far-ranging and sometimes his solution to a dilemma had of necessity been complicated, on top of which I could detect the hand of Ralph Enterkin rephrasing large sections of it, rendering it almost incomprehensible to the layman but indestructible by his fellow lawyers. By ignoring the telephone messages which were accumulating in the answering machine I managed to concentrate for minutes at a time.

Visitors were more difficult to deflect. Several were turned away by Joanna with the news that Miss Hay had returned to university. They left messages of sympathy.

Dorothy Spigatt, however, was a horse of a very different colour, although it was only when she flatly refused to go away without seeing me that I discovered how very appropriate that metaphor was. I saw her close to for the first time at the front door in fading daylight and she had the elongated face that is often regarded as equine, together with a complexion which was either very tanned or the product of mixed races. The Jaguar on the gravel was a recent model and polished to a mirror shine. The rising moon was reflected in its roof.

'I would like to come in and talk to you for a moment,' she said. She spoke very precisely, in an accent which I could not pin down but which impressed me as being both English and educated. I guessed her age to be a well-preserved forty.

In his treatment of his granddaughter's boyfriend, Peter Hay had set an example of excluding undesirables. He had not made an exception in the case of Ms Spigatt so I decided to emulate his example. I glanced down at the card that Joanna had brought me. 'You should see Mr Enterkin,' I told her, without moving aside.

She had started to advance as she spoke so that we collided gently, chest to chest. She recoiled, managing not to look indignant but looked instead surprised. Surely a lawyer must have learned by now that not everybody would withdraw before her? She dismissed the subject of Mr Enterkin with a tiny shrug. 'Is it true that Sir Peter Hay died this morning?' she asked. 'You can surely tell me that.'

'Quite true.'

'And that you are one of the executors?'

'I am,' I said. 'But how did the facts come to your attention so quickly?'

'News travels fast around here and several people knew that I would be interested. May we talk? Inside?'

'I don't think that I know enough yet to be able to

89

talk sensibly about what I assume you want to discuss,' I told her.

'I might be able to add to your knowledge and understanding. And it's very cold on the doorstep,' she added, although it was a warm evening and she was wearing a coat which, in the poor light, I took to be real fur of high quality.

'I'm about to eat dinner,' I told her. 'I suggest that you seek an appointment with Mr Enterkin in the morning.'

'And what are you assuming that I want to discuss with you?'

'All I know,' I said, 'is that your partner embezzled a large sum from Sir Peter's funds.'

She glanced around, looking for eavesdroppers in the gathering dusk. 'That remains to be proved. But if it's true, then it was his own doing and he is no longer a member of the firm. But I, who never made a penny out of it, am being hounded to make good any loss out of my own pocket and I just do not have that sort of money.' Her voice was straying from its measured tone and becoming plaintive. With the change, I thought that I detected a trace of a Midlands accent. 'Is that fair?' she asked me. 'Is it reasonable?'

'Not knowing what part you played in the embezzlement—'

'I had no part in it at all, and no profit from it,' she said furiously.

'But that also remains to be proved,' I said. 'I don't know enough to say whether it's fair or reasonable. But I gather that it's necessary. I have to take my legal advice from my fellow executor.'

'Even if he's wrong?'

'I am not competent to judge between you,' I told her. 'But he is my colleague. If you tell me that he is wrong in law—'

'You could get counsel's opinion on the point.'

'But would you pay for it, if it did not support you?'

She changed the subject quickly. 'The executors represent the interests of the deceased and his heirs. As such, they will have a great deal of discretion. You know about the Scottish Solicitors' Guarantee Fund?'

'Yes,' I said. I saw no need to explain that I had only just heard of it for the first time.

'They will make good the loss. Then they will press you, as executors, to sue me for restitution. But if you insist that the case is not strong and that it would be throwing good money after bad . . .' She lowered her voice until I could barely hear her next words. 'How do you like my car?'

'It's very handsome,' I admitted.

'Less than three thousand miles on the clock. It could be yours. Think about it. Goodbye.' She turned away.

'Offer it to Mr Enterkin. I have a perfectly good car.'

'For the moment.' She settled into the driving seat and started the engine, leaving me to guess whether her parting words related to her farewell or to my car. I ducked through the kitchen and out at the back door to make sure that the garage was locked. I was very glad that the task of dealing with Ms Spigatt would fall to Ralph Enterkin. I judged that she was a tough and tricky lady, and becoming desperate.

*

Mary Fiddler had left for home, leaving for me a dinner of one of my trout with almonds and local vegetables, followed by a crème caramel and cheeseboard. It was a satisfying and delicious meal without tempting an old man to overload his tender digestion. Either Peter Hay's taste or Mrs Fiddler's judgement, or both, met with my full approval. I would have hesitated to make inroads into his cellar (now probably his grand-daughter's – I meant to have another look at the will) but a glass of white wine, a white Bordeaux I thought, appeared with the meal, probably on Mr Enterkin's instructions.

The meal was served by Joanna. Her behaviour was excessively formal, much more so than when Sir Peter had been alive. It was as if she had decided to show that she could be the perfect maidservant when she tried, yet something put it into my mind that we were a man and a woman alone in the house for the night, and I was sure that the consciousness was not originally my own but somehow emanated from her via some trace of body language too faint to identify. Surely, I thought, she could not be afraid of being molested by someone of my years? No, I had to be letting my imagination run riot.

After dinner, I settled again in the study. I had spent enough time on the Trust Disposition and Settlement to have a general overall picture of Peter Hay's wishes. I dipped into it once more, long enough to see that the older wines in Peter's cellar were to be distributed among his more discerning friends but that the younger vintages, those which would only arrive at perfection when Elizabeth Hay would be of an age to entertain guests, were to be saved for her.

My mind was too choked with the ramifications of the will to start absorbing any more detail at that time of night and yet too full for casual reading or watching a television service which seemed to be staffed by and run for the benefit of randy teenagers. I looked for an alternative occupation. Mr Enterkin, quite admitting to being about as technically minded as the Labradors, had taken my nodding acquaintance with Isobel's computer as evidence of complete computer literacy and had made it clear that anything in Sir Peter's computer was, at least in the first instance, my baby. I decided to spend a little time in trying to explore its contents.

I had expected that much of the material would be methodically arranged, like Isobel's, in a family tree of subjects. But Peter had been remarkably unmethodical even for one who must have come, like me, to the computer age late in life and, having initially arranged his files in a garbled and confused fashion, had allowed the same non-system to continue. It had been a workable system only because he knew his way around it. Lacking that advantage and hampered by not always coming up where I expected, I made halting progress. After scanning the directories, I was tempted to discount a great deal of personal or obsolete text but I had a suspicion that many a vital nugget might be found among the dross. When I had at least an outline of the problem I tackled the more confidential material. Here, Peter Hay had been both tidier and more security minded, but he had had the forethought to tell me the codeword which unlocked a list of other codes. Now I had access to the most sensitive items, listed alphabetically from Arnold Drayne to Weimms and Spigatt.

With some interest I pursued the story of the embezzling solicitor. It was much as Mr Enterkin had outlined it except that he had skated rather lightly over Dorothy Spigatt's part in the original fraud. It seemed that the lady's own hands were far from clean; indeed, if the matter ever came before a court she would almost certainly face prosecution. The offer of a £20,000 Jaguar in return for my help began to seem a little miserly.

The evening was slipping away. In my unfamiliarity with the system I was making heavy weather of tracking any subject from document to document and I was terrified that some well-intended move would cause the whole thing to wipe itself clean. I wanted to make hard copies of everything interesting, for later study, but the printing paper was almost exhausted. Some of the material was duplicated on floppy discs, but I could not follow Peter's method of identifying subjects. However, by the time Joanna brought me my usual nightcap of a cup of tea and a biscuit, I had at least a better overview of the tasks ahead.

Joanna's manner was respectful but she brushed my ear with her breast and when she stooped to the low coffee table I was given a view of a pair of very good legs in thin nylon. I was left to wonder whether these treats were due to carelessness or calculation. Surely, I thought as I walked the two Labradors under the moon and whistled for the missing spaniel, her skirt was shorter than the one that I remembered? It seemed unlikely, but possible, that a change of scene had triggered a resurgence of the old pheromones. There was always hope. Perhaps my hormones, too, were making a sympathetic recovery. I sent a little message down my body but received no reply.

Oh well. The age of miracles, after all, is past.

Chapter Six

Sleep, I have been told, was given to us to allow us to digest new experiences. For this reason, or perhaps just because I was tired by so much fresh air and drama in a single day, I slept surprisingly well but roused early. Still in a half-wakened state, I almost expected to hear Peter Hay exercising Spin on the grass outside. Then it came back to me. Peter was dead and Spin had disappeared and instead of Peter's voice and whistle there was the song of a robin – distastefully cheerful until I realized that he was only defending his territory or calling for sex. I was also worried about Spin – not only his loss but that he would not be getting his charcoal biscuit. If somebody had given him shelter, they might well have been driven to turn him out again. I came fully awake and realized that this was nonsense, but by then I knew that sleep had escaped me.

Bathed and shaved and dressed in a more respectable suit as befitted one who was in charge of a house of bereavement and the affairs of the deceased, I descended to find that Joanna was already up and about. There was still no sign of Spin. I gave the two Labradors the short walk that they seemed to expect, whistling and calling in vain for the spaniel, and went in to breakfast. Joanna was still in dark and subdued colours but her skirt was shorter than ever. Just in case there was any misunderstanding, as I made my escape I muttered something about phoning my wife.

I took my second cup of coffee through to the study and tackled the messages on the answering machine, at the same time making notes for Enterkin's benefit. Most left a name and phone number for a return call, but several asked for sympathy to be passed to Elizabeth Hay. It was still too early for me to expect Keith Calder and Ian Fellowes, and far too early for any lawyer of my experience to be in his office or even out of bed.

If I started the phone calls now, offices would be deserted and in the houses I would be fetching people away from their breakfasts. So I decided to take the Labs for another and longer walk and give Spin another chance to make contact.

The sun was well up now, the grass looked dry and we seemed to be on course for another fine day. I took my stick and my mobile phone, which Ronnie had left for me, on charge, in the hall. I told Joanna the direction that I would be taking and that I could be called on my mobile whenever anybody came looking for me. The Labradors came to me readily, already recognizing me as the new dog walker.

I was hardly out of the front door, however, when a large pick-up truck with a canvas cover over the body and a small trailer behind advanced along the drive and came to a halt beside me. A lean and swarthy man who I judged to be near if not actually in his sixties jumped fleetly down. 'You'll be Mr Kitts?' he asked me. I said that I was. He wiped his hand on the rear of his cement-stained dungarees and offered it. 'I'm Jock McAnderton,' he said, 'and that's my nephew Sean.' He glanced towards the cab of the truck where a boy in his late teens was slouched, listening to a Walkman and oblivious to all else. 'Och, never mind him. I keep him on as my helper for my sister's sake. Is it true that Sir Peter's been killed?'

Despite his name, I was sure that I could detect a trace of Irish accent in Jock McAnderton's voice.

'He died yesterday,' I said. 'Whether he was killed or not we'll know after the post mortem.'

'And that you're in charge now?'

'For the moment, Mr Enterkin and I, between us.'

'Well then. It's this way. I've been doing a few jobs for Sir Peter. Just now I'm rebuilding a stone wall that collapsed, at Cartley's Farm.'

'Where's that?' I asked. Cartley's was not among the farms to be offered to the sitting tenants so I had not yet traced it on the map.

'Out beyond the far side of the town. Look, you can see it from here.' He pointed out the farm buildings just beyond where the mist lay in the valley and where the hills rose darkly into the sky. 'It was just a word-of-mouth order. Do I get on with it?'

I considered for a moment. In Scotland, an oral instruction and acceptance can form a binding contract. And putting a builder off the site can be more expensive than allowing him to continue. 'Just carry on for now,' I said. 'I'll come and take a look at it when I have time.'

'And I'll get paid for it?' he asked keenly.

'Whatever you're due, you'll get,' I assured him.

He pulled his forelock, a strangely old-fashioned

gesture, and turned away. As I crossed the lawn I was aware of the sound of the pick-up fading away down the drive. I bent to wipe the cement dust off my hand on the grass.

We went into the wood. So soon after the tragedy, I hesitated before facing the place where it had happened, but with a vague idea of taking a partial step towards overcoming my reluctance I headed in that general direction.

The dogs hung back, as uneasy as I was. I told myself firmly that they could not know where their beloved master had died; they could only be sensing my unease. But when we were in the tunnel under the former railway line, the dogs suddenly perked up. Royston forged ahead and even Old Nick quickened his pace. I hoped that they had caught scent of Spin, but when I emerged into the dappled sunlight I found them fawning around Hamish, who was carrying what seemed to be a wardrobe door complete with full-size mirror.

He seemed glad to put the heavy load down, leaning it carefully against a tree. He looked up at me from a position stooped over the dogs. 'It's only now sinking in,' he said sadly. 'God, but what a loss that man will be! My dad was his keeper and I took over when the old chap retired. I suppose I knew it wouldn't last for ever, but to have him go so suddenly . . . and just when he was so pleased with the wee dog. I was out searching again at first light. Ronnie's out looking for him still, but I had work that couldn't be left.'

'Doing some home improvements?' I suggested.

A twitch of the whiskers and a crinkling of the exposed skin around his eyes suggested the possibility of a smile. He seated himself on a piece of wall forming part of the abutment of the tunnel. 'You could say that. Not my home, though. It's for the pheasants.' For a mad moment I tried to visualize the poults admiring themselves or preening before the mirror, but failed. He saw that I was puzzled. 'On the roofs of the shelters in the release pens. For the sparrowhawks and buzzards,' he explained patiently. 'Best thing. They start to come in for an easy meal, glimpse themselves in the mirror as another predator approaching from an impossible angle and get a hell of a fright. They don't come back in a hurry. Sir Peter aye put the word around that he'd be glad of any big old mirrors left over after a roup. I've another six or seven of them in my store. It's a good trick. It really works.'

'Does it indeed?' I said. 'I must spread the word back home. We're plagued by sparrowhawks. And foxes. They've got wise to the lamp.'

His whiskers hid most of his expression, but in his eyes I could see the glow of the preacher pronouncing a doctrine, or the expert in his subject passing on the good word. So Moses's eyes must have looked as he handed down the tablets of stone. 'For foxes, try hanging a dead hen outside the pen at night. First pour in half a pint of antifreeze wi' a funnel down its throat. In the morn, you'll find a dead fox, like as not. Nothing else, just a fox. They like the taste of the antifreeze fine.' He paused and looked at me thoughtfully. 'What should I be doing next?' he asked suddenly. 'I've been happy here. But what does the future hold? Should I be looking for another job?'

It seemed only fair to set his mind at rest. Peter Hay had left bequests to his personal staff, carefully graduated (with one remarkable exception) in accordance with length of service, but I saw no need to reveal the details until Mr Enterkin decided that the time was ripe. 'There's no harm telling you this much,' I said. 'It will be public soon enough. Sir Peter wanted the estate preserved pretty much as it is, because he still hoped for descendants who would love it as he did but also because he believed in what it stood for. And the shooting is an essential part of the overall management. The syndicate continues.' (Hamish heaved an enormous sigh.) 'Mr Calder takes over Sir Peter's gun in return for running it. Two days a year will be let as before, to help balance the books. You have a job and a house for as long as you want them.'

There was definitely a smile lurking there, somewhere behind the whiskers. 'I'm gey pleased to hear it. This is the only job I know and I doubt I'd be happy anywhere else. Where do these fellows go?' He was still fondling the dogs, to their continued pleasure, and the question clearly referred to them.

I thought back to a section of the will over which I had skipped lightly. Some details came back to me. 'You have first refusal of any dogs in Sir Peter's ownership at the time of his death. If you don't want them they go to Ronnie. Failing which, provision has been made for their retirement.'

'They can come to me.' His voice confirmed the existence of the smile. 'I've aye had the use of them and kept them whenever Sir Peter was away, and we've had good times together. They're tied up with my best memories. And so was Joshua, the Lab before Old Nick. I never needed dogs of my own.'

'You'll get them as soon as we have Confirmation,'

I told him. 'Meantime, fetch them if ever you need them. You'll get a letter soon, spelling it all out.'

With the worst of his fears dispelled Hamish, who, I was to discover, was usually reserved to the point of being considered taciturn, was ready for a chat. It was pleasant in the wood with the sun flickering through the branches above and turning the fresh young leaves to emerald. I found that Hamish was a fund of useful and interesting information. We spoke of releases and habitats, predator deterrence and wildlife generally. Hamish bemoaned the difficulty of recruiting intelligent and obedient beaters. The subject came round again to Sir Peter's death.

'Was it his heart?' Hamish asked. 'It seemed that way.'

'We don't know yet,' I told him. 'There's to be an autopsy today. There were no obvious signs and with nobody having seen him go down . . . Or did anybody pass your way?'

He took my question at face value. 'I heard you go by with Sir Peter. After that, nobody until you called me.'

I was about to tear myself away when the dogs stirred, we heard the echo of voices in the tunnel and Calder appeared with his son-in-law. Time had slipped by while we talked.

Ian Fellowes waved aside my apology. 'Forget it,' he said. 'Joanna told us where you were and we were coming past here anyway. I'm afraid we've no word of the missing dog. I take it that he hasn't found his way back here?'

'There's been no sign of him,' I said. 'If he hasn't been stolen, he may be trying to find his way back to his old home. But with the Firth of Forth lying across his path, I wouldn't give much for his chances.'

'I'll make sure that word gets to the officers in the Lothians. You'll hear as soon as I know anything.' Fellowes glanced at his watch. 'And now, since we've come this far, shall we go on and inspect the place where it happened? I must get a move on. I'm meeting an electrician at the farm at ten-thirty. Come with us, Hamish?'

Hamish looked surprised, but nodded.

We started walking, in single file where the path narrowed. Keith Calder, who was in the lead, groped in the poacher's pocket of his coat and produced a large envelope. 'I have your prints,' he told me. 'Molly says there will be no charge, provided that you come and break bread with us this evening.'

'That's very kind,' I said. 'May I confirm a little later?'

'Don't leave it too late. For some reason, Molly gets uptight about not knowing whether guests are to be expected.'

'Her daughter has the same strange foible,' said Fellowes. 'Perhaps it runs in the family.'

I managed not to drag my feet as we neared the gate, but when the scene opened up it was just a small area of countryside, looking surprisingly bland. I left the dogs, sitting, some yards short of the gate. They seemed relieved not to come any closer to where their master had died and again I wondered whether our body language told them that the place had an unhappy connection. But perhaps they had been stung by the fence in the past. I put such thoughts aside and made up my mind to follow what was going on.

Fellowes looked at the muddy ground, but I could see with half an eye that Hamish and I, followed by the ambulance paramedics and the doctor, had stirred up the mud far too much for any useful traces to remain. He touched the gate cautiously and then opened it. I had never had a shock from the fence but I was very careful to steer clear of the gateposts. Fellowes closed the gate behind us and held out his hand to Calder, who took a slightly smaller envelope out of the larger, handed it to me and gave the larger to his son-in-law.

Fellowes glanced through his envelope. 'I have here a set of the relevant ones,' he told me, 'and I'm hanging on to your negatives for the moment. Do you want a receipt?'

'I'll trust you,' I said.

Fellowes took out a set of large prints in colour – about ten inches by eight, I thought. I forced myself to look at them. I was pleased to note that they looked needle sharp. My camera was a good one and I had trained myself over the years to hold it perfectly still. The light had been bright so that I had been able to use a small stop and obtain a considerable depth of focus. Fellowes singled out a shot of the body with Hamish crouched beside but not obscuring it. 'Was the body moved after you found it and before this shot was taken?' he asked.

I shook my head. 'Not more than very slightly,' I told him. 'Sir Peter was lying on his back and he wasn't touching the fence, so there was no need. We could try mouth-to-mouth and heart massage where he was.'

Detective Inspector Ian Fellowes raised his sandy

eyebrows. 'Why did you say that he wasn't touching the fence?'

'Earlier, Sir Peter had mentioned getting a shock off the fence. And I remembered that once, years ago, when I was nearly electrocuted by a faulty electric lawnmower, somebody else got a bad shock while trying to pull me away from it.'

Ian seemed to have been thinking along the same lines. He grunted without comment and looked down at the photograph. 'So his feet were towards the gate.' He looked vaguely from me to his father-in-law. 'If you were to lie down in the same position . . .'

Keith Calder showed no eagerness to lie down on the damp ground. 'I want to see what goes on.'

'And put in your twopenn'orth, no doubt,' said Fellowes.

Hamish stepped forward. 'Shall I?'

Fellowes regarded him doubtfully. 'You're taller than Sir Peter was. But try it. Lie down the way you remember the body lying.'

Hamish lowered himself to the ground, adjusting his position as directed by Fellowes with Calder adding what I thought was quite a valuable twopenn'orth. When they were both satisfied, Fellowes looked to me. 'Is that how you remember it?' he asked.

It was quite upsettingly close to how I remembered it. I fixed my eyes on Hamish's beard for reassurance and said, 'That's about it.'

'Right,' Fellowes said. 'Where was his gun when you found him?'

'About here.' I laid my stick by Hamish's right hand. 'I moved it over beside the fence because I didn't want to tread on a good Churchill.'

Calder snorted in amusement. 'If it had been a Baikal . . .' he began.

'I'd have walked over it,' I said.

'Obviously a man with a proper sense of priorities.'

'Save the double act for the dinner table tonight,' Fellowes said patiently. 'Either give me your attention or go away. Assuming from what we know so far that he was carrying his gun in his right hand or under that arm, he would have been reaching for the gate with his left. But that's the hinge side of the gate.'

'He could have walked straight up to the gate,' Calder suggested, 'and then turned slightly to reach for the latch with his left hand. Doing that, he might have touched the wire with his barrels.'

'Doubtful,' I said. 'He told me that he got a shock through his gun once before. He warned me to stay well clear and he didn't seem the sort of man to make the same mistake again.'

'Let's try it,' said Fellowes. 'Hamish, you can't fall upwards, but try to get up without moving your feet from where they are now.' Awkwardly, Hamish lurched to his feet. 'Now,' Fellowes said, handing him the stick, 'if that was a gun over your right arm, could you touch the wires with the barrels while reaching for the latch of the gate with your other hand?'

Hamish settled my stick under his right armpit and over his bent elbow in the usual manner for carrying a shotgun and made a few exploratory gestures. 'I *could*,' he said doubtfully, 'if I tried very hard. There's a whole lot of damned, unhandy things I could do if I was daft enough. But my feet's just no' in the right place, by a mile. Can I move them now?'

'Wait a minute,' said Calder. 'Peter wasn't expecting a shot. He could have had the gun under his left arm.'

'Then we wouldn't have found it beside his right hand,' I pointed out.

'I suppose not.'

Fellowes studied the photographs while he thought about it. 'He could have made a convulsive leap when he got the shock,' he suggested at last. 'Then the jolt brought on another heart attack, or caused his pacemaker to malfunction, and down he went.'

'I doubt that,' Calder said. 'I've seen electric shocks – had a few myself, for that matter. Alternating current might throw you back as you say. With direct current, you're more likely to freeze, or go down where you stand. But there aren't any hard and fast rules about it and the shock you get off a cattle fence is probably too quick to have time to alternate anyway. With electricity, the damnedest things can happen.'

'He'd only have had to step back with one foot,' Fellowes said wistfully. 'Well, we'll have to see what the electrician and the pathologist have to tell us.' He looked at his watch again. 'First, the electrician – and I asked the farmer to be available. Coming?'

'Do you need me any more?' Hamish asked. 'If no', I'll awa' and do something useful.'

'You just did something useful,' Ian said. 'I'm grateful. But you can get back to your pheasants, if that's what turns you on.'

'It doesna' turn me on quite,' Hamish said seriously, 'but I like fine to be busy about my work.'

Until Mr Enterkin arrived, I decided, I might as well be learning what I could about the estate and about the demise of its owner. 'Take the dogs with you,'

I told Hamish. 'I'll tag along with them.' He nodded, handed me my stick and patted his leg as he walked back past the two Labs. They fell cheerfully into file behind him.

We set off along the route that I had taken the day before, following the electric fence between the edge of the wood and a strip of kale that bordered the oilseed rape.

'There's one area of Sir Peter's will that I don't understand,' I told Keith Calder as we walked along the edge of the wood. 'Mostly, it's a sensible and business-like document, concerned with giving help where it's needed or rewarding past service and then keeping the estate together. Nothing wild or fanciful. There are none of the eccentric legacies with funny conditions attached to them, which I'd be sorely tempted to include in my will if I were rich enough for anybody to pay any heed. But suddenly there's mention of financing a film, with your name cropping up. That seems totally out of keeping. What's it all about?'

Fellowes fell back so that Calder and I could walk side by side.

'I wondered whether he'd remembered to make provision for that,' Calder said, 'but it might have seemed a bit premature to ask the question before the will's been read. I'll tell you about it. Let me think where to begin . . .

'Peter was very much concerned about bias, politically and in the media, television especially. His view, with which I heartily concurred, was that politicians and journalists are adept at doing the expedient thing and telling people what they think people want to hear, rather than the truth. He believed that most of the papers and networks are owned by big businessmen, so that the editors and staff, who are predominantly left wing, are usually restrained from open class hatred, but they still view the shooting man as belonging to the idle rich and therefore fair game. Did you see that a protest by two hundred anti-vivisectionists made all the top slots while a peaceful march by twenty thousand shooters in central London, protesting against Draconian legislation against them, was hardly mentioned in any news bulletin except one in Australia?'

'I saw that,' I said.

'Peter complained that anything – fiction or news item – seeming to portray the shooting man as a rich and bloodthirsty idiot got immediate coverage whereas anything factual showing him, or any other field-sportsman, as he really is – coming from no particular social or economic level, genuinely humane and concerned about wildlife and usually much better informed about it than the self-proclaimed "experts" – would be spiked and forgotten or edited until the opposite message was all that was left. That is what is now called "political correctness", so help me Jesus! So Peter commissioned a script for a one-hour film from a writer who lives near here, Simon Parbitter.'

It took me a second or two to associate the name with a successful novelist. 'I've read some of his stuff,' I said. 'He's good.'

'I pull his leg mercilessly, but he *is* good. The funny thing is that he's an Englishman and although he's lived in Scotland for donkey's ages, raised a family and merged into the background, he still doesn't shoot or fish. But he isn't above handling a dog to pick up on a shoot and he got so involved in the project that he wrote the script for nothing, with some equally unpaid help from Hamish and myself. And very good the shooting script turned out to be, too. You'll find a copy of it somewhere among Peter's things. Spiral bound with a blue cover.

'The script sets out to be the usual sort of documentary, about the wildlife on a keepered estate, but along the way it brings out the care for wildlife generally shown by shooting interests and their keepers.'

'I take it that you refer to a "wildlife manager" rather than a keeper?' I suggested.

'Once, in the introduction. After that, we decided not to resort to evasions. "Gamekeeper" became a dirty word in Victorian days, when game preservation was taken to ridiculous extremes. Times have changed and the whole aim of the script is to say so. It also brings out how the pheasants and ducks are released, gradually, to grow on under wild conditions and it compares their journey to the table with that of farmed chickens. And it shows the damage that foxes do to farmers as well as to shoots, with actual film of foxes killing lambs and doing all the things that our opponents swear they never do.

'The film would have shown a fairly typical syndicate, consisting of a baronet, a doctor, three shopkeepers, a small builder and two junior civil servants, all turning out for working parties and, later, harvesting some of their released birds – but we've lost the baronet now. Like most of the others, Hamish was going to appear as himself, and very good he'd be.

'At first offering, the script was turned down flat as "too controversial", which wasn't unexpected but it infuriated Peter. I think it's the only time I've seen him genuinely angry. We could have got the project taken on by one of the smaller independent networks, but Peter wanted national coverage. He was just girding his loins for the fight when this happened. He had raised some money and was quite prepared to put a lot of his own into the kitty to provide "consultancy fees".'

'Bribes,' I said.

'Fighting fire with fire,' Calder said firmly. 'It's amazing how some people's scruples become modified at the sight of a nice, fat fee. And how they manage to rationalize the turnaround later.'

The descent into the former railway cutting gave me a breathing space to digest the implications of the project. When we were walking three abreast along the permanent way I said, 'The idea's good. And long overdue. But I don't envy whoever has to kick-start the project. He'll find himself the rope in a huge tug-of-war, with the world and more especially his wife joining in on either side.'

A faint sound of amusement from Inspector Fellowes should have warned me.

'That,' Calder said, 'is you.'

'Me?' I said, or something equally profound.

'Why do you think Peter made you his co-executor? Why did he make sure that we met at dinner? He wanted somebody who knew his way around the world of business but would be sympathetic to the aims of the project. Ralph Enterkin couldn't do it in a thousand years. I said that you would be perfect.'

'Well, thank you very much!' I said indignantly.

'Not at all.'

111

'You do realize that I'm about a hundred years old?'

'You're younger than Peter was,' Calder pointed out, 'and as fit as a flea. And you've been getting restive, vegetating in the countryside, according to Peter.'

I thought of another objection. 'If I start trying to offer bribes to television executives, I'm going to end in clink. Aren't I?' I added to Ian Fellowes, suddenly remembering that he was a middle-ranking policeman.

'Not bribes,' Fellowes said. I could tell that he was hiding his amusement with difficulty. 'You certainly mustn't offer bribes. Consultancy fees. There's a world of difference. And you'll have Ralph Enterkin to keep you a hair's breadth on the right side of the law. That's the sort of thing he's good at.'

'He'd have to be bloody good,' I said.

We walked on in silence, each busy with his own thoughts. A minute or two later we climbed the embankment, reached the road where I had met the ambulance and set off along the verge.

'Peter intended to play himself,' Calder said suddenly, 'the concerned landowner doing a balancing act between the shoot and the farming, putting the brakes on insecticide spraying and insisting on flushing bars on the silage machinery and harvesters. You could read for the part.'

We turned onto the farm road. My interest, already aroused, began to burn. I had always felt that I could have been an actor, even a good one, but had resigned myself to the fact that I had left it too late. But, I decided, it's never too late for talent to reveal itself.

The barns were looming ahead, but first we had to pass a house with a walled garden. From its style and setting one would have taken it for the farmhouse –

which I realized, remembering Peter's words, it had once been.

'This is where that man lives, isn't it?' I asked.

'What man?'

Suddenly I found that my memory for names, usually reliable, had deserted me. It happens, as one grows older. Before I could stop myself I uttered the only name that came to mind, the name that Peter Hay had used. 'Snot,' I said. A furious face fringed with a sandy beard appeared above the wall. I felt cowardice rushing over me. ''Snot that house at all,' I said quickly and hurried onward to the barn without looking back.

Chapter Seven

My improvisation would not have fooled a toddler and had probably made matters worse. I could also sense embarrassment from my two companions. To my relief, there came the sound of a vehicle and a small van arrived. There was a loud exchange of greetings with the electrician, who seemed surprised to receive such an effusive welcome, and I contrived to walk round the corner of the barn without looking back.

The electrician forged ahead and was waiting for us by the big, open-fronted tractor shed as we arrived, a gaunt nervous man of middle age with an early stubble and a thin crop of limp hair. His blue van was crammed with drums of cable, boxes of assorted components and at least one washing machine. The name on the panels read 'J. Flaherty, Electrical Engineer', and I had gathered from the greetings that we were in the company of Mr Flaherty himself.

The farm manager must have found himself a task from where he could keep an eye out for us, for he arrived on foot only seconds after the electrician. Mr Jennings (Geordie, Peter Hay had called him) was a round and cheery looking man, but for the moment displaying anxiety which I put down to the possibility that his employer had fallen victim to an electric fence under his control.

Ian Fellowes took command before the farmer could get overexcited. 'You've heard that Sir Peter Hay died yesterday?' (The two men nodded, wide-eyed.) 'You know me – Inspector Fellowes. And this is Mr Kitts, one of Sir Peter's two executors. We don't know how Sir Peter died yet. The autopsy will be today and we should know more after that. But, for the moment, I'm looking around before things get tidied up, moved, repaired, broken or tampered with, just in case some vital information should get lost. Fair enough?'

'Aye,' said the farm manager. 'As far as it goes.'

'Sir Peter collapsed beside the gate to Langstane Wood, over there,' Fellowes said, pointing to where the wood stood up dark above the green of the fields, beyond the wide hollow. 'The doctor isn't sure of the cause, so the fiscal will probably order an inquiry. The autopsy may show something quite different, but we have to consider the possibility that he may have had a shock off the fence. He was an old man,' Fellowes added quickly before the farmer could begin his protestations, 'with a dicky heart and a pacemaker. It might not have taken much of a shock.'

'There's nocht ill wi' that fence,' Mr Jennings said. 'And it's perfectly legal.'

'I know it's legal,' Fellowes said, 'and I don't suppose there's anything wrong with it. But let's just make sure, shall we? Mr Flaherty?'

'I supplied Mr Jennings with this unit,' said the electrician. 'Right, Geordie? And there was nothing wrong with it then, nothing at all.' In contrast to

115

McAnderton the builder, he had an Irish name but a definitely Scottish accent.

'There still isn't,' the farm manager said gruffly.

Mr Flaherty led the way into the tractor shed and up to the bench, on which stood a white box, the size of a small attaché case. Insulated cables were attached and were led neatly along the walls at high level. The label on the box bore a picture of various farm animals with the legend ELECTRIC SHEPHERD – MAINS ELECTRIC FENCE UNIT and some smaller printing. 'There you are,' he said proudly, as though he had personally designed it or produced it out of a hat. 'Only takes about five watts to run it. That's an eighth of the power of a forty-watt bulb,' he added, in case we were unable to do the sum for ourselves. 'But it can put out more than five thousand volts.'

I was already aware of the principle behind electric fences. Calder seemed equally unimpressed. But Fellowes's jaw dropped. 'Five thousand . . . but that's more than enough to kill a man.'

'Not at five watts,' Mr Flaherty said. 'That's – ' his lips moved silently in calculation ' – that's a thousandth of an amp. Couldn't harm a soul. But they feel it, right enough.'

The farmer was regaining confidence. 'That's right,' he said. 'The idea is that if a beast noses the wire it gets a sharp jolt. It'll not go near the fence again or it might find out that on a dry day most of them could push through the fence without feeling it. Dry hair's a good insulator. But don't tell them that.'

'We won't,' said Fellowes. 'I don't spend a lot of time chatting with farm animals. Not that I wouldn't get more sensible answers than from some I know. Now, that's enough blether. Mr Flaherty, can you tell us what current it is actually producing?'

'No problem.' Flaherty fetched a meter from his van and stooped over the unit. After a minute he straightened up. 'Sir Peter didn't get a shock off this, the way it is now. There's no current coming out of it at all.'

Geordie Jennings jumped as though the absent current had been applied to himself. 'Hey! Look again!' he said.

'You think I don't know what I'm on about? I tell you there's nothing coming out,' said Flaherty. He took a grip of two of the terminals. 'See?'

'Fuse must've gone,' said the farmer, turning away in a hurry.

The electrician was still busy. 'Power's reaching here,' he said. He lifted the casing off the unit and prodded it with the terminals of his meter. 'Secondary winding's burned out,' he announced.

'Can you fix it? Or get me a replacement?'

Flaherty considered. 'Two days,' he said, in a tone that brooked no argument.

Jennings held his head and walked round in a small circle. 'I ken where I can borrow a battery unit,' he said suddenly. He left the shed at the double.

'Damned if I know what he's getting in a tizzy about,' Flaherty said. 'Usually it takes at least a week before they realize the fence isn't live any more.' He picked up his meter and turned away.

'Hold on a moment,' snapped Fellowes. 'You're not finished yet. What could cause the secondary winding to burn out? That's the side that's at high voltage and low amperage, right? Would a short circuit cause it?'

'Not unless the unit was faulty,' the electrician said, pausing beside his van. 'Otherwise, it can't happen. It gets shorted every time the wind blows a wet twig against it. It's supposed to just burn off any vegetation that touches it.'

'Let me get at it another way,' the policeman said. He scratched his neck in furious thought. 'Somebody touching the fence wouldn't cause the winding to burn out?'

'If it did that, the beasts would all be out of the field moments after the first one nosed it.'

'But it *did* burn out. And at that moment, would there be a surge of current enough to be dangerous to a man?'

The electrician frowned. 'Could be. It's possible. I doubt it, but it is possible. There's no telling what can happen, with electricity.'

'I see.' Fellowes was not giving up yet. 'If you took the unit apart, could you tell why it failed?'

'Not to be certain sure. You'd be better sending it back to the makers. Listen.' Suddenly Mr Flaherty became helpful. 'I'll have to get them to send another unit, p.d.q. That means their van will be coming. Why don't I take this one out now and send it back with the van? You can write a letter telling them what you want to know.'

'That,' said Fellowes, 'is more like it. Thank you, Mr Flaherty, you've been helpful at last. Now, are we walking or shall we cadge a lift?' He looked at the electrician.

'The back of my van's full,' Flaherty said, stating the obvious. 'I could take one of you.'

'And have you seen the state Geordie Jennings lets his car get into?' Calder enquired.

'Leave it to me,' I said. My legs were beginning to ache again. I took out my mobile and phoned the house. Mr Enterkin had just arrived, Joanna said, and was looking through the messages while he waited for me. And there was no word of Spin. Had Mr Fellowes found me? I said that he had and asked her to send somebody, anybody, to pick us up from the farm.

As I finished the call, a recent but already battered estate car swung into sight, with Geordie Jennings at the wheel. He braked to a halt beside us and caught my eye, but his windows were closed and whatever he was mouthing at me was drowned by the noise from a faulty silencer. I walked round the car. He wound down his window and, hearing the din, stopped his engine. 'I've just thocht. You're the executor?' he asked.

'I'm half of him,' I said. Looking into the car, I could see what Keith Calder had implied. It seemed that Jennings was not averse to carrying livestock in the back seat.

The farmer's round face remained bland but there was a gleam in his eye. 'Sir Peter was promising me tarmac on the road here and a second bathroom in the farmhouse and a new roof to the drying shed and . . . and . . .'

Behind the farmer's back Flaherty was grinning and Calder, with his face screwed up, was shaking his head violently.

'Bring me Sir Peter's letter,' I said, 'and we'll see what we can do.'

Jennings looked shocked. 'There was no need for letter-writing. Sir Peter was a man of his word.' His tone was intended to imply that I was proving less scrupulous.

'I'll come and take a look when I have time,' I said. 'Then I'll consult Miss Hay. You'll be her employee after the will's proved.'

Jennings glared at me, started his engine and roared off in pursuit of a stopgap energizer for his electric fence.

'He won't be the last chancer to try it on,' Calder said. 'Not by a mile.'

I would have preferred to wait where we were, but I was outvoted and I did not want to be left out of any discussion. We started to walk, passing Snot's house but without a further view of his agitated beard. I might just as well have seated myself and waited, because each of us was busy with his own thoughts. We had covered nearly half the distance to the house by road, as I discovered later, and were arriving at a corner of the pine wood which I had seen from the old railway line, when a car appeared at last in the distance. 'It's your fellow executor,' Calder said sadly. 'We'd have been as quick walking back the way we came.'

'As quick,' I said, 'but more tired. It's all very well for you teenagers . . .'

'You're getting to be as bad as Ralph,' Calder said.

'And that,' Ian said, 'is fighting talk if ever I heard it.'

I was glad to take a front seat when Enterkin pulled up beside us and after a moment's hesitation Calder and Fellowes entered the back of the car. Rather than turn in a narrow gateway, Enterkin insisted on driving to the farm road, so it seemed that we might as well have followed my wishes and taken seats in the shed to wait for him. When his passengers were covering that section of road for the fourth time that day, he said, 'The autopsy is proceeding already. As requested, Professor Mannatoy is carrying it out himself. With the agreement of the procurator fiscal, he has promised to come to the house later and advise us.'

'How did you manage that?' Fellowes asked curiously. 'The fiscal usually hugs these things close to his manly bosom until he's good and ready.'

'The fiscal,' Enterkin said, 'was once my apprentice. Old loyalties die hard.'

We came to a junction with a road which looked familiar. A little further on we turned through the archway and trundled up the drive to the house. A Range Rover in police livery was parked near the front door.

'When do you expect the Professor?' Fellowes asked as we emerged.

Enterkin carefully locked his car. 'He said late afternoon.'

'I'll be with you four-ish.'

As Fellowes's vehicle departed along the drive – at several times the speed at which Mr Enterkin's had arrived – I said, 'What's Calder's interest in this? Don't you find it curious, if not downright suspicious?'

Enterkin led the way into the house. 'I find it neither,' he said severely. 'Apart from the fact that he was a very close and long-standing friend of Sir Peter and knew him better than anyone else, Keith is very knowledgeable about matters rural. Detective Inspector Fellowes, who is, after all, his son-in-law, often depends on Keith to keep him straight. In addition to which, Keith's a remarkable investigator in his own right. He has a nose for anything not quite as it should be, the curiosity to follow it up, a logical and deductive brain and the tenacity of a bulldog. Ian Fellowes would be mad not to make the fullest use of him as an unpaid consultant.'

I apologized. Enterkin, on behalf of the absent Keith Calder, accepted the apology with grace.

Enterkin had already been through my list of messages and had added a note of those which had arrived subsequently. We soon dealt with any business in them, at least to the extent of deciding what action would be taken and which of us would take it. Calder had been right – the tenant farmers were beginning to hear the knocking of opportunity. If Sir Peter had really promised all the improvements which were now being claimed in his name, there would have been little cash in hand left for his granddaughter to inherit. We lunched as before off two trays.

I mentioned the proposed film.

'Sir Peter made some provision in the Trust Disposition and Settlement for its production. When I asked for details, he said that I wouldn't understand but to put it in anyway,' Enterkin said indignantly, spreading pâté on his toast. 'Do you know what it is that I wouldn't understand?' He added thinly sliced tomato.

'In general, yes. I had the explanation given to me only an hour ago.' I explained the bequest, much as Calder had explained it to me.

'He was right,' the solicitor said. 'I don't understand. But then, the uses of propaganda have always been a source of puzzlement to me. Truth is truth.'

'How can you possibly say that?' I asked him. 'You,

a lawyer! To you, truth has no relationship to hard facts, it is whatever a court decides to be the facts, on the basis of the evidence put before it and ignoring all else.'

'And what is your point?' the solicitor asked with dignity.

'My point is that truth, to you, is therefore whatever you can persuade a court to accept as truth.'

'And many generations of lawyers have fought and bled to ensure that it is so. Returning to the *res gestae*, however, the wishes of the deceased are sacrosanct – barring insanity, illegality and impracticability. You will have to deal with the film. All the same,' he added musingly, 'if I understand you aright, it is to be a documentary about real people, and Sir Peter is no longer with us to play himself. I always felt that as an actor I might well have shone. I have often been complimented on my bearing and enunciation in court. Do you think . . .?'

The idea of the fat little solicitor playing the part of the lanky baronet was unthinkable. For a start, he could never have carried a gun in a manner suggesting that he was anything other than totally unfamiliar with it. Besides, I had earmarked the part for myself. I made an evasive answer and then hastened to change the subject. 'I shall have to be taking a day or two at home soon,' I told him. 'When would be suitable?'

'When would suit you?'

'Any time. One day is much the same as another at home.'

He made an extraordinary face. It looked for all the world as though he was about to kiss an unloved and insanitary female relative, but it was, I had learned, his habitual grimace when deep in thought. 'There may be urgent estate or business matters to be dealt with,' he said at last. 'Either, and in particular the first, might see me out of my depth although I would never allow a client to suspect it. But the weekend should be relatively safe. If you could stay on tonight and part of tomorrow – Friday – and go home later in the day . . .?'

'No problem,' I said. 'I could come back early next week.'

'That seems very suitable.'

We settled to work, apportioning the various tasks between us. Broadly, the nuts and bolts of Confirmation were his while, as we already knew, the matters of property and of investments were to be my portion; but I had a feeling that parts of the no-man's land between were being passed to me rather as a magician forces a card on his dupe.

Several more messages had arrived on the answering machine. We dealt with them together. Most required no more than an acknowledgement, but there was one call from a former acquaintance, one of those who I had told of Peter Hay's death. It requested an early call back. I made the call. The outcome made me sit up although Enterkin seemed to take it as a matter of course. The death had left a vacancy on the board of a company. Would I consent to be appointed in his place, at least until the next AGM? I said that I would consider and phone again.

'I've retired,' I said. 'I retired so that I wouldn't have to go to meetings any more.'

He looked reprovingly at me. 'It concerns Sir Peter's investments. It's your duty to go. Besides – ' he twinkled for a moment ' – you will be admirably remunerated for nodding wisely and voting with the Chair.'

'You could do that as well as I could,' I told him.

'Better,' he corrected. 'Much better. In the course of a long career in law I have perfected the art of looking wise while sound asleep but waking instantly when addressed. But they have their own lawyers who will not wish their opinions to be questioned. What they're after is big business know-how. I wouldn't know what the hell they're talking about.' I rather suspected that his reluctance stemmed from neither ignorance nor modesty but from sheer laziness. I was beginning to see through Mr Enterkin.

We were still hard at it, two hours later, when a large Japanese four-wheel drive vehicle pulled up near the front door. It bore several dents and scratches and carried traces of dried-on mud or possibly dung. In rural Scotland, most vehicles soon get into that sort of condition and it occurred to me for the first time that a pathologist must sometimes be called out in any sort of weather to visit bodies in some very difficult terrain. Calder and Fellowes arrived so close behind the Professor that I was sure that they had followed him from the public mortuary.

I had expected a gaunt and morbid figure straight from the pages of a Gothic novel, but Professor Mannatoy turned out to be a rotund and cheerful man, not unlike Mr Enterkin, with whom he seemed to have a nodding acquaintance, but with an even greater capacity for sudden irascibility.

Enterkin, assuming the mantle of host, seated us

in a group with the Professor as focus and introduced me as his fellow executor.

'Detective Inspector Fellowes,' said the policeman, nodding.

The Professor looked at Keith Calder. Enterkin hesitated. 'I shall tell the deceased's granddaughter as much as she should know,' Calder said loftily. I had to admire the man's gall. His statement might be literally true, but it was a prime example of what Mr Enterkin would doubtless have categorized as either *suppressio veri* or *suggestio falsi*, or possibly both, glossing cleverly as it did over the fact that he had not the faintest shadow of a right to be present.

Professor Mannatoy nodded a general greeting. 'If I were to ask what idiot allowed the body to be removed before a pathologist had seen it *in situ*, it would not be with the intention of embarrassing anybody,' he said, 'but purely to satisfy my curiosity.'

The others looked at me with a faint air of withdrawal of the hems of garments. 'There was no one person to blame,' I said. 'I found Sir Peter and called his gamekeeper, who was the only person within earshot. Between us we attempted resuscitation and phoned for an ambulance. A doctor arrived on the heels of the paramedics and they carried him off, either because they thought that he was dead of natural causes or because they still hoped to revive him, I wouldn't know.'

The Professor nodded forgiveness. 'Well, it's a pity. Sometimes a cause of death may be obvious, but more often the only obvious fact is that the body has ceased to function. In such circumstances, such factors as the position of the body or the condition of its surroundings may furnish a valuable or even the only clue. In this instance, there were no significant wounds, none of the usual symptoms of toxic poisoning, nor any signs of organic failure other than death itself. The heart was diseased but could have supported life for several years yet. I have sent samples to the laboratory with a request that they be examined for toxic substances, but I do not expect any to be found.'

'No sign of a heart attack?' Calder suggested.

'A heart attack,' the Professor snapped, 'is an event, not a condition. An infarct might be seen in autopsy, if the patient had managed to live for another forty-eight hours or so. Otherwise not. The heart had ceased to beat. Full stop.'

'In the local surgery,' Fellowes said diffidently, 'there's a sign which says "Nobody with a pacemaker to enter this room", or words to that effect. We wondered whether he hadn't received an electric shock which stopped his pacemaker.'

'I was just approaching that subject,' said the Professor in tones of great patience. 'If you will allow me to speak . . .' (Fellowes muttered a quick apology.) 'Very well. Sir Peter's pacemaker was of the "demand" type, which is only triggered when the heart stops beating. In this instance, the pacemaker was functioning perfectly and still attempting to restart the heart. So,' he added in my direction, 'any attempt which you may have made in the direction of heart massage was wasted effort.

'However, I have seen photographs which confirm that, as I had been advised, the deceased was found near an electric fence and, moreover, that it was his left hand which had been towards the fence. Also, he was wearing leather boots with metal studs or tackets, on damp ground – every one of those factors mitigating in favour of electrocution and against the victim's chance of survival. But electrocution may be very difficult to prove, if it stops short of incinerating the body. Like a heart attack, it is an event.' The Professor was looking past or through us. He had slipped into the mode of the habitual lecturer. The audience had vanished and all that mattered was the orderly presentation of the facts.

'Electrocution kills, occasionally, by paralyzing the breathing centres, so any attempts at artificial respiration might not have been wasted. More frequently, it kills by stopping the heart's rhythm and the only symptom of that, again, is death itself. But there must always be places of exit and entry of the current. Whether these are detectable depends on the area over which the current was diffused, but the signs usually take the form of white spots, often with a pale ring around them. These may be very tiny and difficult to detect.

'I examined the deceased's hands and other exposed skin carefully but his hands in particular were roughened, apparently by gardening, and if signs there were I was unable to find them. However, when I came to the sole of the right foot I found four very faint marks, falling within the definition I have given you and corresponding roughly with the position of the tackets in that boot. I therefore concluded that the deceased had indeed suffered an electric shock and had most probably died from it. That will be the burden of my report to the procurator fiscal and, if called to an inquiry, I shall testify to that effect.' The Professor came back to earth and looked from one to the other of us, apparently surprised to find that he still had a living audience.

'Would Sir Peter's heart condition have made him particularly susceptible to death by electrocution?' Enterkin asked at last.

'In my opinion, no.'

Fellowes stirred again. 'Were your findings compatible with a shock at the voltage of an electric cattle fence?'

For the first time, the Professor hesitated. 'That is getting outside my field,' he said at last. 'Death by electrocution is unusual at less than around a hundred volts. At domestic mains voltage, it is quite common.'

'I have the specification here,' Fellowes said. He opened a brightly coloured leaflet. 'I see that the mains unit can put out up to seven thousand volts.' (The Professor's eyebrows shot up.) 'But that is in a very short pulse about once a second. The overall consumption is only three watts and it stores just over one joule of energy to produce that pulse.'

The Professor shrugged. 'I have forgotten such elementary physics as I ever learned. And, of course, there are far too many unknowns in the equation. If you knew the electrical resistance between the power unit and the gate and how good were the contacts between the deceased and the wire and the earth, somebody might be able to do a calculation, but I would hesitate to count on its accuracy. It is certainly completely beyond me. I will, however, offer you one further fragment of information. The deceased's pockets contained several scraps of newspaper, a toffee paper and a screwed-up yoghurt carton.'

'He hated to see litter,' Calder said.

'Quite so. I inferred as much. It seems that he had just picked up a piece of foil in his left hand, the sort of foil sometimes used to cover over a snack bought for the oven. His fist had clenched tightly around it. That may explain why the current was so broadly diffused that his hand showed no marks. But on the basis of the figures just quoted I would suggest that the pulse of energy would last for far less than the duration of a heartbeat and therefore would be unlikely to interfere seriously with the heart. Moreover, I would suggest that no farmer is going to electrocute his stock.'

'But if the unit developed a fault?' Fellowes said. 'The electrician that we called in found the secondary winding burned out.'

Professor Mannatoy nodded slowly. 'In that eventuality, anything could happen. One of the few facts about electricity that I do remember is that an arc in the system can intensify the current. And in the process of failure the electronic timer or the capacitor, or both, may have failed while current was still passing. The manufacturers may be able to help.'

Enterkin looked from one to the other of us, soliciting questions. 'If that is the full summary of your findings,' he said at last, 'we can only thank you for taking the trouble to come and tell us. No doubt we can call on you again if further questions arise. Perhaps you'd care for a drink before you leave?'

'I rarely drink,' the Professor said, 'and never before driving. I see too many of the consequences on the post mortem table.'

'Very wise,' said Enterkin who, I learned later,

rarely refused the offer of a drink after mid-afternoon, although to do him justice he usually preferred to leave his car and go home by a lift or a taxi if the offer had been overgenerous.

Chapter Eight

We all escorted the Professor to his four-by-four. So much authority seemed to be vested in the pompous little man that we felt we could hardly do less. Or perhaps it was the thought that some day any one of us might finish up under his knife and perhaps, if we treated him with the greatest courtesy, he would be gentle with our poor remains . . .

As the vehicle vanished through the archway, Enterkin said to me, 'I find that my wife will be away this evening. So I'm unable to confirm my tentative invitation. It seems that we shall have to have you for dinner some other evening. I trust that you can face another evening here?'

'Was that why you deferred answering my invitation?' Calder asked me.

'It was. Is it still open?' I asked.

'Certainly. You too, Ralph, unless you'd rather frequent the hotel?'

'And miss Molly's cooking? Never!' the solicitor cried gaily, clearly in a good mood now that he had been relieved of embarrassment.

'What about you and Deborah?' Calder asked Fellowes.

'I'm sure we'll be delighted,' Fellowes said. 'But hadn't we better see what my mother-in-law says first?'

'I suppose so.' Calder seemed surprised that anyone could doubt Molly Calder's ability to cope with sudden guests, but he took the hint. 'If I may, I'll go in and phone both Molly and Deborah.'

He vanished into the house.

'Now perhaps might be the time for that drink?' Enterkin suggested.

'We have things to do,' Fellowes said. 'Another time. If both ladies agree, we'll pick you both up, shall we, at around seven-thirty?'

'But I have a perfectly good car of my own,' I protested.

'Which you would be ill-advised to drive after enjoying Calder hospitality. I speak from experience. Fortunately, while she has a two-year-old to manage, my wife is almost teetotal. I would hate it if duty obliged me to breathalyse myself. I just hope that Deborah can get hold of a sitter at such short notice. Otherwise we may have a fractious infant in the car with us.'

Calder came out of the house. 'Molly says that she'll be delighted to see all of you.'

'In so many words?' Fellowes asked.

'Near enough,' said Calder.

'Until seven-thirty, then,' said Fellowes.

They made their departure. Seen through the back window of the car, they seemed to be arguing.

'We may as well have that drink,' I said.

Enterkin seemed to be on the point of agreeing but he looked at his watch. 'Is that the time? I have one last client to visit. I'll leave you to drink alone. But not too heavily. Our Detective Inspector was correct when he warned you about Calder hospitality. But I must rush. I shall return in the morning.'

'We'll meet this evening,' I reminded him.

'So we shall, so we shall. Until then!' He eased himself into his car and rushed very slowly away.

I returned to the house and told Mary Fiddler that I should be dining out. She seemed to have started work already on the evening meal but she took my defection cheerfully. No doubt Ronnie would benefit to the tune of my portion.

There was time to spare. The absence of company seemed a poor reason not to enjoy sampling Peter Hay's collection of malt whiskies. I found an already opened bottle of a malt that was new to me and drank a private toast to absent friends.

Perhaps I should have resumed work on the Confirmation. Enterkin had asked for a summary of Peter Hay's assets and I thought that I could remember the instructions that Peter had given me on how to winkle the information out of the various files on the computer, springing off from his last return to the Inland Revenue. But I would have to see Peter's accountants next week anyway. It had been a long day and would get longer. All work and no play, I told myself, would make me a very dull old gentleman. So I gathered up my fishing gear, called the two Labradors and set off for the small loch.

There is no accounting for the ways of fish. There was an abundant hatch of insects – until I anointed myself with repellent I was being eaten by midges – yet hardly a rise of fish. One trout was rising within reach of the bank but after a few misjudged casts I had scared him with the line and he had gone deep. They would be feeding below, on nymphs and emergers, I guessed. I took a seat against a tree to change my fly for a suitable nymph from Calder's shop. But I had missed my nap that afternoon and a large malt whisky was no substitute. I closed my eyes for a second against the brightness of the day, and was asleep on the instant.

I was jerked awake by a hand on my shoulder. My eyes snapped open. The light was fading. Hamish was stooping over me. 'Thank God!' he said. 'For a moment, I was thinking I had another corpse to deal with.'

I yawned and stretched and pulled myself together. 'Not this time,' I told him. 'Still no sign of the spaniel?'

'Not a trace. He may turn up yet.' Hamish shuffled his feet shyly. 'Ronnie and I've had a wee crack about the dogs. If we get the spaniel back, he'll take the old Labs on. That way, they'll spend most of their days back at the house where they've lived. You'd prefer that, eh, old ones?' The dogs, aware that they were being addressed in kindly terms, thumped their tails.

'That seems sensible.' I could hear splashes from the water as trout after trout rose to the hatch, but there was no time left for fishing. Hamish helped me to my feet. 'I'll have to go,' I said.

Hamish nodded, but he was not going to let me go just yet. 'You're staying on in the big house?'

I said that I was, meantime.

'And there'll just be you and yon Joanna in the place at night?'

I agreed.

Hamish looked me in the eye. 'I think a lot of

Joanna,' he said. 'Ah weel, you'll be able to see that nothing comes over her.'

'I'll be going home tomorrow for the weekend,' I told him. 'Perhaps you should take a look in, just to see that she's all right.'

He only nodded but he helped me to gather up my things. Hamish and I understood each other. He had made it clear that he had an interest in Joanna while I had assured him that I would not lay a finger on her. On the whole, I decided as I hurried through the calm, luminous dusk, I was rather flattered. At my age, I am not often credited with being a danger to young women. I rather wished that the danger could have been real.

I just had time for a quick shave, a shower and a change into a tolerably presentable suit before Ian Fellowes's car returned to the door, but there was no sign of the policeman. His wife was at the wheel. Deborah Fellowes was very alluring in what I supposed would be called a cocktail dress of elegant simplicity. She was alone in the car so I guessed that a sitter had been obtained.

She drove briskly and competently but had time to talk. 'Traditionally,' she said, 'I thought in-laws were supposed to hate each other. But the curse of my life is that my husband and my father get on too well. With Dad's encouragement – and mine, I must admit – Ian has taken to the country and everything rural like the proverbial duck to water. And Dad never could resist a mystery. Before Ian came along, he was always poking his nose in and upsetting the police. So a detective for a son-in-law was just what he'd have asked for if a genie had popped out of a bottle. In fact, I've sometimes wondered if he didn't mastermind the whole thing. Without our help, to be honest, I don't think Ian would have earned his last promotion, or certainly not so soon. So if the two of them aren't away ferreting or shooting somewhere, Dad's acting as Watson to Ian's Sherlock or more often the other way around.'

She sounded so indignant that I had to laugh. 'That doesn't sound like much of a curse on your life,' I said. 'More of a blessing.'

'I suppose it is, most of the time. But then something like this comes up and the two of them forget common sense and go dashing about the place, getting into trouble. They've vanished now, on some ploy of their own. They'll probably make dinner late, sit down to eat still covered in mud, if nothing worse, and be thoroughly pleased with themselves for having put a cat among somebody's pigeons.'

'Don't knock it,' I said with feeling. 'The opposite, conflict between in-laws, is worse. Is this ploy of theirs anything to do with Peter Hay's death?'

'Damned if I know,' she said.

We collected Mr Enterkin from below his flat near the Square and left Newton Lauder again, travelling northward. But before we came to the main road that bypassed the town, we turned off onto a byroad and turned again between stone pillars, to park in front of a substantial Victorian house. The twilight was almost gone and the light spilling from windows made it difficult to see more than stone walls decked with Virginia creeper and what seemed to be a wide and well-kept garden, in the spread of light from a lamp over the front door.

Molly Calder was as irritated as her daughter by the disappearance of their two men, but I gathered that she was not unused to such treatment. She dismissed the subject in very few words, carried Deborah off to help her and, with another word of apology, left us in the cheerful sitting room to comfort ourselves with the contents of Keith's drinks cupboard. Ralph Enterkin remarked that we could easily enjoy an hour or two in those circumstances and I had to agree. My interest in malt whiskies had been rekindled by the sample from Sir Peter's collection and Keith had a remarkable selection for us to try.

However, I only had time to drink one large one and to pour another when the two wanderers arrived. They joined us in the sitting room within a couple of minutes, washed and tidied and unashamed but looking, I thought, very serious. Deborah and Molly followed them in pursuit of a drink and an apology.

When at last everybody was holding a glass, Molly took her husband to task. 'Where did you have to go that was so urgent?' she asked.

The two men exchanged a quick glance. Some message passed. 'We may as well tell you,' Ian Fellowes said. 'Most of us have an interest in the matter and those who haven't are well able to keep a confidence. The fact is that we think that Sir Peter Hay's death was neither natural nor accidental.'

He had avoided using the word 'murder', but an echo of it hung in the air. I think that each of us had been holding in the dark recesses of our minds a fear that, somehow, Peter Hay had been deliberately killed.

To have that fear dragged out into the light stopped the conversation dead.

Molly Calder broke the silence. 'Not another word!' she said. 'If we start to discuss it here, dinner will burn. Come through to the dining room.'

Keith directed us to chairs in a panelled dining room which, like the sitting room, had been furnished with antiques, some genuine but most, I could guess, reproduction. Nothing had been given a place which would spoil the air of comfort and old-fashioned solidity belonging to the house, and all was very well kept. Molly Calder's love for her home shone through.

When we were seated, I tried to put a question to Keith, but he shook his head. 'Have patience,' he said. 'We'd never be forgiven if we said another word before my wife was here.'

'And mine,' said Ian Fellowes.

So we had patience until a chilled soup was before us. An excellent white wine, which I could not place, medium dry but with a tang to it, was served, unusually, from decanters. Looking back, it seems strange that the news had not spoiled our appetites, but we had already accepted the baronet's death and had our suspicions as to the means of it. Shock would return later when the culprit's identity emerged. For the moment, nothing had changed very much.

'Now,' said Molly. (We were by then all on first name terms by tacit agreement.) 'Who could possibly have wanted to kill Peter? He was the nicest person you could have hoped to meet!'

Deborah looked at her mother with tolerant affection. 'Mum, you're just too innocent. Everybody liked him – well, almost everybody – but a lot of folk will

profit from his death.' (I caught Ralph Enterkin's eye.
We were both thinking of Dorothy Spigatt.) 'Even more,
probably, will think that they'd be better off, because
that's how folks' minds work. And there are others
around with a tumbrel mentality. More to the point,
Ian – or Dad – what makes you think that somebody
killed him?'

Ian put down his spoon. 'The pathologist confirmed
what we had already suspected, that he had died as
the result of a powerful electric shock. Almost the last
thing the Professor said to us was that Sir Peter's left
hand was clamped on a piece of silver foil, of the kind
found covering dishes of food sold oven-ready. Sir Peter
did have a habit of picking up rubbish in order to take
it home and throw it away, but although the pathologist
accepted that as an explanation of why the current
was so diffused as to leave no burn-marks on the hand,
Keith pointed out what I was already thinking, that
metal foil of that sort seemed a strange thing to find
in open countryside. Possible, I suppose, that a dog or
a fox had stolen it out of a dustbin and carried it off,
but unlikely.

'So, on a hunch, we took another hard look at
Henry's photographs.'

'We could do with one or two much bigger enlarge-
ments,' Keith said to Molly. 'Do you think they could
stand it?'

'Easily,' Molly said. 'The negatives are razor sharp.
And there's a good depth of field, so you weren't using
a very high shutter speed.' She smiled at me. 'You must
have a very steady hand.'

'I've practised,' I said modestly.

'Could we stick to the point?' Deborah said. 'What makes you think – ?'

'Cool it,' said her husband. 'We're telling you. And yes, the photographs are razor sharp. On one of them in particular, taken from the other side of the fence and showing Peter with the spaniel and Hamish, you can see the metal gate and there's nothing untoward there at that time. But that was while you were on the outward journey?' He looked at me and I nodded. 'A later shot, taken when you were on the way back, shows the place. It's a very distant shot, but there's a tiny blink of light near a hinge of the gate. And it's not caused by dust on the negative because under powerful magnification the negative shows a distinctly dark spot in the emulsion. On the print it looks silver rather than white. That's one that we'd like pulled up bigger.'

'It set us wondering if the metal foil might have blown against the fence,' said Keith. 'When Peter came back, he would have seen the stuff on the fence and reached down to take it off, got an electric shock and clamped on it before going down. We haven't heard back from the manufacturer of the unit, and I don't suppose that we will for a week or more, but it seemed possible that the sudden earthing caused the unit to blow, momentarily releasing a higher current. Apart from the fact that Mr Flaherty said it wouldn't happen, there's only one other thing wrong with that for a theory.'

'That there wasn't any wind,' I said.

'Exactly,' Keith said. 'So we hurried back to the place, to have a good look before the weather breaks and traces are lost.'

'And?' said Deborah.

'And there are definite traces of something greasy on the gate and one of the wires,' said Ian. 'I've taken samples for analysis and comparison with the grease on the foil, but it looks like beef gravy. It's lucky that one of the dogs didn't happen along or they'd have licked it clean.

'So now we're guessing that somebody put the foil there, twisted round a wire and the post or the hinge of the gate, so that the gate would be live. They could have waited in the tractor shed and used jump leads to send mains voltage along the wires when they saw Peter arriving at the gate. Instead of getting the shock when he touched the gate he went to pick up the foil instead, but the result was the same.' He blew out his cheeks and made a helpless gesture which nearly knocked his glass over. 'You may well think that it's a piece of wild guesswork, a tower built on sand, a coat sewn onto a button and all the other expressions for a wild speculation. And maybe it is. But we've been cudgelling our brains, such as they are, and we can't come up with a better explanation.'

'You have to assume that somebody knew that we'd be going that way,' I objected.

'He always went that way into Home Farm,' said Deborah thoughtfully, 'when he was at home and meant to go and potter about with a dog and a gun. If you wanted to intercept him, you waited at the gate. And I think that everybody for miles around knew it.'

The soup was finished. Telling us to remain seated, Molly got up. We passed her our empty soup plates and she served the main course, a game pie. I learned later that during the season it was her habit to collect any badly damaged birds and, with Deborah, to turn them all into a very savoury stew which could be bagged and put away in the freezer as pie-fillers, ready for instant production in the event of unexpected guests.

'I'm enjoying the wine,' I said, 'but I don't recognize it. Do you mind if I ask what it is?'

'Not at all,' Deborah said. 'It's Vintner Number Three, fermented slowly at a very constant temperature, racked with great care and given just enough time to mature.'

'It's from a concentrate?' I was impressed. Mother and daughter were ladies of talent.

'It is. And it has a kick, so beware,' Ian said.

Molly resumed her seat. As the vegetables circulated, she said, 'What else have you found out?'

'From the gate,' Ian said, 'we went to the farm and took Geordie – Mr Jennings – round to his tractor shed. He told us that he was across the fields on foot at the crucial time, using a herbicide spray beneath the fence to keep the weeds from growing up and shorting the wires.'

'That's right,' I said. 'I remember Peter giving him a wave.'

'He also said that he might or more likely might not have seen somebody going into his tractor shed but he definitely couldn't have seen them once they were inside. But somebody inside could still have seen the gate and known when to switch on the power.

'We took a good look at where the energizer unit had been. There was a pair of jump leads at the other end of the bench, but nothing like long enough to reach from the nearest mains outlet to the unit, nor to the fence or any wiring connected to it. The cables which run to the energizer are clipped to the wall and there's no sign that they have been unclipped and fastened up again. But, of course, the place is a workshop and there was any amount of cable lying around. Any ingenious handyman could have rigged up a connection to put mains current into the fence wires. According to Mr Jennings, nothing had been touched – by which he meant that it all looked familiar. In a guddle like that, he wouldn't have known if the junk had been turned over by a bulldozer. So, really, we're not much further forward.'

Ralph Enterkin had been listening in silence while doing justice to the food. 'What happens next?' he asked.

'I'll have to make a report to the fiscal,' Ian said, 'and to my bosses in Edinburgh. Much will depend on their reactions. They may be understandably sceptical. We may not be able to take it much further until we have the report from the manufacturer of the energizer and another from the lab. I'll have to assemble a team and go over the ground with a fine-tooth comb, metaphorically speaking, and try for prints on the foil, on the gate and around the junk in the tractor shed. And I could do with larger blow-ups of all Henry's film, if you'd be so good,' he added to Molly.

'Yes, of course,' Molly said. 'And if you don't mind, Henry, I'd like to make prints for myself. Your photography's good and you've made a record of Peter's last few hours, showing him being himself and . . . happy.' Her voice broke on the last word but she pulled herself together and dabbed her eyes. 'If somebody killed him on purpose, Ian, you must catch the beast and put him away.'

'I'm glad you included the "if",' Ian said. 'We don't know anything for sure yet. But we won't let anyone get away with murder if we can possibly prevent it, I promise you that.'

'You'll keep us fully posted?' Ralph asked sleepily as Deborah drove us through the darkness. Ian hesitated. 'As executors, we have to walk with care,' Ralph added.

Ian, in the front passenger seat, turned his head. 'I don't quite see – '

'Let us suppose, to take one possibility among many, that Sir Peter was indeed helped out of this vale of tears. If the guilty party, or any accomplice, was to be given access to the house, he or she might not only profit from the crime by removing valuables from it, but in addition it might open the possibility of some tampering with evidence. Yet we can't exclude everybody. Nor can we expect you to tell us who you suspect. But we are capable of drawing our own conclusions.'

'If there was a crime,' I put in, 'it seems quite likely that the motivation for it stems from Peter Hay's business interests, in which case it may very well lie within the material held in his computer. If that were to crash, in the electronic sense, or to develop a virus, we could lose the evidence and a huge amount of other information besides, and we could never prove how it happened. So we need to know who we can and can't admit to the house.' I was pleased to note that I still sounded quite lucid.

'Heavens, yes!' Ralph said. 'Good that you thought of that.'

'I've had it in mind all along,' I said. 'Peter used his e-mail facility quite a lot. I'll have to see if any messages are waiting for him, but I've been putting it off because that's one medium by which a virus might get into the system.'

Electronic mail was beyond Ralph's experience and therefore did not exist. He had, however, accepted the existence of computers just as he accepted that their manipulation was beyond him. 'We can hardly exclude the granddaughter from what is now, subject to Confirmation, her own house,' he said, 'and I would not put it past her to introduce her undesirable – er – inamorato into the house while everybody's back is turned. I'll get hold of an expert and have him visit the house over the weekend and copy everything in the computer onto – what do they call them? – floppies? Damn silly name!'

'Almost as silly as inamorato,' I said.

'Early next week,' Ian said drowsily, 'I shall probably – if my superiors back me – want to see you both and get a list of everybody you know of who benefits, or thinks that he or she benefits, from Sir Peter's death.'

'You can't expect that, surely,' Ralph said sharply. 'There could be the most appalling conflicts of interest. Just suppose – and I'm not saying for a moment that it's the case – but just suppose that one of my clients happens to obtain a business advantage from the death.'

'You're probably right,' Ian said. 'And, come to think of it, it would be most improper of me to update you on the progress of my enquiries.'

Ralph was ready for that one. 'In which case, we might admit quite the wrong person to the wrong information or place, unwittingly allowing him or her to hamper your investigation. However, this discussion seems premature. You have no further progress to report while for all I know my clients are one and all beyond suspicion. We must consider and discuss. Meantime, I will take advice about protecting the information on the computer. Floppies, forsooth!'

Ralph was still grumbling to himself about modern jargon, quite forgetting that he was a member of one of the world's most jargon-prone professions, when we dropped him off in the Square. Deborah looped around several small residential streets to deposit her husband at a neat modern bungalow, so that he could relieve the sitter.

As she left the street lights behind, she said, 'Is Joanna looking after you all right?'

Something in her voice suggested that she was not just concerned that I was being adequately fed. 'She seems anxious to please,' I said carefully.

Deborah drove for half a mile in silence. 'That's what I was afraid of,' she said at last. 'I'd better tell you something about Joanna. I've known her since she was a child. She was illegitimate. This was back when it mattered more than it does today. Her mother couldn't cope. Joanna was taken into care and I think, reading between the lines, wasn't treated any too well. The point is, ever since then she's been . . . odd. Sometimes she'll flirt with the older men. I think she's looking for a replacement for the father she never knew. She certainly set her cap at Dad once. God knows what she'd do if one of them took her up on it; my personal hunch is that she'd scream and run a mile, but I could be quite wrong.'

'That's very sad,' I said.

'Yes. I wouldn't have said anything except that she's also inclined to fantasize. I thought I should warn you that, given the least trace of encouragement, she may invent stories and not care where she repeats them. It happened once before and then, of course, they did the rounds and got believed. This place is like a gossip factory, with scandalmongers on every corner.'

'I'm glad that you told me.'

I was set down in my turn at the front door of the 'big house'. Ian's two warnings, one about Calder hospitality and the other about the strength of his wife's wine, had not been enough to save me from feeling my drink. Frankly, I was sure that I was glowing in the dark, a sensation which I had not felt for more years than I could remember.

But the evening was not yet quite complete. I managed to recall what was missing. A cup of tea seemed superfluous – I was neither hungry nor thirsty. On the other hand, I knew only too well that an evening of indulgence was likely to be followed by a night rendered sleepless by indigestion. When Joanna followed me into the sitting room I asked her to bring me a large glass of milk. While I waited, I managed to ignore the ranks of bottles but I indulged myself to the tune of one of Peter's cigars. After all, they would soon become so desiccated as to constitute a fire hazard. I could not see young Elizabeth appreciating their excellence and I hated the idea of them falling into the hands of her present boyfriend.

Joanna returned with the milk. 'Have the dogs been walked?' I asked her.

'Hamish came up and walked them,' she said.

There was no point asking whether Spin had been

found. She would have been dancing on the doorstep with such news.

I had been avoiding eye contact in case she should build that up in her imagination into a sexual advance but her voice had sounded choked. I looked and saw that her eyes were inflamed and her cheeks smudged with weeping. 'What's wrong?' I asked rashly. My first thought was that Hamish had done something to upset her, or that there was something wrong with one of the dogs.

She put down the milk hurriedly, spilling a little. Tears came back easily to her eyes. 'It's been getting to me,' she wailed. 'I'm only now beginning to believe it. He's really gone. I'll never see him again. The dear man! Oh, the dear man!' She covered her face, swaying dangerously, shaken by sobs.

I got to my feet. 'You'd better sit down,' I said. I was careful to get behind a chair as if to hold it for her although some of those chairs would have needed a crane to shift them. Joanna was looking for comfort. If she wanted a father-figure then that was exactly what she would get; but the impersonation would not include cuddling an indiscreet, twenty-year-old sexpot. To my relief, she collapsed into the chair, took the handkerchief that I offered and bubbled into it.

'I think perhaps you'd be the better for a drink,' I suggested. 'Would you like a whisky?'

She was rocking backwards and forwards but I thought that I detected a nod. I poured her a good double anyway, sternly denying myself the relief of joining in the debauch.

She took a long pull at the drink, almost emptying the glass, and covered her face again. I poured more whisky, this time watering it. After a few minutes she began to recover. She blew her nose loudly. 'I'm sorry,' she said in a thick voice. 'I'm ashamed of myself. But Sir Peter was very good to me.' She hiccuped once and put her hand out for her whisky, swallowing half of it at a gulp and without blinking.

I found myself lost for words. 'It must have been a shock, losing a good employer,' was all that I could manage.

'Aye. But he was more than an employer,' she said. She swallowed the rest of her drink. The tears were back in her eyes, although whether they were due to emotion or the whisky I was uncertain. 'You're very kind, letting me run on like this. I think that you're a very kind and considerate gentleman.' She regarded me with the eyes of a devoted spaniel while toying meaningfully with her glass. I refilled it. I had decided that I would prefer her comatose rather than affectionate.

I nearly said something trite about a shoulder to cry on but decided that she might take it literally. Instead I muttered about lending a sympathetic ear. Ears seemed somehow less suggestive.

'He was sympathetic like you,' she said. Her voice was already beginning to slur. That made two of us. She took a pull at her drink.

'You're not alone in the world, you know,' I said. 'You have friends. There are good people around here. I was very impressed with Hamish. And I know that he thinks a lot of you.'

Her eyes had lost their focus but they seemed to brighten for a moment. Then the light faded. 'Well, I don't think a lot of him. He's nice enough. But I could never kiss a man with all that beard.' She giggled suddenly. 'It would be like pushing my face into a straw bale.'

Off the top of my head, I could think of no other unmarried older men to put forward as a distraction. 'You'll find somebody,' I said. 'Everybody has somebody waiting to come into their life. Or already there.'

'Not like Sir Peter. He was very good to me,' she said again. She made a gesture which knocked over what was left of her drink. The whisky seemed to have found its way to her head very quickly. 'But I was good to him too. After her ladyship died . . .'

The implication was clear. If I had had a grain of sense I would have left it there. But my tongue, like hers, was loosened by drink. 'Oh, come now,' I said. 'He was an old man.'

She drew herself up, as well as she could in the deep chair. Evidently I had insulted her feminine powers. 'He was old but he was still alive,' she said. She paused and I could almost see the wheels turning. She was wondering how far she dared go. 'He was past the real thing,' she said at last. 'His years with the old biddy had seen to that. But he still had his needs. He liked to do what he called ninety-six.'

She closed her eyes as though picturing the act. Her head went back. One moment later she gave vent to a ladylike snore.

I would not have touched her for the world. I would probably have to make my own breakfast in the morning, but that would be a small price to pay. I left her where she was, made my way unsteadily upstairs, drank a lot of water, dosed myself with my indigestion mixture and went to bed.

As I lay waiting for sleep which was not far away, I wondered how much, if any, of what she had said I was to believe. Not much, I decided.

An anomaly suddenly struck me for the first time. I was aware of the practice that the French call sixty-nine and I knew that it was so called because of the shape of the two numerals. But ninety-six? I tried to visualize it. But no, it was physically impossible.

All the same . . . there was no smoke without fire. I caught myself up. I was beginning to think like the rumour-mongers. And yet . . . Peter had left Joanna a legacy quite out of proportion to her length of service. But, I decided as sleep began to take over, if she had brightened his last few years she deserved it. Elizabeth would never miss it.

I woke suddenly in the middle of the night with another and more likely explanation for the legacy clear in my mind. Perhaps Peter had been her father. But would she invent a sexual liaison between herself and her own father, always assuming that she knew who her father was? On consideration, I thought that she might if she equated love with sex.

There had been a time when such ruminations would have kept me awake, but those days were far behind me. I subsided again into sleep.

Chapter Nine

Saturday dawned grey, in tune with my feelings. My head was one dull ache, I had a cough and I could sense that my bowels were bent on trouble. If I had been at home I would have risked Isobel's attentions and stayed in bed.

But there were things to be done and home itself was calling. I dragged myself up, showered, managed to shave without cutting myself and got dressed. I had been gathering my dirty laundry in a bag for taking home but somebody had abstracted it all and replaced it, neatly laundered, in my luggage, so at least I was fresher on the outside than within.

Joanna was not still snoring in the sitting room, I was relieved to see. There were sounds from the kitchen but I was not yet ready to face her or breakfast. I went outside, puffing gently, and gave the two Labradors their morning amble. I took them into the wood in the hope of bumping into Hamish but there was no sign of him. The clouds were dry but the trees still managed to drip moisture. Breathing deeply of the cool fresh air and feeling rather better, I returned to the house.

The dining table was laid for my breakfast and Joanna appeared as I sat down and helped myself to cereal. Her face was puffy but otherwise she looked much as usual and almost as desirable. 'Just toast and coffee,' I said.

She nodded sympathetically but carefully. 'And will you be here for lunch?'

'I have to meet somebody in Edinburgh,' I told her. 'I'll leave here elevenish and have lunch with him. And I'll be back here on Monday morning, fairly late, or I'll phone. Oh, and Mr Enterkin is sending somebody to attend to the computer.'

'That'll be Mr Paterson from the TV shop,' she said confidently. 'He's a whiz with computers. They say that he's doing very well for himself with inventions and things. And I think he's quite good-looking.'

'Well, apart from him and Miss Hay, and staff of course, nobody is to be admitted to the house until I come back. Nobody at all – unless possibly a plumber or electrician if you have an emergency. In which case somebody stands over them until they've finished. You understand?'

She nodded again. 'I'll tell Mary.' She shuffled her feet. 'And, please, forget what I said last night. I said too much. I shouldn't have said anything at all. It was the whisky talking.'

'It's forgotten,' I told her. My handkerchief, I noticed, had been washed and ironed and left beside my napkin.

'I shouldn't have let you give me so much to drink,' she said. Shuddering, I hoped that she was not going to broadcast that sentiment. The implications would be too awful to contemplate.

I settled in the study, meaning to print out certain documents for reading more carefully at home over the weekend, but while the computer was still loading the word processor program I heard a car and then the doorbell. Joanna announced Jake Paterson.

Paterson was a man of around fifty, with greying red hair and a prominent nose. Ralph had outlined the problem but without understanding it, so that Paterson's grasp of what was wanted was patchy. I explained it again. 'No problem,' he said cheerfully. 'I'll transfer everything onto floppy discs as a backup, sweep the machine for viruses and leave it loaded with any e-mail that's waiting. You realize that it will take a lot of floppies?'

'I accept that. It'll be cheap compared to the sort of sums involved if it crashes. I dare say somebody will be glad to get the discs when we've finished with them.'

'Can I take the computer away with me? I'll see that any material remains confidential.'

'I'm going home for the weekend,' I said. 'Could I get it back on Monday?'

I expected him to jib at working over the weekend, but shopkeepers expect to work on Saturdays. 'Certainly. I'll bring it back on Monday morning.' He paused and looked serious. 'I was sorry to read that Sir Peter had popped his clogs. He was one of my favourite people. He was also my landlord. Can I take it that my tenancy of the shop remains? Or can I buy the freehold?'

'Either,' I said. 'He seems to have hated to part with property during his lifetime, but for his grand-daughter's sake he wanted things simplified after his death. The main body of the estate is to remain intact. Outlying farms and various other properties are to be sold, but not until it suits the present tenants, and they get first refusal at valuation. You come within that category.'

'Thoughtful to the last. And the disposal will be your job?'

'One of them.'

'Sir Peter always was the most considerate of men,' he said. 'I hope that his granddaughter becomes as much of an asset to the district. When will the funeral be?'

'That I can't tell you yet.'

'There's not a kirk big enough to hold the crowd that'll want to come.'

He gathered up the computer and such discs as Peter had filled. There would be no point reduplicating material. I saw him off the premises. He drove off in a very sporty and expensive turbo-charged fastback. Business had to be good.

As I re-entered the house, the phone was ringing. I took the call in the study. A deep baritone asked to whom it was speaking and I explained my existence.

'I see,' said the voice. 'This is Adrian Hastings of Swinburn and Hastings, Surveyors, Edinburgh. I saw Sir Peter's death in the papers and was very sorry. We did a lot of work for Sir Peter over the years. To whom should I write a letter of condolence?'

'To his granddaughter, Miss Elizabeth Hay, at this address.'

'Thank you.' There was a pause – while he made a note, I supposed. 'I had a phone call from Sir Peter a week ago, to ask whether we would be available to do some more work for him. He was going to write to us, giving more details, but the letter never arrived.

I was in the office this morning, clearing my desk, and it occurred to me to follow it up. Do you happen to know what the work would have been?'

'I've no idea,' I said. 'I may come across an explanation as I go through his papers. What kind of surveyors are you?'

'General practice.'

Valuations would be needed in connection with the Confirmation and also before the properties outwith the main estate could be offered to tenants. 'Would you be available to undertake some valuations?'

The voice perked up. 'Certainly.'

'Can you pay me a call next week?'

'Of course. Let me look at my diary. How about Tuesday morning?'

'That would suit me,' I said. I paused. Here came the crunch. 'Would you bring examples of the work you did for Sir Peter?'

If he was a chancer, phoning in the hope of picking up some lucrative work in connection with a rich man's estate, that would have cut the ground out from under his feet. But, 'By all means,' he said. He sounded amused. 'I'll see you on Tuesday morning, then. Perhaps around eleven, but that might depend on the traffic.'

'I'll expect you when I see you,' I said.

There was little more to be done in Newton Lauder. If I set off soon I could take my time to Edinburgh. A little mental arithmetic suggested that I would by now be just on the right side of the breathalyser. My case was already packed, including such of my laundry as remained dirty. No doubt Mary Fiddler or Joanna would have dealt with it as a matter of course but it would have felt presumptuous to leave it for them. I had more than enough clothes at home to keep me going.

Ronnie, dragging his feet, intercepted me on the way to the garage. 'If Sir Peter was alive,' he said, 'he'd tell me to drive you to your home.'

'Very likely,' I said. 'But I'm making a stop in Edinburgh and then I want my own car at home.'

'Ah well! But if you want fetched back,' he said hopefully, 'because maybe your wife wants the use of the car, you've only to phone.'

'Thank you.'

'Sir Peter and I was always out and about,' he explained. 'Now he's awa', I'm just kicking my heels.'

Ronnie had my sympathy. Enforced idleness could only worsen a sense of loss. 'You've got his share of the gardening to get on with,' I suggested. 'And we're still by no means sure what happened. You could pick up as much as you can of the local blether. Anything about anyone not liking Sir Peter, or owing him a debt. And anybody whose plans have changed suddenly since the death.' Already, Ian Fellowes's enquiries had set off more than enough rumours, so I was hardly adding fuel to the flames of gossip.

'I'll do that.' He spoke stolidly but his eyes were brighter and there was a new spring in his step as he turned away.

'One moment,' I said on an impulse. I lowered my voice in case my next words should carry to the kitchen. 'You should know most of the gossip around here. A small matter has arisen . . . Would you happen to know who was Joanna's father?'

His face drained of all expression. 'I wouldna' ken a'thing like yon,' he said.

'Would it have been Sir Peter?'

Expression, startled and concerned, returned to his face in a hurry and he dispensed with the dialect that he had been using as a screen. 'No,' he said. 'Not that. Certainly not. I know that for a fact.' He turned again and hurried away.

I got on the road and, without unduly hurrying, I was parking in a multi-storey car park off Princes Street by lunchtime. The hotel where I was to meet my former acquaintance was a short walk away. The rain was holding off but a stiff breeze was whisking through the grey streets.

The acquaintance himself, Gordon Bream, was waiting in the foyer. Speaking with him on the phone, I had had only a vague recollection of his appearance but now that I saw him again – tall, hollow-chested, with a thin, humorous face – although his hair had silvered he became as real to me as if we had never lost touch. He had been promoted to senior accountant on my strong recommendation after the two of us had been responsible for investigating a complex fraud on the bank and later for briefing advocates in preparation for several prosecutions and a whole string of lawsuits seeking to recover the money, most of which were ultimately successful. Gordon had shown an almost intuitive ability to put his finger on discrepancies, or on the flaw in a culprit's story.

We had a drink at the bar while each told the other mendaciously how little we had changed. He had left the bank eventually, I learned, and was now Managing Director of one of the companies in which Peter Hay had had an interest and a seat on the board.

Over lunch, he explained.

'Agrotechnics,' he said, 'grew out of Agromech, which was set up to make and market a new range of tractor attachments, aimed at letting the farmer do more and more tasks mechanically, with less and less time wasted on side issues. I think you know something about it.'

'I helped Peter Hay to set up the original company,' I said.

'I thought I remembered something of the sort. That makes your presence all the more appropriate. The company's grown a lot bigger since those days, of course. We're into grain dryers and spray-bars now and we make a lot of the components for combine harvesters. We have three factories in the Borders. All good agricultural stuff for men with muddy boots and straw behind their ears. I don't pretend to understand the technicalities, I leave all that to the boffins and concentrate on keeping management efficient and the finances on the straight and narrow. It seems to be a successful working arrangement.

'Last month, we were approached by a much bigger concern with an offer of a takeover. It's a friendly offer at a fair price, there's no denying that, though it's only a little more than the business is worth. But, although they won't confirm or deny, there's a strong suspicion that they want to close down those sections which are in competition with their own products. Which means that three-quarters of our production would go and about the same proportion of job loss.'

'Peter Hay's original intention in starting the business was to provide jobs in and around his territory,' I said.

'Quite so. He always made that clear.'

'The board had five members. Of those, three were shareholders – the only shareholders. Sir Peter was vehemently against having anything to do with the offer. The other two – one private individual and the representative of a pension fund – wanted to accept, quickly before the buyers changed their mind. Of the other two members, the chairman was appointed because he represents the local authority. The other is myself. We, naturally, sided with Sir Peter.'

'Naturally?' I said. 'I would have expected any good accountant to vote for the best financial deal.'

'But the best financial deal for which party? When he confirmed my appointment, Sir Peter was quite clear. My responsibility is divided between the shareholders and the workforce. It's not an unusual division but it can introduce all the inherent dangers of divided loyalty. If the offer had shown a very high profit element, I might have had to take a different view, even if my job vanished in the process.'

Thinking over what he had said, I discounted his modest disclaimer. He would never have been appointed to his present post if he was ignorant of the agricultural technicalities. 'I seem to remember,' I said, 'that we made special provision for the death of a board member.'

'You remember aright. All other decisions are taken on a straight majority, but in the event of the death of a board member, which would otherwise leave the board with an even number of members, the chairman

161

has his personal vote as well as a casting vote in the election of a replacement.

'So the chairman agreed that I sound you out. As an executor of Sir Peter's will and one who was involved in the initial negotiations, you're the obvious person. I take it that we could count on your support?'

I thought about it while I finished an excellent steak. 'My duty is to the wishes of the deceased,' I said. 'But as a trustee I also have to guard the interests of the residuary legatee, his granddaughter. Like yourself, I might fall for the kind of offer that can't be refused. However, the heiress won't be short of the appropriate bob or two and in the long term it will be in her interest to support employment in the area while allowing the investment to appreciate. You'd better let me have the figures and if the offer is, as you say, acceptable but nothing to get excited about, you can count on my support. I take it that there's no likelihood of their upping the offer? We could always take the money and set up again in some other line. Sir Peter had several irons in the fire.'

'I think it unlikely.'

For the next few minutes we were engaged in making selections from the sweet trolley. Those important decisions taken, I said, 'Do you by any chance have any contacts in the upper echelons of television?'

He looked startled at the sudden change of subject but, 'As it happens,' he said, 'I do. I play golf most weekends with one of the top brass at the Beeb. We were colleagues at one time. He shares a flat near here with one of the top programmers at Scottish TV – they too used to be colleagues until one of them was headhunted. My pal works in London and comes up here at the weekends for the golf. The STV man works here but has a wife and family and all his interests in the Smoke. It's an arrangement which suits both of them. They hardly ever even meet and yet the flat's never empty for long enough to attract burglars. Their planes pass each other around Newcastle. I expect they wave to each other.'

'The estate has an interest in financing a TV documentary,' I told him. 'Might either or both of them be interested in a fat consultancy fee?'

'I'll ask. I'll be seeing my pal either tomorrow or in a week's time. Off the cuff, my guess is that you'll have both of them on your doorstep within a very few days, each determined to undercut the other.'

'Yes,' I said, 'I think you can almost certainly count on my support over the takeover.'

Gordon had got the message. He was glad to return to the main item of business. In his satisfaction, his manner regained the flippancy which I remembered of old. 'That's hunky-dory,' he said. 'I'll give you a copy of the audited figures before we part, to pick holes in if you can. When you confirm willingness, I'll call an emergency meeting of the board. Your election should be automatic. The man from the pension fund will take it phlegmatically – it's an appreciating investment and there may be other offers in the fullness of time. But the other can be expected to throw a real, knicker-wetting tantrum.'

'But surely,' I suggested, 'he could realize his investment, if he really wants to, for almost the same figure?'

'He could, of course,' Gordon agreed hastily, anxious not to sow any doubts in my mind. 'But he seems determined to suck the last drop of milk out of the corporate tit. Yes, I can quite see Mr Synott doing his nut.'

'Who?' I said.

'Synott. A neighbour of Sir Peter's but a great disappointment to him. Sir Peter always referred to him as Snot, sometimes to his face.'

Over the last few miles, I detoured slightly from the shortest route in order to pass our house. It was still standing, roughcast, traditional, two bay windows and two dormers, neat and tidy, very ordinary and looking more so and smaller than before, but very definitely home. There had been no fire, no obvious break-in, and the garden was only slightly shaggy. I was relieved. I felt as though I had been away for months. There was no sign of Isobel but I could guess where I would find her. I had lingered in Edinburgh to go over the figures with Gordon Bream, so I was later than I had intended.

At Three Oaks, doors were open and I could hear the sounds of movement and the occasional bark of a dog. Daffy, wheeling a trolley full of empty feeding dishes, came from the direction of the kennels. Although she now considered herself to be a respectable matron, reserving to herself only the right to dress eccentrically when so inclined, she sometimes suffered the recurrence of one symptom of her early rebellion against repressive parents and resumed paraphrasing scurrilously some of their old and favourite ballads. There was Northern Irish on both sides of her family tree but, being a hardened atheist, she supported neither side in the Troubles but disapproved strongly of both.

'When Irish eyes are smiling,' she sang, 'you pass on the parcel quick. / In the lilt of Irish laughter you may hear a trigger click. / When Catholic hearts are happy, someone's run out of luck / and when Proddy eyes are smiling, jump out of the car and duck.' I shuddered at the image but nevertheless I felt comforted. Nothing had changed.

Daffy paused beside me as I locked the car. 'Welcome home,' she said. 'I was sorry to hear about your aristocratic friend. I rather liked what little I saw of him. Has Spin turned up yet?'

'He hadn't, up to the time I set off.'

Her face lost its customary look of being eager to break into a happy grin. 'I hate to think of a dog lost. They have such a capacity for being miserable. Emotional creatures! But they do usually turn up in the end. Are you here to do a useful job of work?' she asked.

'I doubt it very much,' I said, laughing. 'You can wash your own dishes. Where's Isobel? In the surgery?'

'She was doing accounts and VAT on the kitchen table,' Daffy said, 'but Mr Cunningham was heading for the sitting room and muttering something about needing a drink.'

'So the vultures are gathering?'

'I'm one of them,' she said. 'Excuse me. I'll join you when I've put these in hot water.'

From all of that, I gathered that I was in time for the customary round of drinks and discussion in the sitting room, taken when the main work of the day was done. I headed in that direction. At the front door I met young Sam.

The Cunninghams' son was very proud of his school uniform and, in contrast to most of his peers, had to be ordered into more suitable clothes for helping around the kennels at the weekend. In what was virtually the uniform of the business – washed-out jeans and a T-shirt – his resemblance to his father was stronger than ever although, despite being skinny by reason of growth and nervous energy, he was obviously bursting with health whereas John, in the interminable aftermath of serious illness, always looked underweight and usually tired.

'Hullo, Henry,' Sam said, grinning. 'Dad was just asking when you were coming.' He always called me by my first name despite his mother's protests. Personally, I liked it, as Sam well knew.

'Is Isobel in the sitting room?' I asked him.

'Plobably.' He took me by the hand and tugged me towards the sitting room door. As we entered, Beth, already seated, gave him a warning look. 'Here's Mr Kitts,' he announced carefully.

A log fire was adding a cheerful flicker to the room. Isobel and Hannah were in possession of the sofa. John was already pouring drinks. While the usual babble of greetings flowed over our heads, he nodded to the vacant chair, raising his eyebrows and a can of beer. But I still felt full after my heavy lunch and Peter Hay's hospitality had reminded me how well a whisky could go down at the right moment. I shook my head. John lifted his eyebrows and the whisky bottle. I nodded. A whole conversation was embraced in five gestures. The knack of silent communication was, I supposed, one of the legacies from the days of man the hunter-gatherer.

John handed me a generous whisky and took a seat on the arm of Beth's chair. Sam sat on the floor and leaned back against her knee. Daffy came in and pulled up a small, tapestry chair. 'Mr Kitts says that there's still no sign of Spin,' she said.

'Stolen, you think?' John asked.

'It seems likely. Perhaps he ran off when Sir Peter collapsed and some opportunist decided to latch onto him. After all,' I said, 'if he'd just run off and lost his way, we'd have heard something by now. The local DI has an interest and he's been in touch with all the appropriate bodies. The farmers have all been notified. I've put advertisements in all the local papers for miles around, offering a reward, and sent notices to all the dog and fieldsports magazines.'

'Make sure that all the dog clubs know over at least the same area,' John said. 'The dog-walking brigade know each other's dogs and they'd soon notice if some-body had suddenly acquired an adult springer.'

'Can I come and help look for him?' Sam asked.

His mother gave him the same pat on the head that she would have given a friendly spaniel. 'It's a long way away,' she said. 'We'll just have to hope for the best.'

'It would have broken Peter's heart to lose him,' I said. 'They'd only just learned to live with each other but they were getting on like the proverbial house on fire. But it could have been worse. Spin goes to the 'keeper, along with the two elderly Labs, and Hamish – the 'keeper – hadn't had time to form a relationship with him. And he has some money coming under the will, so he can afford a replacement. I'll see if I can point him in this direction,' I added quickly as the three partners began to speak in unison.

'You do that,' Isobel said, 'although I'm sure we all hope it won't come to it. Spin will turn up. Has the question of Sir Peter's death been settled yet?'

In my regular phone calls, I had given Isobel a brief account of the enquiries into Peter Hay's death, as much for lack of anything else to sustain a conversation than any other reason. I had a feeling that more detailed discussion of the subject should be held without Sam's ever-open ears absorbing such nightmarish talk. I glanced down at him and made a face. Unfortunately he looked up and caught me at it. 'If you're going to talk nasties,' he said with dignity, 'I'm going to go and see the dogs. Aren't I not?' His grammar had improved by leaps and bounds since he started school but he still sometimes clung to the double negative.

Beth looked unhappy. It was dusk now and the unwritten rules required that Sam be accompanied, but Beth had no wish to undertake escort duty and miss whatever revelations might still be to come.

Hannah understood immediately. 'I want to see that they're settled,' she told Sam. 'I'll come with you.'

When the heavy doors had closed behind them and John had moved into the vacated place on the couch, I said, 'It's still very much up in the air, or it was when last I heard. The pathologist – a professor of clinical pathology, no less! – was certain that Peter Hay had had a powerful electric shock, and fairly sure that he'd died of it although he hedged his bets slightly.'

'They're good at that, pathologists,' John said.

'Yes. And the unit feeding electricity into the cattle fence had developed a serious fault. We don't know yet whether, in doing so, it could have passed enough mains voltage to cause a death. The unit's been sent back to the makers for a report. Anyone with a few yards of electric cable and a little electrical knowledge could have led mains current to the cables supplying the fence. The makings were all there in the tractor shed. And there are overhead cables wandering around the place. But so far, the only physical evidence pointing towards anything other than a tragic accident is that there was a piece of aluminium foil stuck to the gatepost and forming a connection between the fence wires and the metal gate. I don't remember feeling any wind, but one can get localized gusts. It could have blown there, I suppose.'

'It could,' Isobel said. 'And pigs could fly. Whichever way you look at it, something unlikely happened. Either a piece of foil blew, on a calm day, right onto the place where it would convey electricity from a faulty power source to where it would do most damage. Or else somebody put it there, which I find rather less incredible.'

'I feel the same,' I said. 'As it happened, Peter was a very tidy soul who hated to see litter. He went to pick up the foil before touching the gate, but the result was the same. Ian Fellowes, the detective inspector, was to speak to his superiors today. They may feel that the metal foil is a little too much of a coincidence, or they may think it a very feeble reason for embarking on the expense and publicity of a murder investigation.'

At my last words Isobel frowned, although it seemed to me that she had herself been suggesting the probability of murder. 'Was there anyone around who wished him dead?' she asked. 'He seemed such an . . . an *unhateable* man, if you know what I mean.'

I knew exactly what she meant. 'Not as far as we know,' I said carefully. 'But there were plenty who will be better off. He was extremely well-heeled and he made generous provision for his staff, his tenants and his granddaughter.' I decided not to make mention of embezzling solicitors, undesirable boyfriends or bereaved cat-fanciers just yet. Comments can be repeated and slander is definitely slander.

Beth always reserves her lowest opinions for her own sex. 'Would the granddaughter know enough to be able to rig an electrical connection?'

'She's studying for a degree in Electronics and Computing,' I replied, 'so we can assume that she understands the rudiments of electricity. In point of fact, although she argued rebelliously with her grandfather she told me that she had loved him and her grief was convincing.'

'But could it have been due partly to guilt?' Beth asked.

'I can't be sure, but I don't think so.'

In the course of a long marriage, Isobel has learned to read me. 'Come off it,' she said. 'There's something you're holding back.'

I decided to be a little more frank. 'In confidence? Her boyfriend is another matter.' I went on to describe the unsavoury Roland Chatsworth.

'I don't believe that name, for a start,' Isobel said. 'And you seem to have become one of her trustees as well as an executor. The things you get up to as soon as I take my eye off you! Can't you restrain her?'

'We could threaten to apply financial pressure,' I said, 'but she seems to be going through a left-wing phase at the moment so it might only be pushing her into her lover's arms. And Ralph Enterkin – my co-executor – said that a court might well come down on her side if we were too restrictive. Interference from beyond the grave, he says, is generally considered not to be in the public interest.'

'What's needed,' Beth said thoughtfully, 'is an impoverished nobleman – some handsome young man on the lookout for an heiress. How about Freddy Crail? He's single at the moment, flat broke and quite capable of cutting out the sort of graceless Romeo you've been describing.'

Lord Crail was all that Beth had said, but he was rather a friend of mine and I would not have saddled any of my friends with Elizabeth Hay, money or no, until her attitude had abated. 'For heaven's sake!' I said. 'Things are complicated enough without any scheming matchmakers.'

'You mean,' said Isobel, 'that if there's any match-making to be done, you'll do it.'

'I don't mean anything of the sort,' I said indignantly, but that night, in my own bed, I found myself conducting a roll-call of eligible but impecunious bachelors. Sadly, each one that I could think of was either charmless, gay or infectious. One of them was all three.

Chapter Ten

In what was left of the weekend, and despite demands on my time to throw dummies, feed puppies, chauffeur Isobel to the shops and hold onto a spaniel which was determined that no way was he ever going to accept another injection, I managed to pick Isobel's brains to the extent of being given a lengthy lesson in the use of the computer. I had been struggling and fumbling my way around Peter's machine, terrified that one careless error might wipe its memory clean; but Isobel extended my basic knowledge of the first elements into a general understanding of the methodology behind what had been a total mystery, in particular the occasions for what is known as 'double clicking', which tiny event makes all the difference between triumph and frustration. I found that, on Isobel's machine, I no longer needed to go in and out of the File Manager to find what I wanted and frequently arrived at my target without any abortive journeys in and out of various modes, the purposes of which were too obvious for even the 'As Told To Idiots' sort of manuals to bother to explain. I felt ready to tackle Peter's beast with enthusiasm rather than trepidation.

Thus I arrived back at Newton Lauder on the Monday, in the early afternoon, with the car full of clean clothing and my head so filled with good intentions that I hardly noticed the presence of an unfamiliar small sports car in the big garage.

Joanna met me at the door. Her manner still subtly suggested that there were delicious secrets between us. She had been too well trained to keep me talking in the hall. She brought me a cup of tea in the sitting room before making her report. There was still no word of Spin, but another wanderer had returned to the fold. Elizabeth Hay had moved back into the house.

'But not . . .?'

Joanna shook her head emphatically. 'He was with her when she came but we wouldn't let him over the doorstep. We thought that that would be the right thing to do.'

'Absolutely right,' I said. 'Where is she now?'

'She's in her room. Studying for her exams, so she said. And there were messages. Mr Enterkin will be here at about four and Inspector Fellowes will be meeting him here. And Mr Paterson phoned. He sent his apologies. The computer isn't quite ready but he'll send or bring it out this afternoon.'

Another matter was intriguing me. 'Did Hamish come here during the weekend?'

She looked at me in surprise. 'Aye, he did, about nothing in particular. I think he fancies me, that one.' The idea did not seem to displease her, beard or no beard.

I moved into the study. Alone with my teacup, I wondered what to do until the computer arrived. I checked the answering machine but most of the few messages were mere formalities. There was a call, however, from Mr Synott – Peter's Mr Snot – asking me to call him back. I had not liked Mr Synott and, following my gaffe, he was the last person I wanted to speak with. I decided to put off returning his call indefinitely. I skimmed through the mail but there was nothing that I could answer without Mr Enterkin's help or approval. I thought of fishing, but there was a blustery wind which would have made casting difficult and, among the trees, very possibly expensive. Instead, I decided to go and see Hamish. There was a question which I had not thought to ask him. But, hard behind the thought, the mountain came to Mohammed. Joanna brought him to the door.

Hamish had brought some accounts, for feed and fuel and grit, to be settled. I said that I would approve them and pass them to Mr Enterkin for payment.

'Hamish,' I began, 'you said that you saw nobody in the wood that morning. But did you hear anyone?'

He shook his tousled head. 'Not a soul.'

'Not even outside the wood?'

'The sound of my working was in my ears,' he said. 'I never heard Sir Peter coming, though I wasn't far away. I mind that I heard a heavy vehicle in the distance, on the road it would've been, but that was all.'

I decided to leave it there and move on. Beth's words were still fresh in my mind. They had referred to Elizabeth Hay but they were just as applicable to Joanna, so while I had Hamish at my mercy I decided on a little unforgivable interference. I would have invited him to sit down except that his clothes were sprinkled with sawdust.

'Hamish,' I said, 'Joanna thinks that you fancy her.'

He drew himself up to his considerable height. 'Is there any reason why I should not?'

'None at all,' I said hastily.

'Well, I'm ta'en up wi' her, right enough,' he said. 'But she hardly knows I'm alive.'

'She knows you're alive all right,' I told him. 'But . . . tell me, Hamish, how long have you had that beard?'

'A' my days.' He seemed unsurprised at my question. Evidently his late employer had shown similar unexplained curiosity.

'Oh, come on!' I said. 'You can't have had it for the first fifteen years. What do you look like underneath it? I only ask because Joanna dropped a hint about not being able to fancy you with all those whiskers. She said that kissing you would be like pushing her face into a gorse bush. Something like that – I don't recall the exact words.'

'That's close enough,' Hamish said. I could have sworn that the area of skin that I could see around his eyes and nose was blushing. 'She said that, did she?'

'Something like it.' I was curious. 'What do you look like under the whiskers?'

He shrugged and shifted from foot to foot in embarrassment. 'It's been a long time. She really said that? About kissing me?'

'She really said it. But you didn't grow the beard to hide a birthmark, a hare lip or a bad scar?'

'Nothing like that. My dad had a fine beard and I always fancied looking like him.'

'Then why don't you think about taking it off?'

'I'll think about it.' Hamish stroked his beard fondly. 'Of course I will. But it's been where it is for a good few years now. I'd be taking a chance. I can't call to mind what I looked like and anyway I was in my teens the last time I saw myself without it. Suppose I look

175

real daft? I could have the whole town laughing at me. They'd ken fine why I did it.'

He had a point, but there was another side to it – if a point can have a side. 'What you think you look like doesn't matter,' I pointed out. 'It's what Joanna thinks that matters. And who can predict what kind of looks will take a woman's fancy? You'll just have to place your bet. After all, you can always grow it again if she turns you down. As for the whole town laughing at you, that's the way people always think, being a self-conscious species. But it's seldom if ever true. Hamish, if some other man took off his beard to please some girl, you wouldn't point the finger of scorn at him, would you?'

'That's true,' he said. 'But, man – Mr Kitts, I mean – it's a big step to take. And a girl can't think much of a man if all she wants is to change him.'

He wanted to be persuaded but I had already assumed enough responsibility. 'It's up to you, Hamish,' I said. 'If you feel that the chance of winning Joanna isn't worth the risk of being laughed at, that's your business.'

'Aye,' he said unhappily. 'That's so.' He became businesslike again. 'I was wanting to get Geordie Jennings to plant trees on his set-aside land, but he says he'd lose the grants.'

'I'll have a word with him,' I said. 'When shooting continues on much the same basis as it was before the trees were planted, there's no problem.'

Hamish brightened, already envisaging new game coverts on large tracts of Home Farm. In his mind, the new trees were as good as planted and matured. He switched tracks. If the shoot were to continue as before, he pointed out, it was not too early to be considering the first advertisements of the 'let days'. We settled down to discuss the wording.

As he prepared to leave, he returned to the subject of Joanna. 'She really said that? About kissing me?'

'Yes,' I said. 'She really did.'

As he left the room, he was stroking his beard affectionately.

After Hamish made his thoughtful departure, I had ten minutes to myself. I meant to put them to good use, but I had again missed my doze of the early afternoon. I relaxed for a moment in the wing-chair and within seconds I was away.

I was woken by the arrival of another visitor at the front door. I managed to achieve full wakefulness before Joanna, almost fawning, brought in a young man. He was dark and well built and he had the modelled cheekbones and jaw muscles of the classically handsome. He had brought back the computer and, with it, Mr Paterson's further apologies. Paterson, who was electronically talented far beyond the call of a local TV shop, or so Keith had told me, had been called into Edinburgh to deal with a problem in the automation of a small factory, leaving the young man to return the computer, deliver a large box of computer paper and induct me into the mysteries of computer viruses.

He settled in the swivel chair. 'You chose the right moment. There was a virus waiting in the pending e-mail,' he said, with all the solemnity of a surgeon explaining that he had operated just in time to save the patient's life, 'and when Jake had swept the entire memory with an anti-virus program he keyed for any more incoming e-mail. A whole lot more mail arrived and he traced another virus in that lot. He couldn't be sure which message it was in. Somebody seems determined to crash this computer. You do know what I'm talking about?' he asked solicitously.

'I know roughly what a computer virus is,' I said. 'But just to be clear, a virus will infect and eradicate everything in a computer's memory? Not just the electronic mail bit?'

'The lot. But the whole system's clean now and I've brought you a printout of the waiting messages. If you want to go on using the e-mail facility you'll have to keep on disinfecting it – with this program.' He produced one of the rigid squares known as a floppy disc – I had to admit that Ralph Enterkin had a point when he complained about the jargon – and he began to explain the use of the program but, despite Isobel's coaching, in the first ten words he had left me far behind.

'Hold on a minute,' I said. It had occurred to me that Elizabeth Hay had no discernible motive to erase information from the computer. I left the room, headed for the stair and met Joanna on the landing. 'Go and knock on Miss Elizabeth's door,' I said. 'Ask her to come down to the study and help me with a problem.'

'She's not in a very good mood,' Joanna said doubtfully.

'When was she ever?' I asked. 'If she won't come, just let me know. I'll deal with her.'

I thought that the time was probably ripe for a showdown. But Elizabeth Hay was in an improved mood or else Joanna had reported the implied threat, because the heiress came clattering down the stairs while I was recrossing the hall and dead-heated with me at the study door. She preceded me into the room and stopped dead. 'I'll be damned,' she said. 'Duncan Ilwand!'

'Miss . . . Hay!' my visitor retorted. 'Elizabeth Hay, isn't it?'

'You two know each other,' was all that I could find to say. I tried not to let it sound like a question.

'We're fellow students,' Elizabeth said. 'Duncan's a year ahead of me.' I noticed that she had lost her sulky scowl and instead, for once, was looking and sounding almost shy. 'Whatever brings you here?'

'I work for Jake Paterson when I'm at home – vacations, weekends or whenever he needs help,' young Mr Ilwand explained. 'It's good experience and it supplements my grant.'

'He was trying to explain to me how to disinfect and protect the material in your grandfather's computer against viruses,' I told her, 'but it's rather above my head. If you're going to be here for a few days, perhaps you'd look after that side of it for me?'

'Yes, easily,' she said. She pulled up another chair beside the swivel and the two of them were immediately lost in a huddle from which the occasional word which escaped was meaningless to me. I relaxed in one of the easy chairs and glanced through the newly printed-out messages. There were some items of mere gossip from correspondents all over the world and a few business communications of little importance. None of them stood out as being probable vehicles for delivering a virus.

179

When Duncan Ilwand got up to go, Elizabeth jumped to her feet. 'I'll see him to the door,' she said. Such courtesy and consideration were not a normal part of her repertoire. She returned, looking slightly flustered, and settled behind the computer again. 'Oh,' she said, recollecting herself. 'Is this all right? Or do you have secrets locked up in it?'

We seemed to be making rapid progress towards at least minimal observance of the courtesies. 'No secrets,' I told her. 'It will all be yours soon anyway. In fact, you could be of even more help. I've tried to look at anything that might be important, but God alone knows what I've missed. You could sort out the material and give me a note of everything you think your executors ought to be aware of.'

She eyed me impishly from under an errant lock of hair. I began to see that her sex appeal was not entirely due to her financial prospects. 'I could do that,' she said. 'But, if I do, will you let Roland into the house?'

'Don't push it,' I said lightly. 'I can always hire somebody at what would eventually be your expense. Help me, and we'll take a more liberal view of finances as your trustees.'

'I suppose,' she said. She pecked absently at the keyboard.

'Tell me something. Who would know enough to be able to introduce a virus by way of the electronic mail?'

She looked at me with that air of amused superiority that makes me want to slap any youngster who patronizes me on the subject of computers. 'Almost anybody computer literate,' she said. 'Which means

180

almost everyone from twelve to twenty plus anybody older who's taken the trouble to bone up on computing.'

I had hoped to narrow down my suspects, but it seemed that the field remained wide open. 'He's a very good-looking young man, isn't he,' I suggested. 'Duncan Ilwand, I mean.'

She shrugged but without her customary air of contempt for the world in general and her company in particular. 'I suppose so. Some of the girls at uni go weak at the knees when he's around.'

'But you're above that sort of thing?'

She glanced up at me again from the keyboard. The gleam of mischief was back again. 'I don't know anybody who's above that sort of thing,' she said. She smiled suddenly. 'Not even the very old.'

'Like me?'

'You said it, I didn't. The real reason I came back here was to chaperone you and Joanna.'

She was only trying to needle me, I thought, to exact revenge. Or perhaps not. *Keep it light*, I told myself. 'I'm much obliged, you young dog in the manger,' I said. 'I shall call you Gooseberry from now on. What else do you know about young Ilwand?'

She focused on the computer and keyed into one of the directories. 'Not a lot. He's some sort of connection to the Earl of Jedburgh. Umpteenth cousin. Third son of a fourth son, so there isn't a penny in it for him. I suppose that's why he has to work for Jake Paterson. He's supposed to be brilliant.'

'That's good,' I said.

'Ilwand's the family name,' she said absently. She was studying the screen. 'It's an old, alternative spelling of Elliot. Duncan gets invited to Aikhowe

181

sometimes, for the gatherings . . .' Her voice faded away, leaving me free to pursue my own thoughts.

Her sudden gasp jerked me back to the here and now. She was staring at the screen as though it had shown her a vision of hell.

'What's wrong?' I asked. But she shook her head, cleared the screen and switched off the computer, then jumped to her feet and ran out of the room. I followed her, uncertain what to do. When I reached the door of her room it was shut tight.

I knocked. Her voice invited me, in less than delicate terms, to go away. Under no circumstances would I have entered her room uninvited but I listened at the door for a minute or two. I could hear her crying as though her heart was already broken.

As it happened, I had only a minute or two to hesitate on the threshold. Then Joanna's head appeared at the top of the stairs.

'Please,' she said, 'Mr Fellowes is here. And Mr Enterkin's car just came through the archway.'

'Put Mr Fellowes in the study, and Mr Enterkin when he eventually turns up.' I resumed my approaches to the unresponsive door. 'Won't you at least tell me what's wrong?' I asked it. 'I can't help if I don't know what's wrong.'

In a voice distorted by tears, Elizabeth Hay again invited me to go away, although she expressed herself even less politely than before. It seemed that our little truce was over. 'You'd better come back and wait here in case she suddenly needs a confidante,' I told Joanna.

'A what?'

'Someone to talk to.'

In the study I was joined by Ian Fellowes. He took

a stand at the window, watching Ralph Enterkin's car, which by then was nearly halfway along the drive. When he turned I saw that he looked tired. I invited him to be seated and asked, 'Tea, or something stronger?'

'Tea will do for now,' he said. 'Ask me again later.'

I nodded to Joanna. 'Three cups,' I said.

'Right away. Mrs Fiddler just made a pot,' she said.

I decided that I could come to like being the master of a substantial house staffed by willing slaves. With Isobel so busy, I was more often the slave. I sat behind the desk and, to fill the gap while we waited for the solicitor, toyed with the computer.

Enterkin arrived and endorsed the majority vote for tea. Joanna wheeled in the trolley, poured and left us. A plate of buttered rock cakes, still warm from the oven, passed round.

'Right,' Ian Fellowes said a minute later, emptying his mouth with difficulty. 'Now I feel strong enough to bring you up to date.' He looked at me. 'And free to do so. Mr Enterkin has furnished me with a list of those who may expect to benefit from Sir Peter's death and no doubt he'll let you see it. I don't think it's for me to broadcast it.'

'I scanned it carefully for my own clients and found none who were not already too obvious to merit mention. The list consists primarily of those who gain under the will,' said Ralph. 'Plus of course a lady of whom you know and a gentleman ditto. The list is headed by our own two names.'

'*What*?' I said incredulously.

He seemed surprised at my surprise. 'But of course.

Each of us can expect to earn a substantial fee. One of us was on the actual scene. I do not seriously suspect myself but the Detective Inspector should certainly do so. We must be considered.'

'I was hardly in a position to electrify the fence,' I pointed out. 'What's more, I didn't know at the time that Peter had already signed his revised Trust Disposition and Settlement.'

'It was hardly for me to omit names because of my own interpretation of the evidence,' Ralph said stiffly. I let the subject drop. The legal mind has its own logic.

'Don't worry about it,' advised Ian Fellowes, hiding a smile. 'You both come rather a long way down my personal league table of suspects or I wouldn't be having this discussion with you at all. I'll give you the facts in systematic rather than chronological order. First either way, I spent Saturday morning in Edinburgh, reporting to my superiors. As usual, they saw this as a splendid opportunity to eat their cake and have it too. They quite agreed that the circumstances were suspicious and I was to look into them with all my might; but, because there was no real evidence of foul play, they would support me neither from above nor below. In other words, I have a free hand, unsupervised, but no more help than I can beg or borrow locally.

'So a small and motley crew of uniformed PCs, some cadets and a very few DCs have spent a lot of the weekend on a supposedly methodical search. The snag, of course, is that the place where Sir Peter died was never very likely to reveal anything for the simple but sufficient reason that, apart from the depositing of a piece of foil, nobody committed any evil deed there.

The territory in which some such deed was committed lies within an unknown distance of the whole length of the farm boundary and we are very unsure what we are looking for anyway, so not surprisingly they have found a great deal of material, none of which is so far of any evident significance. The search continues.

'Meanwhile, the makers of the energizer unit have also been busy over the weekend. From experience, I was resigned to getting a report long after the case had been closed and even then saying very little, but I owe them a mental apology. In fact, I received their report just after lunch today. I only wish that they were as lucid as they are prompt. The only part of the report that comes over loud and clear is where they hedge themselves around with ifs and buts. For the rest, I had to get Keith to interpret it for me. He seems to understand electricity as he does other matters of engineering. As interpreted by him, the report suggests that the primary winding – the coil into which the mains electricity is fed – is undamaged. Therefore a substantial current must have arrived via the side which normally stores the energy and releases it at high voltage and low amperage for a very brief period about once a second. This input current, they think, must have been full mains voltage at least. It fused the timing electronics, creating an arc which then destroyed the secondary winding.'

I could see that Ralph Enterkin was flagging, so I said, 'That doesn't seem to take us any further. It already seemed almost certain that somebody had fed mains electricity into the fence wire.'

'And now we have it confirmed,' Ian said. 'Which makes it murder – barring a remarkably unlikely

185

accident, and if an overhead power line had blown down onto the fence we would surely have heard about it by now. So to that extent it's a major step forward. Next we need to know where the deed was done.

'Mains power could have been fed into the fence from almost anywhere, given two requirements. One is the availability of power near the fence, which almost certainly means a building or a power line. The other is that the gate would have to be visible from the place or nearby. It's not to be supposed that somebody fed mains electricity into the fence and then wandered off, hoping that Sir Peter would come to the gate before some other poor soul or Jennings's cattle brushed against the fence. You'd think that that would narrow it down but in fact, if you allow for the second condition being met by somebody climbing a tree or standing on the roof of a vehicle, a preliminary look suggests a surprising number of buildings and several power lines. You see, the power source may not be right against the fence. We've had one small stroke of almost luck.

'The Local Authority is laying street lighting cables in Denbigh Street and there was a drum of cable left overnight, the night before the death. By the morning, although they've only just got around to reporting it, some cable had been stolen off the drum. Not as light as domestic cable nor as heavy as the mains in the street but conveniently in between. Ideal for the job.'

'What sort of length?' I asked.

'The nearest estimate they could give me was "quite a lot",' Ian said disgustedly. 'That's why I referred to it as a stroke of almost luck. I suspect that they only noticed the theft at all because the end had been left stripped ready for making a connection and when they came back they found it severed cleanly, apparently by hacksaw. Not that an exact figure of the length stolen would have helped us. The most casual of murderers would surely think of cutting off a little extra rather than present us with a valuable piece of evidence.

'I stood again today on the spot where Sir Peter died and used my eyes.

'It turned out to be a revealing exercise. Looking to my right, the ground rose slightly to the fence above the old railway cutting and the conifer wood beyond. An overhead cable carrying a high voltage follows a ride cut through the wood and ends up at a substation at the farm, from where power is distributed at domestic voltages through other overhead lines. I've asked the electricity board to take a look at the high voltage lines and at several other overhead cables that pass over or close to the boundary. One of the constables, who claims to have some knowledge of electricity, will go with them. He's been briefed to look out for the marks of climbing irons on timber poles, strips of cable showing brightness and anything else suggesting unauthorized abstraction of power. But I'm given to understand that unless the culprit works for the Electricity Board he'd have to be mad to interfere with the high voltage cable.

'In front of me and slightly to the right were Mr Synott's house and the farm buildings. Away beyond the barns is the farmhouse. Beyond again and left, the farm boundary follows the crest, but the village of Bellafield lies beyond and I could see the upstairs rear windows of six houses.'

Ralph Enterkin, who had been listening with a glazed expression on his plump face, stirred suddenly. 'One of those houses, you may care to note, is occupied by Ms Dorothy Spigatt.'

'I had already discovered that fact for myself, thank you very much. Left again, the farm boundary vanishes behind Langstane Wood and a small hillock, reappears for a moment beside a pair of houses in so far unknown ownership, vanishes again behind the trees only to emerge and return to the gate along the side of the wood.

'My spying out of the land led me to two conclusions,' Ian Fellowes continued sadly. 'First that there's a lot of work to do. And second that the most likely place remains Mr Jennings's tractor shed, with Ms Spigatt's house a close second.

'But.'

'I knew that there would be a but,' Ralph Enterkin said.

'Buts, like the poor, are always with us,' Ian replied. 'This particular but is that Mr Jennings is becoming more and more sure that he would have seen anybody going into his tractor shed.'

'Unless Mr Jennings himself is the culprit,' Ralph suggested.

'He claims to have been spraying weeds along the line of the fence,' I reminded them both. 'And Peter Hay waved to somebody who seemed to be doing just that, a long way from the tractor shed, a minute or two before Peter died.'

The Detective Inspector nodded. 'So tomorrow starts with a search around those vicinities and at any place where mains electricity is available within fifty yards of the fence and a view can be obtained of the death site.

'What else can I tell you? The local supermarket has been very helpful in providing samples, and the lab technicians now state that the metal foil came off the top of one of their frozen shepherd's pies and that the grease on the wire and the gate stems from the gravy in one of the same pies.

'Meantime, a borrowed sergeant, temporarily removed from uniform but quite intelligent for all that, has been busily checking on where every apparent suspect was that morning. I have my own list of suspects but you can't expect me to tell you who they are.'

Ralph Enterkin, who had been working his way through the plate of rock cakes with small, appreciative noises, swallowed quickly. 'If you are gauging the qualification of a suspect by the degree of motive,' he said huffily, 'we probably have as good an idea of who they are as you have, and probably very much better. On the other hand, I know, as you should know by now, that murders and other crimes have been committed for motives which you or I would consider trivial beyond belief, which is why courts do not always require motive to be proven.

'We, not being committed to secrecy for secrecy's sake, will continue to feed you the information as we come across it. However, in return we ask you to bear in mind that we are not only the executors of the estate but the trustees of Sir Peter's granddaughter. Accordingly, it is vital that we know of anything suggesting that her present boyfriend, as well as being undesirable, is a physical threat and a dangerous person to have around.'

Ian hesitated. 'Would you consider his motive that strong?' he asked at last.

'I certainly would,' I said. 'Give me a moment.' I fed paper into the printer and set it going. 'Just before you arrived, Miss Hay came across something in the computer which upset her to the extent that she rushed upstairs and shut herself in her bedroom for a good cry. It only occurred to me a few minutes ago that I could find out what it was. In the File window of the word processor program there's a small panel showing the last four items referred to. While we were waiting for you, I keyed up the most recent one. It's a copy of an incoming e-mail.'

The printer finished its gentle muttering. I got up and handed the paper to Ian. Ralph leaned across to share the reading of it.

'What is the firm?' Ralph asked. 'I seem to know the name.'

'You should,' said Ian. 'They're the best detective agency in Scotland.' He read aloud.

As instructed, we enquired into the identity and ante-cedents of the young man known as Roland Chatsworth. At first some difficulty was experienced because he seemed to have no history going back more than eighteen months and no student of that name had ever been registered with the university. However, by following the lines of enquiry outlined in the Appendix, we uncovered the following facts.

The man's real name is Arnold Drayne although he has also used the names Ross Pemberly, Harvey Hamilton and others. He was born in Paisley and is 34 years old but looks and claims to be younger (copy birth certificate attached). At 18, he left home, taking with him his father's credit cards and cheque book, etc. Since then he has supported himself mainly by mingling with students at various universities and passing himself off as one of their fellows. He then seeks out girls of good family, courts and, when possible, seduces them. On several occasions the girl's family has paid him off. On others his bluff has been called and he has shown no reluctance to go through a form of marriage, deserting the bride only when the pickings seemed to be exhausted.

'The report,' Ian said grimly, 'seems to go on and on, with chapter and verse, but I think that's enough for the moment. His movements will certainly be investigated. I'll keep this copy and I'll be obliged if you'll print out the appendix for me.'

'Of course,' I said, wondering where in the computer's diverse memory to look for it. I could hardly ask Elizabeth Hay.

'Poor child!' Ralph Enterkin said. 'A terrible shock for her! And, not least, the narrow escape from having become Mrs Drayne. But what a mercy that Sir Peter thought to commission that report.'

'And that Henry found it,' Ian said.

'Yes, by Golly!' Ralph said, giving credit at last where it was more or less due. 'Is there anything we can do to soften the blow?'

My mind went immediately to the eligible Duncan Ilwand. There is no better cure for a broken romance than a fresh one. 'She should be kept occupied,' I said. 'For the moment, exams are looming. But the long

191

vacation will follow. I suggest that we might release an allowance to her, proportionate to what she can earn.'

'Restrict her allowance to doubling her wage?' Ralph queried.

'Treble it,' I said. 'Make it worth her while. Do you think that your friend Jake Paterson could find work for her?'

'I'm sure that that could be arranged,' Ralph said. 'Given a little encouragement, if needed.'

'Encouragement?' Ian echoed.

'When you have an estate of this size to manipulate, there are always little pressures that can be brought to bear. I am sure that Mr Kitts is aware of that. But perhaps Sir Peter's faith in your acuity was misplaced?' he added in my direction. 'Mr Paterson, for instance, is very anxious about his lease. And you might well find that one of the businesses in which Sir Peter had a stake is overdue for having its burglar and fire alarms updated.'

I said that the point had not passed me by.

Joanna came in to enquire who would be staying to dinner. Ian said that he was leaving to resume his investigations, and did so. Ralph Enterkin let his business face drop for the moment. 'To set aside sordid commerce and teenage heartbreak for a minute or two, would this be a suitable day for me to renew my dinner invitation?'

'I think not. I wouldn't want Elizabeth to have to dine alone. After losing both a grandfather and . . . more,' I said carefully, mindful of Joanna's presence, 'any kind of company would be preferable to that.'

'Of course,' he said. 'Clumsy of me.'

'Perhaps you'd care to dine here?' I suggested.

He shuddered elaborately and shook his head. Joanna left the room. 'Among my preferences for dining company,' Ralph said, 'a bereft teenager falls somewhere between a deaf mute and a convicted poisoner. Back to business.'

'Yes. Is Joanna Sir Peter's daughter on the wrong side of the blanket?'

Enterkin jumped as though I had bitten him. 'No she is not,' he said firmly.

'And you don't know who her father *is*?'

'As it happens, I do know. But that sort of information is on what they call a need-to-know basis and you definitely do not need to know.'

'His legacy to her is surprisingly large,' I reminded him. 'If it should turn out that Sir Peter was helped on his way, that could furnish the mysterious father with a motive. The police should know.'

'If that should be the outcome of this afternoon's discussion,' he said haughtily, 'I will make sure that the police do know if they do not, as I would suppose, know it already. That would still not entitle you to know so . . .' he paused, 'so delicate a fact.'

'I shall find out.'

'Not from me. Our duty ends with paying over the legacy to the girl.'

Between matters thrown up by the estate and my rather random scanning, I might almost say 'surfing', of the computer files, I had collected a file of material requiring consultation. An hour later, we had worked most of the way through it, deciding who would do what about which, when we were interrupted.

Joanna arrived again at the study door. 'Mr Synott's here. He wants a word with you.'

'With which one of us?' I asked her.

'He is hardly likely to aware of my presence,' Ralph pointed out. 'But never mind. We may as well see him together. Show him in.'

If Mr Synott bore me any ill-will for having put my oar in during the altercation over the death of his cat, or for referring to him as Snot within his hearing, the only sign of it was a certain stiffness of manner which could equally have arisen from embarrassment. His skinny frame was dressed more formally than before in a charcoal suit and sober tie, his sandy beard had been trimmed and he accepted a chair in which he sat rigidly upright, as if to relax would be to concede something.

'You never returned my call,' he told me sadly.

I nearly reminded him that the first rule of business is to assume that nobody ever calls you back. Instead, I said, 'Not yet,' and waited.

'We have decided to move house,' he said. 'And the recent sad events were the last straw. As it happens, a house that we have always admired, within walking distance of my sister-in-law, has just come on the market.'

'And, of course,' Ralph said, 'your lease obliges you to give the estate first refusal, at valuation.'

'That's why I'm here.'

I said, 'Mr Hastings, of Swinburn and Hastings, is coming to see me to discuss valuations for probate. I'll ask him to put a value on your lease. If you don't like his figure, you can engage a surveyor of your own. If there's still a dispute, we'll refer the two opinions to an adjudicator. That's satisfactory?'

'If that's how it's usually done. I hope that we can

194

move quickly,' he added. 'We're anxious to complete the other purchase before somebody else enters the bidding.'

'Does that mean that you're giving up your director-ship of Agrotechnics?' I asked him.

If he was surprised at my omniscience, he hid it. 'I would like to get my money out,' he admitted. 'And that, I suppose, would mean resigning my directorship. But there is still the question of the offer of a buyout.'

'I'm afraid there isn't,' I told him. 'I have been put forward for the directorship made vacant by Sir Peter's death and, with the chairman's casting vote, I have a majority behind me. And the buyout will not happen.' I nearly said that it would happen over my dead body, but suddenly the implications of the phrase hit me and I bit the words back. 'And, just as with your house, the Articles require you to offer your shares first to the other directors. I'm sure that we can find you a buyer at market price – which will show you a very good profit on your original investment.'

'The duty of the Board is to the shareholders,' Synott said in a high, quick voice, looking at the ceiling. 'And I'm a shareholder. The Board has no right to refuse an offer which would benefit the shareholders.'

'The Board members *are* the shareholders,' I pointed out. 'And they have every right to take into account employment in this area, which is what the company was set up to safeguard in the first place.' I waited until his eyes came down and met mine. 'Were you under the impression that Sir Peter's death would change that?'

'I hoped that it might.' Suddenly the implication of

my words got home to him. 'What the hell are you suggesting?'

It was too early to start throwing accusations around. Before I could formulate a compromise answer, Ralph asked, 'What do you know about Sir Peter's death?'

'Nothing. Well, almost nothing. Nothing in the sense . . . Nothing that isn't known to everyone. The police have been asking questions. There was something not right about the death. The word going around is that he got a shock off the cattle fence and that it stopped his pacemaker.'

'That is indeed one of the words going round,' Ralph said. 'You had words with Sir Peter not long before-hand. Where did you go after that?'

'I went home and stayed there,' Synott said coldly. 'I was quite shaken by the death of my cat and the arguments that followed it. The police have already asked the question and my wife confirmed my answer.'

'As wives are wont to do,' the solicitor murmured.

I jumped in quickly before Synott could take offence. There was already a danger that he might become an aggrieved board member, exploiting every opportunity to make a nuisance of himself. 'We would like to have the question of the board membership settled quickly,' I said, 'just as you would the purchase of your lease. Perhaps we can hustle the two things along together. I suggest that you go home and write us a letter, offering your shares and also the lease of your house for sale. Then we can move rapidly on both.'

'I'll do that straight away,' Synott said. He seemed relieved. From being defensive, he became curious. We managed to send him away, in the end, little wiser than when he had arrived.

'The reaction of an innocent man, you think?' Ralph asked me.

'Or a very good actor. I'd like him to be the guilty party, if there is one,' I admitted. 'He certainly seems to have had both motive and mains electricity. And I had an impression that he was . . . not guilty of murder, perhaps, but in some way vulnerable. He was more nervous than he wanted us to believe and he made too much eye contact. But I really don't see him as desperate enough to kill.'

Ralph made his funny, thinking face. 'I'm not so sure,' he said. 'The rest of his money was with the World Bank of Industry and Commerce, which went hugely bust last year. There was no secret about that – he went around telling anybody who would listen to his tale of woe. So a modest percentage added to the price of his shares might look like a lifeline to him. Well, at least you have some leverage if he makes a nuisance of himself to the board. Dawdle over the valuation and purchase of his lease and he'll soon come to heel.'

We managed a further half-hour of consultation before Ralph announced that it was time for him to 'go back to his office and sign things', as he put it. 'You'll have to manage without my advice and encouragement tomorrow,' he said. 'I have a meeting in Edinburgh.'

I lingered to tidy some papers, make a few notes and shut down the computer before going out for a breath of fresh air and to give the two Labradors a walk.

The earlier drizzle had passed, leaving a cool, fresh day with all the colours of spring washed clean.

We went as usual into the wood. If I was still clinging to the last vestige of a hope that Spin would suddenly return, looking as if he wondered what all the fuss was about, I was doomed to disappointment. There was a pleasing absence of the midges which, later in the year, would have made such a moist day into a penance, but trout were jumping in the little loch. The light was already almost gone but I made up my mind to try my luck within the next day or two.

When I turned away, I almost bumped into a tall man. A stranger. Yet his working clothes looked familiar and he seemed to know me.

'Hamish?' I said faintly.

Hamish made a strangled sound. 'Aye,' he said at last. He seemed ready to flee at the first sound of laughter.

With his beard removed and his hair trimmed, Hamish looked younger. I guessed his age as mid-thirties. If I had hoped, for Joanna's sake, that he would be revealed as an Adonis, I was to be disappointed. True, he was almost good-looking, but at a second glance his nose was a little too large, his lips a little full, his cheekbones and eyebrow ridges a little too prominent. But it was a strong face and masculine. He would pass, in a crowd.

'Has Joanna seen you yet?' I asked.

Wordlessly, he shook his head. I decided to provoke a confrontation before he lost his nerve altogether and fled the country, to grow another beard far from the haunts of those who knew him. 'I want to discuss the shooting programme,' I told him. 'Come up to the house and see me in the morning.'

Hamish nodded miserably.

Back at the house, I felt that Elizabeth had had long enough to mope in decent privacy. It was time for a bracing, avuncular approach. I climbed the stairs and knocked on her door. There was no answer. Perhaps she had gone out. On the other hand, she had just been disappointed in love. She might have taken an overdose of something or other. I knocked again and then, daring, opened her door and looked inside. My great fear, that I would surprise her in a state of undress, was not realized. The room, which was plainly, almost severely furnished and not at all girlish, was otherwise empty.

Joanna met me in the hall, to say that dinner would be served in about twenty minutes.

'Where's Miss Elizabeth?' I asked.

'She went out. I waited, just as you said, in case she wanted someone to talk to. But she came out suddenly and said that she didn't want dinner but she'll be home tonight, late.'

I dined alone.

Chapter Eleven

If I had guessed at the stresses the next day was to bring, I would have eaten a heartier breakfast. There had been signs that a prolonged exposure to Mrs Fiddler's catering would necessitate a letting-out of waistbands, so I had managed to persuade her that I was quite satisfied with a little cereal and one slice of toast and was no longer coaxed to take bacon and eggs, tomato, mushrooms and venison sausages.

Elizabeth Hay arrived at the breakfast table in her old, surly mood, tempered with depression and the defensive touchiness of the recently humiliated. I decided that I had liked her better in tearful vein. 'Did you put an e-mail message into the computer about Roland?' she asked as soon as we were alone.

'Definitely not,' I said. 'And nor did your grandfather. You'll be able to find it duplicated in the autofile, and I don't think you can fake that.'

'Somebody could have sent it in for you. Roland swore that it was a fake.'

'Well, what did you expect him to swear?' I asked her.

She shrugged. Her mouth was full at the time, which I took to be a good sign.

'Do you believe him?'

She shook her head. 'I wanted to. But . . .' She paused, wrestling with herself. 'I could see that it was true,' she said at last. 'The report, I mean, not the denial.'

'I'm sorry, Gooseberry,' I said. 'You're bound to be sad that it turned out this way but be thankful that your grandfather had him figured out before you got deeper into the mire.'

She sighed. 'Maybe I'll be able to look at it that way in a year or two,' she said. She paused and then added, 'You can call me Gooseberry as long as nobody else is there. And, listen, I know I said that I'd sort out the computer for you, but after the time I wasted yesterday I've got to put in some studying.'

'That's all right,' I said. 'I'm getting on better with it now. I think it's getting to like me.'

She snorted and left the room, only to return a minute later. I noticed that she was meeting my eye as though I had become a real person to her rather than a figment of her imagination. 'If you like that computer, you can keep it when the work's done.'

'But – '

'Look, I have two other ones, both more powerful than that. If you don't take it, somebody else will.' And she disappeared again.

The return of the fine weather was continuing and I would have liked to be out in it. I intended to do the rounds of the houses and farms shortly, reassuring his tenants about the effects of Sir Peter's will, taking note of any repairs required and, out of sheer curiosity, keeping an eye open for the proximity to Geordie Jennings's fence of mains electricity together with a viewpoint overlooking the metal gate. But I had told

Hamish to come and see me, and I was expecting Mr Hastings a little later. So I gave the two Labradors a stroll along the edge of the wood and then settled in the study to fill in the time by continuing my reading of the material in the computer. I had now mastered the knack of flicking from file to file and of having several files open simultaneously. The fact that the computer would some day be mine, provided that Ralph Enterkin could see no ethical objection to my accepting it, added satisfaction to each small triumph.

As was to be expected, much of the material was outdated and very dull, but it had to be scanned because of the occasional nuggets of live business to be found. One file, simply titled UFL, turned out to have been reserved for unfinished letters and I was soon scratching my head over the contents. These comprised two items – a list of half a dozen farm buildings, and a letter addressed to Ralph Enterkin.

The letter read:

Dear Mr Enterkin,

I have been trying to reach you by telephone but your line was permanently engaged. In any case, this may be better dealt with by letter for the sake of a formal record, with discussion to follow.

Unfortunately I have come across another instance of fraud, smaller and yet in its way just as serious. I think that I shall ask Swinburn and Hastings to carry out a preliminary investigation, but I feel that you should be kept informed from the beginning.

The attached list

The letter broke off at that point. It was undated but I had no difficulty in guessing that it had been started just before we set off on our last walk and was then put aside in favour of the much more interesting venture of putting Spin to work.

A knock on the study door signalled the arrival of Hamish and put an end to my attempt to slot this new piece into the puzzle. I set the printer to work and gave my attention to him.

It was much easier to read his expression now that the whiskers were removed. He was looking unhappy. He did not sound any happier. 'Damn't to hell!' he said.

'Did Joanna not prefer you shaven and shorn?' I asked.

'She laughed!' Hamish said indignantly. 'Laughed at me! Bloody women!'

It was a reaction which I might have foreseen. 'She shouldn't have done that,' I said. 'But calm down and have patience. Many people laugh when they're surprised. See how she reacts second time around.'

He shook his head angrily. 'She'll not change. I might ha' kenned it. I'll be a laughing stock. Well, that's that, then. What was it you were wanting to discuss?'

I had asked him to come to the house so that Joanna would see the new and improved Hamish and I had nothing in particular to say to him. 'We'll leave it for now,' I said. 'You're upset. But don't go away. I have a surveyor coming in connection with the valuation of the estate for Confirmation of the will. You may as well show both of us your cottage and sheds.'

'I'll not be far away, then.'

He nodded and left the room and my mind went back to the mystery surrounding Peter Hay's death.

There seemed to be more than a sufficiency of people with motives. Motive, I reminded myself, did not make a case and indeed was not necessary in law. But it seemed to me that a study of motives must give the investigators their best pointer towards those who should be checked for alibi, fingerprints (genetic and manual), contact traces and all the other means of scientific investigation. Ian Fellowes's study of the geography would produce another list. Comparison of that list with the list of motives would prove enlightening.

Or would it?

A half-formed thought at the back of my mind refused to take shape and yet from somewhere in that subconscious reasoning a conscious thought surfaced. There was one question which Hamish, as far as I knew, had not been asked. I got up willingly from the chair. I had my excuse to go back into the sunshine.

The two Labradors greeted me outside the front door, hoping that this was going to be the occasion for a proper walk instead of a token stroll, but they settled down again grumpily to rest their old bones when I shook my head and gave the stay-there signal. There was no sign of Hamish. I walked round the end of the house and into the yard behind. The garage doors were open and my car stood on the tarmac. A hose lay abandoned on the ground. The car was freshly washed and on the bonnet were a couple of cloths and an empty tin which had held wax. Either Hamish or Ronnie had been giving my paintwork an overdue polish and had gone in search of more wax.

Well, I could wait. The sunlit side of the car was perfectly dry. I leaned against it and enjoyed the sunshine while resuming my cogitation, but the errant thought still refused to surface. There were, I thought, plenty of overhead power lines. One tended not to see them until finding that one's best photographs were spoiled by the lines crossing the sky. But most of those lines were at very high voltage – the figure of 11,000 volts came to my mind, rightly or wrongly. One did not throw the end of a cable over them to purloin a little electricity – indeed, I recalled reading about a vagrant who had been electrocuted while attempting just that. But, in the country at least, between the transformer substation and the houses the supply lines were usually still overhead, and not even at mere 220 volts. Double that voltage could be obtained between two adjacent houses . . . I tried to recall the technicalities of three-phase supplies, but I had never found it easy to envisage what I could not see or feel.

How long I mused in that semi-soporific state is uncertain. I was jerked out of it by a shadow across my feet and a rough push to the shoulder.

Arnold Drayne, alias Roland Chatsworth and sundry other names, stood glaring at me. He was dressed in full motorcycling gear complete with helmet but I could recognize his rodent features behind the visor.

'You bugger!' he shouted, his voice half muffled inside his helmet. 'You showed her that message.' His accent had lost the upper-class drawl and was frankly Glasgow.

Perhaps because of the implied machismo, motorbike leathers and helmet radiate menace and invulnerability. There was no doubt as to his temper. He was quivering with anger. I tried to keep the atmosphere cool. 'She found it on the computer for herself,' I said as calmly as I could. 'I didn't even know it was there until after she saw it. I wondered why she was so upset and looked at it for myself. It was just your bad luck.' My voice had gone husky.

The leather and studs did nothing to disguise his mounting fury. 'Bad luck? And I suppose if you'd found it first you'd have said nothing?'

'I don't know,' I said honestly. 'Did you send messages with computer viruses in them, hoping to wipe it off?'

'If I'd known it was there – '

'Then you'd have known that Sir Peter knew all about you and the jig was up,' I said. Then I realized that I was crediting him with a powerful motive for having committed the murder and I shut my mouth quickly.

Fortunately, he was too angry to search for implications. 'Like hell! You deliberately shopped me. It was going to be my once-for-all. I would have married the little bitch. Bloody hypocrites, the lot of you. Who the hell are you to judge . . .?' He was going to go on and say more, much more, but the rush of furious words was more than his voice could cope with. The result was a traffic jam of words and an explosion of rage. He lashed out at me. I just got a shoulder up in time to save my face.

I had no time for logical thought and yet in retrospect I can recognize a combination of reasoning and instinct at work. Some men may punch and the blow is barely felt, but this punch was like a hammer-blow. As an elderly man with arthritis and a heart problem, I knew that I must not get embroiled in a lengthy scrap. If I had had a weapon to hand I would have used it ruthlessly, but there was nothing. I thought of a swift kick to his crotch, but my kicks were less swift than they used to be. The sensible course seemed to be purely defensive and to hope that his fury had already run its course. I went with the blow and sat down, rolling onto my side.

My hope was misplaced. Arnold Drayne, it seemed, had no inhibitions about hitting a man when he was down. He swung a heavy motorcycle boot and I just managed to curl up in time and get my soles to his shin. The impact hurt him but it drove my knees against my chest, knocking most of the wind out of me. He moved round and came at me from the back and I knew that I was done for. I closed my eyes.

There came the sound of voices and the expected kick never arrived. I opened my eyes again. Hamish had arrived out of nowhere and Joanna was crying out something unintelligible in the background. Both men looked almost incredibly tall from my low viewpoint but Hamish seemed to tower over the other. They were shouting but I never absorbed the words. They closed and wrestled. The helmet went bouncing away across the tarmac. Then something mirror-bright sparked in the sunshine and span away after the helmet, rattling on the ground. Hamish said a rude word and jumped back, a dark line across his jaw spilling blood down his neck.

There was an inarticulate roar. Ronnie had returned, carrying a tin of wax polish. At the same moment, Hamish recovered and closed in again. Outnumbered and intimidated, the intruder sought the only haven open to him, my car. He stepped over me quickly without further assault and dumped himself in the driver's seat, slamming the door behind him.

Ronnie had left the spare key in its slot and if my assailant had been quick he could have driven off; but he wasted a few seconds in locking each of the doors by hand against the vengeance of Hamish and Ronnie and another second in taunting them with a rude gesture through the glass. Then, before he could put his hand on the key in the ignition, I had managed to fish the premier key out of my pocket, pointed it at the driver's door and pressed the button. My car was fitted with the latest security equipment. The remote locking device deadlocked the doors and also triggered the engine immobilizer. The attacker had become a prisoner.

Ronnie put his tin of polish down carefully on the bonnet. From his belt he produced a much larger knife than the lock-knife now lying in the corner of the yard. 'I've just washed this bloody car,' he ground out. 'You damage it, you bugger, and I'll fillet you like a fish. Aye, and then kipper what's left.'

I was concerned for my car but I was more concerned about Hamish. In the heat of the moment I thought that his throat had been cut but a second glance assured me that it was little more than skin deep and placed relatively harmlessly along the jawbone. Hamish might hope to be left with a romantic scar, but his life was in no danger. Joanna, however, who had accompanied him into the yard, was in no mood to assess degrees of wounding. He had galloped to the rescue and his blood had been spilled. That was enough for her. She threw herself at him, nearly bowling him over, and, heedless of the blood, flung her arms round his neck.

My breath had more or less returned to me. With a little assistance from Ronnie, I got to my feet. My mobile phone seemed miraculously undamaged. I keyed the Emergency Services and asked the police to pass a message to Detective Inspector Fellowes to come at once because we had something very interesting to show him.

I dusted myself down and breathed deeply. Apart from an aching shoulder I seemed to be more or less unhurt. Hamish, I decided, was in need of sticking plaster and fatherly advice rather than an ambulance. On the other hand, while we were waiting for Ian Fellowes seemed to be as good a time as any to ask the burning question which had brought me out of doors in the first place.

'Hamish,' I began.

But he and Joanna were in a world of their own, looking deep into each other's eyes and so exchanging messages of love and lust. But for the blood which was being spread around they would have made a prettily romantic picture, fit for the lid of a chocolate box.

'Hamish,' I said again, louder.

There was no reaction. Clearly each had been pricked by a tranquillizer dart from Cupid's bow.

Although I considered myself in large part responsible for this new romance, I was not prepared to be ignored in favour of it. I put my hand between their faces.

This was a mistake. I had intended merely to interrupt their eye contact and so perhaps gain Hamish's attention. But at that very moment the pair closed their eyes and moved in for a long, first kiss. It was a second or two before either of them realized that my fingers were not the expected lips. The sensation of having my hand kissed on both sides simultaneously, with tongues, was highly erotic. For a minute or two I wondered if there might not be life in the old dog yet.

I would have left them to it but Ronnie, stopping just short of throwing a bucket of water over them, took charge and almost wrenched the two apart. Hamish, his cut plastered, was dispatched in the Land Rover to the doctor's surgery, at my insistence and just to be on the safe side. Elizabeth Hay's former love was released from my car and removed, to be charged with assault with a deadly weapon, to wit one knife. A more serious charge, I supposed, might follow.

Twenty minutes later I had washed, tended to one or two scrapes and scratches and was changing my slightly damaged clothes when Ronnie tapped on my door. He seemed to have switched into his butler role, in that he was carrying a silver salver bearing glasses of whisky. Two glasses, I noticed. I assured him that I was uninjured, accepted one of the glasses and invited him to join me. He subsided with a grunt into the one comfortable chair.

'D'you think yon wee bugger killed Sir Peter?' he asked abruptly.

'I don't know. It seems possible. But that's not our business any more,' I pointed out. There was another matter on my mind. 'Ronnie, you're Joanna's father, aren't you?'

His eyebrows shot up. On any face less craggy than

his, I would have interpreted the look as stark horror. He put down his drink and looked out of the door, closing it carefully behind him. 'Why do you say that?' he asked hoarsely.

'I saw your face when she was kissing Hamish,' I told him. 'It had disapproving parenthood written all over it. Don't you want Hamish to marry her?'

'It's Hamish not marrying her that racks me. I've just been speaking with her. She's willing. If Hamish . . . Och, but he's a good lad. He'll do right by her or he'll ha'e me to reckon with. But you'll not say a word outside this room, about me being her dad? No' that I'm ashamed,' he added quickly. 'But I'd not like my sister to know and Mary'd never let me hear the last of it. See, I was going wi' Mary at the time. Then we lost touch and it was years later we met again and married.' He sighed. 'We never had a child of our own, except one that was stillborn.'

'I won't say anything.'

He raised his glass to me and then drained it. We went downstairs together.

Elizabeth, still subdued, joined us in the sitting room to hear the story. And Joanna, sponged but still slightly bloodied, had managed to provide Ian Fellowes, Elizabeth and me with soothing tea and sweet biscuits in the sitting room. Joanna had a private smile and the secret air of one whose mind is miles away and already indulging in intimacies too delicate for ordinary folk to understand. Peter Hay had asked me why the young always thought that they had invented sex. Joanna, I thought, could have told him.

Ian Fellowes, on the other hand, was very much all there and walking a fine line in manner between being a friend and an investigating officer. 'No,' he said, 'no and no. I'm obliged to you for offering me a villain caught literally red-handed. But, while the nasty Mr Drayne may be guilty of seducing maidens, of assault and quite possibly of polygamy, if he has murdered anybody it was not Sir Peter Hay. His alibi for that morning is beyond reproach.'

Elizabeth had flinched at the tactless reference to maidens but she was still game. 'He had a tutorial,' she said, nodding.

'Do try to remember that he was not actually enrolled with the university,' I told her.

'That's right,' Ian said. 'Universities have a large and ever-changing population. It would be very rare for anyone of apparently suitable age and carrying a few books or papers to be challenged. In fact, he was in the Students' Union of the *other* university, on a stolen membership card, having coffee with the daughter of Lord Bonnyrigg. So whatever else he may have been guilty of, murdering your grandfather, Miss Elizabeth, was not one of them. The attack on Mr Kitts must have been an ill-advised explosion of anger at having one of his more hopeful ploys spoiled. He may have extra cause to regret it, because there will almost certainly be enough publicity to cramp his style for good and all and, if he really has been going through forms of marriage, bring one or more of the young ladies to us. You really have been very lucky, Miss Elizabeth.'

'I don't feel very lucky, just at the moment,' she said in a choked voice, and got up to leave the room.

'Poor girl!' said Ian with what seemed to be genuine

sympathy. 'Between loss and humiliation, she must feel terrible. But it could have been very much worse.'

I had had more than enough of young and not-so-young love for the moment. 'What other alibis have you managed to prove or disprove?' I asked him.

He regarded me reprovingly. 'You know I can't tell you that. If somebody were to assure you that they had been elsewhere and you knew that we had proved the alibi false, you'd be almost bound to let slip that you knew. And you will certainly be a prosecution witness. I could be put in an impossible position. You must know how defence lawyers operate. But here's one little snippet that I can offer you in compensation. What seems to be the missing length of street-lighting cable has turned up. We were lucky. One of my men spotted the local scrap dealer with it on the back of his lorry. He swears that he found it on some waste ground by the canal. It may even be true. But if we'd missed him, the cable would have been cut up within the hour.

'The street-lighting foreman is prepared to identify it because one end was still finished exactly in accordance with his technique. The snag is that the other end was hacksawn cleanly and couldn't possibly have been attached to anything while in that condition. So perhaps it wasn't used after all. Perhaps it was stolen and discarded to mislead, I don't know. On the other hand, the cut end doesn't seem to be a perfect match for the cut end on the big reel, so the thief may have used it and then cut off a piece, just to make it difficult for us – or a jury – to draw any inferences from the length he'd needed or the connections he'd made. For what it's worth, the length was just under thirty metres.'

As a clue, I decided, it was not worth very much. If the length of the cable had been significant, it would surely have ended up in the canal, not alongside it. Somewhere, perhaps in the canal, there would be another piece. I suggested this to Ian. He thanked me politely but said that a frogman was already at work.

'How far is it from the Spigatt woman's house to the fence?' I asked him.

He regarded me pityingly. 'Please get rid of the idea that you can point out suspects to me,' he said. 'Miss Spigatt has been considered. Any cable from her house to the fence would have had to cross the public road. And, in case you're thinking that she might have had the use of a neighbour's house, I may as well tell you that we have spoken to Mr Enterkin's secretary. Enterkin was speaking to Miss Spigatt while you were shooting rabbits with Sir Peter.'

'But – ' I began.

He rode over me. 'But she could have phoned from home, you're about to say. Well, she didn't. She made the first call and left a message asking him to call her back, which he did. The number is still in the secretary's notebook. It is the Edinburgh office.'

While I had him in this peevish but semi-confiding mood, I intended to ask Ian whether he had ever put to Hamish the question that I had been forgetting to ask. Hamish had remembered hearing the sound of an engine at around the time that Peter Hay had died. Of course, it might have been the sound of some perfectly innocent vehicle going past on the road, but the driver might have witnessed something and I was curious to know how the engine had sounded. Large or small, petrol or diesel, most men could tell at least that much from the noise.

But, before I could work around to the subject, we were interrupted. I had heard the sound of the doorbell without really noticing it. Now Joanna arrived at the door with the news that Mr Hastings had arrived.

Ian made his escape and I asked Joanna to bring Mr Hastings to the study.

Adrian Hastings turned out to be a man of around fifty with a calm, expressionless face spoiled by broken veins. He was dressed in good and apparently new clothes, his suit tailor-made for him and cut to accommodate the beginnings of a portly belly. He was accompanied by a younger man who he introduced as his assistant, Jim Frazier. Frazier was the more suitably dressed for scrambling around in old farm buildings and I guessed that any mucky jobs would fall to his lot. He was also, it transpired, along as Mr Hastings's driver. Mr Hastings was quite open about the reason for this. He had lost his driver's licence as a result of 'one of those dinners that the professional man can't avoid and so boring that he can't get through without a good dram in him.'

Hastings had brought with him a file of correspondence with Peter Hay, but I had come across several of the letters in the course of my wanderings around the computer's unfamiliar filing system, so that I knew the documents to be genuine. Sir Peter, it seemed, had trusted the firm and made extensive use of them. Jim Frazier sat silently as his employer and I skirmished and haggled over the Conditions of Engagement sponsored by the RICS.

'This is what I propose,' I said at last. 'I'll engage you, at first, job by job. If we get along, you can do all the valuations required for Confirmation and for disposing of certain properties. And if we're still on speaking terms by the end of it, we'll probably leave the factoring in your hands.'

'In that event, we would open a local office.'

'That could be sound business,' I said. 'We've already severed relations with the previous factors and I suspect that others will do the same.'

It seemed that Hastings knew about the Weimms and Spigatt debacle. 'Yes,' he said, 'that was a sad business. I quite understand. And the arrangement you propose will be satisfactory.'

I looked at my watch. The morning had almost gone. 'If you'll stay for lunch,' I said, 'you could meet Sir Peter's granddaughter, who will be your client in the long run, and then look at the first two tasks that I want you to undertake.'

Adrian Hastings accepted for them both. I rang for Joanna and sent her to Mrs Fiddler with the news of two guests for an early lunch.

'Now,' I said. I took the two pages of printout from my pocket. 'You phoned me about an approach from Sir Peter which he had failed to follow up – for the obvious reason. I think that this may have had a bearing on the subject, but the information is again incomplete. Can you shed any light?'

Hastings read the unfinished letter and ran his eye down the list of buildings. 'Not a glimmer,' he said. 'I can imagine several possible answers, but I'd be guessing.'

'The only possible link that I can see,' I said, 'is

that at least four of the farm buildings, maybe more, had work done on them within the last few years. But I'd like you to take a look at one or two of them after lunch and advise me.'

'We can certainly do that.'

Joanna returned to say that soup and an otherwise cold lunch would be on the table in five minutes. Miss Elizabeth would be joining us.

Mary Fiddler's talent for coping with sudden guests was noteworthy. The broth, followed by cold venison with salad and then a cheeseboard, seemed to be appreciated, as was only right. I was beginning to wonder for how long I could spin out my tasks in Newton Lauder. Adrian Hastings joined me in a glass of chilled white wine.

Elizabeth had made at least a partial recovery from her megrims and fell into mildly animated conversation with Jim Frazier who, after maintaining a proper silence while his chief talked business, was now discovered to have the gift of amusing chat and a knack of coaxing sulky girls out of their shells. We finished with the coffee, after which Elizabeth went back to her studies, leaving me satisfied that there would be no objection on her part to Swinburn and Hastings acting as factors for the estate.

'Two tasks, you said,' Adrian Hastings reminded me.

'That's right. We'll go and look at them. No need to take two cars,' I said. 'I'll come with you if you'll drop me back here when we've finished.'

With Jim Frazier at the wheel I directed the big Japanese four-by-four back down the drive and out along the minor road that led to Home Farm. The car was remarkably glossy and undented for one of that type in that environment. We halted outside the Synott residence.

'You walk on as far as the farm,' I told Frazier. 'The drying shed was supposed to have a mostly new roof two years ago but the farm manager's complaining. I'd appreciate your comments. You and I,' I said to Hastings, 'will call on Mr Synott. He's moving away and the estate has first refusal when he decides to sell his lease. I want a valuation. I was supposed to give notice before any visit, but he's in a hurry to move so he may be accommodating.'

But at the front door we met with a snag. The bell was answered by a lady who I guessed to be Mrs Synott. She was angular and rather masculine in appearance, dressed in a faded print smock. I introduced Adrian Hastings and myself, apologized for the lack of warning and asked that Mr Hastings be allowed to see over the house for valuation purposes.

For some reason, Mrs Synott looked perturbed. 'It's most inconvenient,' she said. 'The house is in a mess.'

'He will be looking at the fabric of the house,' I said firmly. 'He has no interest in the contents or the housekeeping.'

'All the same, I was told that we would get some warning.'

I felt that one apology was enough. I had conceived a dislike of both the Synotts and felt inclined to match any bloody-mindedness that was offered. Adrian Hastings, I was sure, was on the point of saying that Jim Frazier could carry out the valuation whenever it suited her, so I spoke quickly. 'It may be some considerable time before Mr Hastings will be back in the area.'

'I only need to make a few notes about the rooms and their condition,' Hastings said, following my lead. 'My assistant can run a tape round the outside when he rejoins us.'

Mrs Synott took a few seconds for unhappy thought. 'Would you wait here, just for a minute or two?' she asked and without waiting for an answer she slammed the door.

Hastings had learned to take such treatment in his stride. He studied the outside of the house and made a few notes in an electronic notebook. 'An attractive property,' he said, 'and a good outlook.'

There was no denying either comment. The house, which was stone built, was spacious and well proportioned. It had been built around the time of World War One and stood in a well kept if severely set out walled garden. It looked over a small patchwork of farmland to the gate where Sir Peter had died. The front garden was not yet at its best, being mainly given over to roses – the resort of the unimaginative gardener.

I thought that I heard a car's door close. Surely Mrs Synott could not be getting rid of an inconvenient lover? But there was no sound of an engine and after another minute the front door opened again. 'You can come in,' she said sternly. I thought that she seemed flustered.

We entered a hall and then a living room which were furnished in a tasteful if old-fashioned style although becoming overdue for decoration. But I was not concerned with visual effect. I was too busy sniffing the atmosphere.

I had intended to accompany Adrian Hastings on

219

his guided tour in the hope of seeing some sign of non-standard electrical connections, but I changed my mind. 'You won't want to be bothered with two of us,' I said. 'I'll wait in the car.' Hastings handed me the key without any more comment than a raised eyebrow.

I would have liked to walk round the house but there would be windows overlooking the rear. Instead, I returned to the car and shut myself inside. Safe from eavesdroppers, I called the police from my mobile and for the second time that day asked for a message to be passed to Ian Fellowes. If he joined me quickly I might be able to show him something of interest.

My afternoon lassitude was creeping up on me, but my shoulder was stiffening where I had been struck and a bruise on my hip was nagging at me. I opened my eyes. I could see Mr Synott in a door mirror, walking from the direction of the road. He was swinging a stick and lugging a plastic carrier bag, from which I deduced that he had walked into Newton Lauder for some minor shopping. Any temptation to sleep departed in a hurry. I could not be sure what he would do when he discovered that his house had been invaded, but I preferred to have Ian Fellowes at hand before I found out. I got out of the car and greeted him affably.

He hid his surprise at my sudden friendliness, came to a halt and wished me a cautious good day.

'I was just admiring the house,' I said. 'You'll be sorry to leave, I'm sure.'

'In a way,' he admitted. He put his shopping down by the gate and rubbed his fingers. 'We've been contented here. But it's quiet. Rather isolated, in fact. And the locals keep themselves to themselves.'

I considered the locals to be more forthcoming than any other Scots except, perhaps, Glaswegians. If the Synotts considered them stand-offish, the reason lay within themselves. But I pretended to agree, offered a little sympathy and led the discussion round to his directorship at Agrotechnics. 'I thought that, while I was passing, I might call in and collect that letter,' I said.

'I haven't written it yet.'

From that point on, our communion became less friendly. He avoided my eye. I concluded that he only forced himself to make eye contact when he was lying. His expression became crafty, his tone wheedling. He did not say so aloud but I was left in no doubt that he still hoped to be recompensed for the might-have-been profit from the buyout, either through the company or by way of an adjustment to the value of his lease, failing which he was going to be as obstructive as he could manage. I was even more determined that he would receive no such special benefit, but I was equally reluctant to say so outright.

'I thought that you were in a hurry to sell your lease,' I said.

He looked me in the eye for once. 'And I thought that you were in a hurry to settle the matter of the directorship.'

Ian Fellowes must have been pursuing his investigations nearby. Before I could lose my temper and say something which would have had Synott hurrying into the house, I was relieved to see the blue Range Rover which was Ian's usual official transport turning into the farm road. He parked nose-to-tail with the Swinburn and Hastings vehicle and dismounted.

'You have something to show me?' Ian asked me. Synott, I noticed, had turned white. Keith Calder followed Ian out of the car. Synott and I looked at him in surprise. 'Mr Calder is my civilian adviser,' Ian said grandly.

'I can go away, if anyone objects,' Keith said.

Neither of us said anything. For my part, if my suspicion was right I wanted as many witnesses as possible. If I was wrong I would rather be alone, but I had set my foot on the path and it was too late to retreat. 'There is evidence,' I said, 'that either Mr or Mrs Snot – ' I was past caring for his wounded feelings ' – visited the place where Sir Peter died within a few minutes of his death. And, of course, the other could have fed mains electricity into the fence, from the house or from the tractor shed. Anyone could slip from this garden and round the end of the gable of the tractor shed without much risk of being seen, whereas anyone arriving across the fields or along the farm road would be visible for miles.'

A sizzling silence was broken at last by the shaking voice of Synott. 'You're mad,' he shrilled. 'Stark mad! I'll sue you! None of it's true. I don't even know what you're talking about. I'll see you prosecuted for . . . for . . .' He came to a halt, uncertain of his legal rights. I gained confidence. There was no doubt that Synott felt vulnerable.

'Come round to the back of the house,' I told the others. 'I want to show you what Mrs Synott was in a hurry to shut in the boot of the family car when I asked her to let a surveyor see through the house.'

'I don't have to take this from you,' Synott yelped. 'You were supposed to give us notice before bringing in a surveyor. This is entrapment. You'll hear from my solicitors. If any one of you sets foot inside this garden, I'll prosecute.'

'You can't,' I said. 'There's no law of trespass in Scotland and I represent the superior of the feu.'

Synott glared at me for a second. Then, forgetting his shopping, he scuttled to the door of the house.

'Come on!' I said. My sprinting days are past but I managed a respectable jogtrot, following the grass rather than the gravel drive round the gable of the building so that we arrived without excessive noise at the corner. I slowed down, panting but with a great relief spreading through me. Had I been several decades younger, I would have leaped for joy.

Behind the house, a polished but slightly rusty saloon stood outside a concrete garage. Synott, who must have bolted through the house like a whippet, was lifting Spin out of the boot.

The man turned, snarling. I called softly to the dog. Spin took a second or two to recognize me and then began to struggle. A struggling spaniel rivals an eel for evasiveness. He jumped down and ran to me. His tail had been docked at birth, but he wagged the remainder so hard that he nearly fell over. He jumped up against my leg and then lay down and rolled over. When I bent and patted his stomach, he squirmed in ecstasy. He seemed to have been well looked after. He had even put on a little weight although I thought that the difficulty of exercising a stolen dog in the area of the theft might in part account for that, and also for the hurry to move house. When I straightened, slightly dizzy from bending down, Spin sat up and leaned against my leg.

I said, 'I identify this animal as the dog that was the property of Sir Peter Hay and was with him at the time of his death.'

'This – ' Synott began. He stopped. Whatever unlikely story he had been about to concoct, perhaps disputing the identity of the dog, he must have seen that it would never pass muster. He began again. He had assumed a new dignity and I was sure that this time we might get the truth. 'All right. If I don't tell you, you'll think that I had to do with something worse.

'You remember – ' he looked at me ' – I came across Sir Peter and his gamekeeper that morning. One of them had shot my cat.'

'Marauding after young birds,' I agreed. 'Detective Inspector Fellowes has been informed.'

Synott flinched but went on. 'That's as may be. I'm making no admissions. I went home, but I was angry. Frankly, I was furious. I told my wife about it and she was even angrier than I was. I suppose that we were working each other up into a state. You know what I mean?' he asked me. He seemed to have fixed on me, as his accuser, to be the recipient of his explanation.

I nodded. That is how riots are fuelled. Even two people in concert will act more rashly than one alone.

'Anyway,' he resumed, 'when I had been suddenly confronted with the corpse of my old friend – my cat – I was upset and I went off without expressing my true feelings.'

'What were your true feelings?' Ian asked softly.

'I've just said that I was furious. Of course I was. I . . . I did nothing to harm Sir Peter but in honesty I'll admit that I was seething with rage and . . . and contempt.' He paused and glanced away. 'I had every right to be. Anyone would have been. I saw that I had been cleverly bluffed. But I had no thought of . . . anything physical. I decided to give Sir Peter a piece of both of our minds, that was all. I had thought better of him. Now I realized that he was no better than a murderer and I meant to tell him so. I could see the two of you coming back over the hill and I knew that he always went back through the iron gate, I'd seen him often enough in the past. So I set off to meet him. I went by way of the old railway line – not to be secretive but because it's the only logical path if you don't want to be climbing fences and picking your way along the edge of crops.

'I was hurrying to catch him, but I was almost too late. If he'd still been moving, I'd have had to follow you through the wood.'

'You'd have been in time,' I said. 'We stopped to have one last rabbit hunt in the bottom of the wood.'

'I see. I never got that far. I reached the place where you have to climb a stile, about fifty yards from the gate, but I was still hidden in the old railway cutting when his dog – this dog – came through the fence and circled around me. He was whining. I couldn't make any sense of it.'

'Peter must have collapsed by then,' Keith said. 'The dog was looking for somebody to go to his aid.'

'Well, I didn't know that,' Synott said. To his credit, he sounded more defensive than he had over the dog.

'It was already too late,' Keith said.

Synott glanced at him gratefully. 'I'm glad of that small mercy. I wouldn't want to think that I'd removed his last chance. You see, the way I felt, he owed me an animal. He'd killed my cat and I thought that it would be no more than justice if I took his dog and let him see what it feels like to lose a much-loved pet. So I put my belt on the dog as a lead and brought him home. Then I waited for the hue and cry to start. I was going to take the dog back to him and say, "How did you like it, losing a friend?" But later that afternoon I heard what had happened and that the police were asking questions. I felt that I couldn't own up without inviting all sorts of suspicions.'

'What sort of suspicions?' Ian asked him.

'Oh, not that I'd killed him. That never entered my mind. But it might have been thought that I'd found Sir Peter dead and decided to steal his dog. Or even that I'd found him dying and left him to die. I wouldn't want that said of me.

'Anyway, my wife had fallen in love with the dog. I suppose that I had, a bit, too – he's a well-mannered animal, I hadn't realized before what character a dog can have, quite different from a cat. I've drawn them often enough, for the children's books, but somebody else wrote the stories and I never had one as company before.' Synott looked round our faces and seemed relieved to see that we could understand his senti- ments. 'And Sir Peter wasn't going to be missing him after all. We had already been considering a removal to the other house to be nearer to our relatives and this made up our minds for us. I suppose . . .' he added sadly, 'I suppose you'll be taking Kinnock away now?'

'Who?' He had caught me flat-footed.

'We call him Kinnock, after Neil Kinnock. We very much admired him.'

I swallowed a sarcastic remark. One of the vaunted freedoms of democracy is that you can admire whoever you like. 'He isn't yours,' I pointed out. 'Under Sir Peter's will, he will belong to the gamekeeper, who has no cause to love you.'

'Perhaps he'd sell him. What would the value be?'

I quoted John Cunningham's price for a fully trained male springer and Synott's face fell. 'But the dog would never be happy in a non-shooting home now,' I told him. Synott looked so miserable that I felt almost sorry for him. 'And most of that price is in the cost of keep and training while turning a puppy into a working dog,' I said. 'You could buy a young pup of similar breeding much more cheaply.' I nearly went on to suggest that he approach Three Oaks, but remembered in time that John never sells his puppies for pets.

Ian Fellowes had been waiting impatiently for us to finish with what he considered to be a complete irrelevancy. 'You can't have been very far from Sir Peter when he died. Did you see or hear anything, usual or unusual, when you were walking along the old railway line?'

Synott frowned. 'I wasn't paying much attention,' he said. 'Going, I was too angry; and, coming back, I was pre-occupied with the dog. But – let me think . . . There was something . . .' He paused. My legs were tired and I sat down on a front wing of the car. 'I remember,' Synott said suddenly. 'I don't know whether it has any significance. On my way out, there was something, a rope or thin hose or a piece of electric cable or something like that, lying across the track. I'd never seen it there before and I don't think it was still there when I came back. If I thought about it at all, I thought that children had been playing about in the wood.'

Synott paused, wondering why we had frozen. He seemed quite unaware of having said anything remarkable.

Chapter Twelve

Ian stirred and straightened his back. 'Could you show us exactly where it was?' he asked.

'I think so,' Synott said doubtfully. He turned on his heel. 'Come with me. This is the easiest route.'

Frazier and Hastings were waiting at the corner of the house, but I knew that Ralph Enterkin would make my life a misery if I was unable to report every detail of what was coming. Also, I was curious. 'Hold on for a few seconds,' I told Ian. 'I want to come with you. I may be able to contribute something.'

Ian hesitated but then nodded.

I called Spin to heel and went to join the surveyors. 'We'll be sending you a written valuation and a report on the drying shed,' Hastings said. 'But I thought that you should hear what Jim has to say.'

I listened to a brief report on the drying shed roof, promised to send further instructions and hurried to catch up with the others, who had started to drift away along an earth path between neat vegetable beds towards a clump of overgrown rhododendrons. A small caravan stood nearby and I thought that, if Snot had been given more time, Spin might well have been tucked away there while the surveyors inspected the house. The trees – they were too large to be called shrubs – were hiding a small gate into the old railway cutting between two bridges. On our left the railway was tunnelled under the local road. Rough steps had been cut or worn in the banking and we made our way down, in my case with some care. We turned right and our footsteps rang as we walked beneath another bridge and passed under the farm road.

The cutting curved gently but steadily to the right so that we could see ahead for only a couple of hundred yards or so. There was little wonder that, whether on purpose or fortuitously, Synott had made his way to and fro unobserved. Our view was limited to the blue sky, a few small white clouds and to the banking on either side which was clad with heather. Atop the right-hand bank ran the farm boundary, identified by the black rubber insulators in the electric cattle fence. We had no landmarks to tell us the distance we had covered until, above and on our left, the tops began to appear of a plantation of tall conifers which, as I had noticed when we passed the other side of it on the road, had been thinned once and then left to grow. Over the past few hours I had been presented with so many subjects for thought that much of my mind was taken up with wondering which to think about first, but I made a mental note to have Adrian Hastings value the standing timber on the estate.

With that out of the way, my mind threw up the question which had been nagging me, on and off, all morning. I hurried to catch up with Ian – rather painfully, because my morning's antics were beginning to catch up with me. 'Hamish said that he heard an engine running. Did you ask him what sort of engine?'

'He had the impression of a diesel-powered van or

small truck on the road. The local coal merchant was as near as he could guess.'

'You asked the coal merchant?'

'His lorry's being overhauled, not before time. Jennings says that nothing came to the farm. But, of course, the road goes on round to Bellafield.'

Synott stopped dead and then walked on. 'But that's reminded me,' he said. 'I heard a motor running while I was walking in this direction. It wasn't running along the road. It could have been a lorry ticking over, perhaps. I don't remember hearing it while I was coming back, but I was pre-occupied with the dog.' He glanced down at Spin, still walking faithfully at my heel and looked away quickly. 'I think we're getting near the place now.'

'Come another fifty yards,' Keith's voice said from somewhere ahead of us among the trees. 'This is the place.' Ian looked wildly around. Neither of us had realized that Keith had climbed the bank and entered the wood.

'How do you know?' Ian called.

'Marks of a vehicle.'

We walked on. Keith's head appeared at the top of the bank, above a clump of gorse in full yellow bloom. 'This is the place, true enough,' Synott said. 'I tripped on the whatever-it-was and looked up. The gorse was just coming out.'

Ian studied the bank. 'I can't imagine this heather holding any useful tracks,' he said. 'All right. Thank you Mr Synott. We needn't keep you any longer.'

Synott nodded. He stopped to give Spin a farewell pat but the spaniel's attention was all on me. The man's face dropped and I thought for a moment that he would break down. Suddenly, I was sorry for him, knowing too well how a dog can wrap itself around your heart. 'You can always get another spaniel from the Rescue Centre,' I suggested.

'Another dog wouldn't be the same. We'd always be making comparisons.'

'Sometimes,' I said, 'a young dog fails in training – turns out to be incurably gun-shy or hard-mouthed, or something like that, and gets sold off cheaply. If you let me have your new address I'll let you know, the first time that it happens to one of identical breeding.'

'Thank you,' he said. 'I – we'd appreciate that.' He paused, trying to think of some stronger expression of friendship or at least gratitude. 'You can call me Snot,' he finished bravely.

I climbed painfully up the bank after Ian. The heather alternately dragged at my feet and gave me a good purchase for the next step, but the tough stems were undamaged. Ian was right, there would be no discernible tracks after the passage of the intervening days. At the top, I crawled through a fence of plain wire with a barbed top strand and dragged myself upright. The heather gave way to a surface formed by many years of fallen pine needles. At least it was easier walking than the uneven metalling of the former railway.

Keith was drawing Ian's attention to a hole beside the nearer fence. 'He'd need a good earth,' he said. 'He seems to have hammered in an angle-iron, probably poured water onto the ground as well, but it's dried by now.'

I could see a faint impression of wheels, hardly

discernible in the shade beneath the trees. Otherwise, I thought, the surface was about as impervious to tracks as the heather had been.

'Don't touch anything,' Ian said sharply. 'I'll get the search team down here. Come away now.' He hustled us away to what he regarded as a safe distance. He fumbled for his personal radio but put it away again. 'Before I make an idiot of myself, let's be sure we know what we're talking about. The nearest overhead power cables are the other side of the road. Right?'

'Perfectly true,' Keith said patiently. 'But we are not talking power cables. Why do you think anybody would bring a heavy vehicle into the wood?'

I was beginning to catch up, but Ian was still floundering. 'To stand on the roof? To reach overhead cables? Or to see over obstructions?'

'Or to tow something,' said Keith. 'Put overhead cables out of your mind. And take note that you can see the gate from the edge of the trees without even standing on tiptoe. We're talking generators.'

Ian frowned. 'I did think along those lines. Several people have portable generators around here – the Synotts among them, for when they go caravanning. But Mr Flaherty assured me that one of those could never push a lethal current along a stretch of fence wire.'

'Jim Flaherty must have been dreaming,' Keith said. 'Or else he didn't want to point the finger at a pal. I'm not suggesting one of those suitcase-sized two-strokes. They're all right for powering a television set but not for running machinery. I'm talking about a substantial diesel-powered generator capable of putting out ample three-phase current.'

'But who'd have a thing like that around here?' Ian asked plaintively.

'Jock McAnderton. The builder. That's who. For Pete's sake,' Keith said impatiently, 'what do you think he tows around everywhere behind that truck of his?'

'I assumed that it was a compressor, for powering pneumatic tools.'

'So did I,' I admitted.

'Well, it isn't. Jock used to be in a bigger way of business and that generator could power and light a whole building site. But then came the recession and much stiffer competition and the big contracts weren't there any more. He sold off most of his plant but kept the generator and a selection of tools. Now he makes do as a jobbing builder, usually a one man band plus what little help that nephew deigns to give him, though he re-hires some of his former employees when he needs them. And,' Keith added, 'I don't suppose for a moment that they sign off at the labour exchange each time.'

Ian glanced around. He looked tired and I realized for the first time that he must have been on his feet since before I left my bed. There was a fallen tree nearby, mossy side down. Ian took a seat on the trunk and Keith and I settled on either side of him. It was very peaceful in the wood.

'I don't see an occasional fraud on the Benefit Office as being a motive for murder,' Ian said. 'Not even if Sir Peter stumbled on evidence of it. Who else might have obtained access to Mr McAnderton's generator? And his truck, unless they have a towing vehicle of their own?'

Looking past Ian, I saw Keith frown. 'That will take

a little thinking about,' he said. 'And probably quite a lot of legwork by your boys. It would have to be a very close friend. Jock's very wary about lending or hiring out his plant. He said to me once that he might make a pound or two hiring it out but it could cost him his livelihood if it came back knackered.'

'He'd know about electricity,' I said, 'but would he know about computer viruses?'

'That nephew of his would,' Keith said. 'He was offered a place at the Technical College but his uncle had work for him and the lad has a lazy mind.'

'This has the makings of a long haul,' Ian said, 'with no certainty of a positive result at the end of it. My chiefs in Auld Reekie will not be happy.'

I was not happy either. 'Motive doesn't make a case,' I said. 'We keep telling each other so. And lack of motive doesn't damage it.'

'That's the theory,' Ian said. 'But it tells you where to look. And juries don't see it your way.'

I sighed and felt like a supergrass. 'I can hand you a motive,' I told him. 'From what's just been said, I take it that Mr McAnderton has financial problems?'

'The recession caught him with a lot of plant bought but not paid for,' Keith confirmed. 'I know that he borrowed off Peter to settle his more pressing debts but I gathered that he's been repaying the loan. Peter's death wouldn't do him any good. Or does the will cancel the debt?'

'And, if so, did McAnderton know it?' Ian put in.

'There's no mention of it in the will,' I said. 'But I've no record of the loan either, so far. I think it must have been a personal arrangement between the two of them, off the record and in cash. But even that isn't the whole motive. When we met Jennings, the farm manager, at the tractor shed, he was complaining about the roof of the drying shed.'

'He was trying it on,' said Keith.

'He tried it on about several things,' I said. 'The roof of the drying shed was the one genuine article. In Sir Peter's files, I came across a receipt for re-roofing by Jock McAnderton about two years ago. The surveyor has just reported to me that the roof is leaking badly and seems to have been replaced reusing second-hand materials.'

'About two years ago,' Keith said slowly, 'I remember Peter complaining that he was getting too old to hop around on ladders. I think that he trusted Weimms and Spigatt to do the inspecting, but the shit was about to hit their fan and I don't suppose they were too fussy.'

'Can you think,' I asked, 'of anything more certain to put Peter's back up than to discover that the very money being used to pay back the debt to him had been gathered by frauds against himself? I think that the wall where McAnderton's working now may have been the first of them to come to light – it collapsed and Peter told him to rebuild it properly at his own expense. And,' I added indignantly, 'the cheeky beggar came to me as soon as Peter was dead, asking me to confirm that he would be paid for the work. Peter had warned a firm of surveyors that he would have some work for them and on his computer I found the beginning of a draft letter to Ralph Enterkin, listing seven or eight farm buildings. The letter reads as though, when finished, it would have instructed the solicitor to bring proceedings. I'll have to get the other buildings on the list inspected, but I've no doubt the result will be much the same. Is that motive enough for you?'

'Ample,' Ian said. 'And it's also enough grounds for holding him in custody while we look for evidence in connection with the murder. If you wait for a few minutes while I get the search started, I'll come and get copies of the evidence from you.'

As always at a time of breakthrough, new thoughts were coming thick and fast. 'But why would he need to steal cable?' I enquired. 'He must have had miles of it.'

'He did,' said Keith. 'He still does. But he got fed up with it being stolen and with his men tripping over it, so just before the recession began he had one of his men paint the whole lot white with chlorinated rubber paint left over from some job or other. If he'd had to abandon it, or if somebody had noticed it in place – as Synott did, you remember – the jig would have been up.'

The time for talking seemed to be over. Keith and his son-in-law set off back towards the farm, to collect Ian's Range Rover and for Ian to transfer the searchers to the new venue. Ian offered to collect me from the nearby roadside, but could not commit himself as to when. I was not far from the house and I was anxious to get Spin home and settled. I continued along the former railway line and scrambled down the bank to the track through the wood. Spin knew where he was. As we got nearer, the spaniel began to dance.

I met nobody along the way and there was nobody in sight, yet, by that inexplicable beating of the jungle drums which can happen in close-knit communities, Mary and Joanna emerged from the kitchen premises (which looked in the opposite direction), Ronnie and Hamish appeared out of nowhere and even the two Labradors joined the welcoming party.

Spin was revelling in the attention, capering and offering himself for petting, but my joints were aching. Rather than stand around on the gravel I collected a pocketful of charcoal biscuits and then led the way into the sitting room, ignoring all questions and taking all the dogs with me, letting the staff follow on. I seated myself comfortably and made a small fuss of the Labradors, dispensing charcoal biscuits all round rather than risk allowing jealousies to develop.

It was not for me to spread the tale. I parried a hundred questions. The true facts, or a reasonable approximation, would do the rounds soon enough; but what I did not realize was just how soon this would be. I had not seen Mary Fiddler leave the throng, but she came back in with an air of triumph. 'That was the fish van,' she told Joanna, and to me, 'So it was yon Mr Synott who had the wee dog all this time.'

'The bugger!' said Hamish. Joanna frowned reprovingly.

Mary's two statements seemed to be something of a non sequitur. 'Where did you get that idea?' I asked her cautiously.

'Duggie Scott, who drives the fish van, told me. He was just pulling up at the Old Farmhouse when he saw you leaving with Mr Fellowes and Mr Calder and the wee chap. And when Mrs Synott came to the door, he could see that she was gey upset. He asked her did she want fish for the cat and that nearly set her off.

And Duggie said another thing. He went on up to Bellafield and when he was coming back just now he says that it seemed like every policeman in Lothian and Borders was gathering at the fir wood between the Bellafield road and the old railway line.'

There was a sudden outbreak of nodding and grunting. Any speculation about that latest development was likely to wander too close to the real facts and, if bruited about, might well damage Ian's chances of an arrest. The garrulous fish-van driver might well put the same spoke in Ian's wheel, but that would not be my fault. I broke up the party and sent the four about their various businesses, only asking Joanna for a cup of tea and suggesting that Hamish, as his future owner, should attend to the feeding of Spin.

My mind was too full for humdrum estate business, but I set about advising the various bodies who had been contacted about Spin that the spaniel was now back in residence and cancelling any advertisements which had not yet appeared, after which I leaned back for my post-prandial rest.

After a day already filled with incident I had expected sleep to evade me, but I jerked awake to find Joanna stooped over me and peering anxiously into my face. It seemed that the staff had become aware of the mortality of the elderly. She jerked back when my eyes opened.

'Please,' she said. 'Mr Enterkin was on the phone. He can't come here this afternoon, but would you care to dine with him and Mrs Enterkin tonight, don't dress, seven-thirty for eight? I said that you were tired and I wouldn't wake you but that I thought you'd be glad of the invitation and I'd call him back when you woke up

if you had some other arrangement,' she finished all
in one breath.

'What about Miss Elizabeth?' I asked her, conscious
of my duties as an uncomfortable compromise
between guest and guardian.

'Don't you worry about Miss Elizabeth. She's been
working away at her books all day,' Joanna said approvingly, 'but Mr Ilwand phoned, the laddie that works
with Mr Paterson, and she's going out to dinner with
him tonight. She's in the bath now,' Joanna added as
evidence that she had the facts straight.

'In that case I'll be delighted to go to the Enterkins,'
I said. 'No doubt you've told Mrs Fiddler?'

I had time in hand so I took all three dogs with me
and managed a quick visit to the loch, where I landed
a handsome brownie of nearly three pounds. Then
back to the house to make myself tidy for dining out.

A taxi arrived at the door before I could get my car
out. It had been sent by Ralph Enterkin and the driver
assured me that this was his habit when expecting
guests from not too far away. I assumed at the time
that this signified that Enterkin hospitality was to be
as bibulous as that of the Calders, but Keith suggested
later that Ralph's real motivation was so that he would
have control over any guest's time of departure.

I was admitted to the Enterkins' large flat, one floor
up in a quiet street just behind the Square, by a plump
lady who seemed familiar. Penny Enterkin had a neat
little apron over a cocktail dress. I decided vaguely that
I must have bumped into her during one of my few
forays into the town. I was more interested in studying

the Enterkins' home. The flat was remarkably spacious and freshly decorated. In contrast with Peter Hay's old-fashioned solidity and the Calders' carefully matched antiques and reproductions, the Enterkins had opted for an unexpected modernity, Scandinavian pine mingled with glass and chromed tubes.

Mrs Enterkin withdrew into a kitchen, opening directly off the huge living-dining room. She left the door open, allowing delicious smells to emerge, because, she explained with a sweet smile, she didn't mind cooking the meal but she was damned if she was going to be left entirely out of the conversation. Her accent came from somewhere in the far south-west, Devon I rather thought, which almost but not quite triggered my memory.

Ralph gave me a ferocious gin and tonic complete with ice and lemon, poured a sherry for himself and took another through to his wife, but his mind was not really on such courtesies and comforts.

When he had the pair of us seated opposite one another in a couple of not uncomfortable steel and leather chairs, he demanded, 'What in hell's been going on this afternoon? I was back in my office, preparing a brief for counsel who will be attempting to convince a jury that one of the sons of Newton Lauder did not after all press the pursuit of a certain lady's virtue beyond the point at which courtship becomes harassment. In this, I fear, he will fail, but don't quote me. Thus I heard nothing until Penny, who had been in the hotel since eleven a.m., returned in mid-afternoon laden with gossip and rumours which had been flying around the town. And it would seem that you were at the heart of the business.'

I did not answer immediately. Four or five hours seemed to be rather a long time for a respectable lady to have been hanging around the hotel, absorbing gossip and rumours. But then, belatedly, I put together the length of that visit, my recollection of the Devonian accent and the attractive if comfortably upholstered lady and realized at last that she had been the plump barmaid who had served us when we lunched with Sir Peter at the hotel and with whom I had thought Ralph had been on surprisingly familiar terms. All things considered, he had carried it off very well, perhaps from long-standing habit. Some might have found it socially problematic to introduce the barmaid to a fellow-guest as his wife and he had evidently decided to postpone introductions altogether. I mentally reviewed such words of social chit-chat as I had exchanged with Ralph and decided that I had not dropped any serious bricks. 'Which business are you referring to?' I asked cautiously.

'Any and all of them,' he said. I gestured with my eyes towards the open kitchen door. Ralph snorted. 'My wife is privy to almost every secret in the town,' he said, 'but she disgorges them only to me. And not always to me, I strongly suspect,' he added in the direction of the kitchen. 'I would have every objection to my wife working at all, let alone as a common though skilled barmaid, were it not that she picks up every morsel of tittle-tattle and usually relays it to me. Not that I am interested in gossip per se, you understand, but its value when litigation or prosecution is pending may be beyond rubies. So you may speak freely.'

'I see.' Again, I took a few seconds for thought. 'I've been holding my tongue,' I said at last, 'because, though the driver of the fish van seems to be spreading a version of the facts all over the town, it wasn't for me to add to the confusion and maybe make Ian Fellowes's job more difficult. But if Ian was prepared to take you into his confidence as an executor of the estate, and you share the same confidences with Mrs Enterkin, I suppose I can do the same.'

'Then, instead of prating about it,' Ralph snapped, 'I suggest that you do so.'

'Now, now,' came Penny Enterkin's voice. 'Manners, Ralph.'

'Quite right,' Ralph said gruffly. 'I apologize. Now get on with it.'

Between their insistence on hearing every detail and the necessity of filling in those parts of the story not yet known to Mrs Enterkin, the telling took some little time. Indeed, we were called to the table before I had even finished with the recovery of Spin. From that point on, the insistence of my hostess that I should not allow my food to get cold delayed the story still further. We had finished the soup course, complete with garlic bread, before I had revealed Synott's bombshell and we were through the roast beef, which was accompanied by an excellent claret, before I was able at last to arrive at Keith's unmasking, if I may be permitted the cliché, of the villain.

At that point, Ralph put down his wineglass with a haste which must have endangered the Edinburgh crystal and said, 'Oh dear! Oh dear! Oh dear!'

'Friend of yours?' I asked.

'By no means. But here I have been, consoling myself with the thought that no regular client of mine appeared to be suspect and it turns out that a man who

I have steered through physical injury suits, financial disaster and a charge of driving while under the influence is right at the forefront of suspicion.' Ralph refilled his glass but only held it up to the light. 'Is he guilty?'

'That's not a fair question,' Penny said. 'Surely it's up to a jury to decide.'

'I'm not asking for a decision. Once a jury decides, their decision will become fact. But an opinion at this stage might be invaluable.'

'It might mean that you can't take the case,' I suggested. 'Or not without pleading him guilty.'

He shook his head. 'It would only be your opinion. I'm entitled to believe that you might be wrong. But if he killed Sir Peter, I wouldn't want the case anyway. Sir Peter was my client too.'

'My opinion,' I said, 'for what it's worth, is this. There's no shadow of a doubt that he was ripping off Peter Hay in circumstances which Peter would have had every right to resent. I think that a jury would accept the draft letter and list of properties as indicating that Peter intended to take him to court, which would have spelled his ruin. As to whether he did kill his patron, I wouldn't know for sure. Personally, I think it probable. But no doubt Ian Fellowes and the forensic science laboratory will be able to settle the matter.'

'No doubt,' Ralph said. The thought seemed to pain him. He turned to his wife. 'Has Inspector Fellowes spoken with Jock McAnderton yet?'

'The last that I heard,' she said, 'no.'

'Still in confidence,' I said, 'Ian was going to spend the rest of today on the search of the area and in asking certain questions. As, for instance, does McAnderton buy the supermarket's frozen shepherd's pies.'

'Oh dear, oh dear!' Ralph said again. 'I shouldn't think there was any doubt about it. I know that, being a widower and often working out in the country, he has a small microwave in the cab of his truck. He runs it off that generator of his to heat himself up a meal.' He stopped fiddling with his glass and drained it. 'Even if I don't eventually take on this case, I think that I should have a word with him. I'm the nearest that he's got to a solicitor at the moment.'

'You can't,' I said.

'I must. He's entitled to legal advice.'

'You would be queering Ian Fellowes's pitch,' I said. 'I only told you as my fellow executor, and in confidence.'

Ralph combined a frown with his pouting expression of deep thought until his wife told him that he was in danger of getting stuck that way. 'I don't remember anything being said about confidence,' he said at last.

Penny got up to serve the sweet course. 'I do,' she said. 'I remember it being said several times. But Jock must have heard the rumours by now. Maybe, if he has any sense, he'll contact you himself.'

'But he doesn't have any sense,' Ralph said. 'He never did. I'm going to phone young Fellowes. The least I can do for McAnderton is to go along when the police visit him, make sure that he has his proper rights and then fix him up with other representation. Excuse me.'

He left the room, taking the cordless phone with him and leaving Penny and me to discuss the weather and how much Peter Hay would be missed. He returned after ten minutes.

'Ten a.m. tomorrow,' he said to me. 'And young Fellowes wants you to come along too. He expects to start off on the subject of the frauds. He'll fetch you himself.'

I awoke to more sunshine, birdsong, the comfortable realization that Spin had been retrieved and a sensation of unease when I remembered that today was the day when I would help confront a suspected murderer – strongly suspect but just possibly innocent. I comforted myself with the thought that I was not required to accuse him of anything more than fraud, of which I could be reasonably certain. I walked the dogs and ate breakfast in a mood of mild apprehension.

My breakfast was served by Mary Fiddler, who was not usually at work so early in the day. She explained that there had been some rearrangement of hours between Joanna and herself so that Joanna and Hamish (each perhaps wanting to tie the knot quickly before the other could change their mind) could go shopping for an engagement ring.

'I'm pleased that they're following the conventional path,' I remarked. 'Most couples these days move in together first and get married later if at all.'

'That's so,' Mary said comfortably. 'But Ronnie had words with the pair of them. She's his daughter, ye ken. He thinks I don't know.'

Ian arrived just after nine-thirty in the police Range Rover, sitting beside the sergeant who was driving. I joined Ralph Enterkin, who was already installed in the back.

As we emerged from the archway I asked, 'Where are we going?'

'Cartley's Farm,' said Ian. 'He went to work as normal. He can't have got word, despite all the rumours that have been buzzing around.'

'He's still working there? There's one thing I don't understand,' I said. 'The complaint at Home Farm was in connection with a roof renewal and second-hand materials. But that surely couldn't apply to rebuilding a wall, could it?'

'Something very similar could,' Ian said. 'I was making some enquiries last night. In recent years, someone told me, you could engage Jock McAnderton to do some building work using your materials, and he'd do a fine job. I'm told that his masonry could ring like a bell. But if you got a lump sum price from him, so that he was responsible for buying the materials, he grudged every grain of cement that went into it.'

'An old story,' I said. 'And a sad one.'

We turned off the road to Newton Lauder and began to climb the other side of a shallow valley. The land was farmland, all part of the Hay estate, and seemed to be in good heart. We passed a figure plodding up the roadside, carrying a paper bag.

'The nephew,' Ian said. 'He'll have been down to the town for their lunch.'

Thinking back to when Jock McAnderton had pointed out Cartley's Farm to me, I thought that we must be there; and when we drove on I decided that either I had misunderstood him or my sense of direction had deserted me. But then we turned off through a farmyard and round the back of some barns to where one wall of an old stone-built cattle-court was half down and half rebuilt and Jock McAnderton was cleaning and arranging his stones and hoisting them onto his scaffolding ready for a day of masonry work. Beside him, his lorry was parked and the generator in the trailer was ticking over.

The Range Rover drew up, nose to nose with the lorry. We dismounted. I saw McAnderton's eyes go from one to the other of us.

Ian said, 'I am Detective Inspector Fellowes and I have some questions to put to you.'

McAnderton nodded. 'I'll just put this thing off, so's we can hear ourselves,' he said. He turned to his generator. It was done so naturally that I suspected nothing until Ian jumped forward. But he was too late. McAnderton stopped, flipped back a lid and made a grab at a pair of terminals. I heard the note of the diesel deepen and accelerate as an electrical load came on. For a second or two his back arched and all his muscles were in spasm. Then he collapsed. He seemed to be living still, but I was sure that only the continuing current through his body was responsible for the ceaseless muscular tremor.

The sergeant was about to lay hands on the body, but Ian shouted at him to keep back unless he wanted to go the same way. 'For God's sake,' Ian said, 'how do you stop this thing?' The sergeant found the right control and the maddening mutter died away. McAnderton's body relaxed and fell to the ground.

I turned away quickly to face the wall. I found that Ralph was still beside me. Neither of us wanted to look at the still twitching body. Behind me I could hear Ian's voice, summoning help by radio. I put out a finger and scratched at the mortar in a section of rebuilt wall that must have been a day or two old. It came away as powder. 'Almost pure sand,' I said. 'Some people never learn. But he knew what was coming and he was ready to kill himself. We should have guessed. The generator was running although nothing was connected to it.'

'Yes. Oh dear, oh dear!' said Ralph. He sounded desolate.

'Perhaps it's best this way,' I suggested.

'You think so? But consider. What will the Inspector of Taxes make of his debt to Sir Peter? Will he let us write it off before Inheritance Tax? Or only the balance after recovering what we can? Or what? You'll have to get quotes immediately from a reputable builder for repairing or replacing the faulty work. And you'd better have all his plant and materials impounded, before some other creditor thinks of it. In theory it makes no difference but I believe the old adage about possession being nine points of the law, does have a foundation of truth.'

It was clear that Ralph's distress was not on behalf of this former and now late client.

My story is almost done. The procurator fiscal brought both deaths before the sheriff in quick succession and the burden of his decision was that Jock McAnderton had murdered Sir Peter Hay and then died by his own hand.

There is one final point. On rereading what has gone before, I see that I have tried to give at least some physical description of each character of importance, excepting only myself. If any reader should be curious as to my appearance I may say, beyond the fact that I look elderly to the point of decrepitude, that any regular viewer of television may have seen me on the Scottish news, giving away the granddaughter of Sir Peter Hay in marriage, and also playing the part of the late baronet in the documentary *Syndicate Year* and still later its successor *On The Moor*. I suppose that it would be rather late in life for me to embark on a fresh career as an actor, but you never know.